Stand in the Box

Noël F. Caraccio

Black Rose Writing | Texas

ISBN: 978-1-68513-044-2
PUBLISHED BY BLACK ROSE WRITING
www.blackrosewriting.com

Printed in the United States of America
Suggested Retail Price (SRP) $22.95

Stand in the Box is printed in Baskerville

*As a planet-friendly publisher, Black Rose Writing does its best to eliminate unnecessary waste to reduce paper usage and energy costs, while never compromising the reading experience. As a result, the final word count vs. page count may not meet common expectations.

"You can be brave, especially when you are fearful.
In fact, that's the measure of bravery."

Acknowledgments

A huge thank you to Richard Lavsky for his help with all the technical and IT issues. I always know that I can call him for help when I have a computer issue, and there were plenty of times I called for help.

Thank you to Sandy Schoeneman for giving me an idea, and then I ran with the ball.

Thank you to Annalinda Ragazzo for all her good work in proofreading the manuscript for mistakes and typos. Such a necessary but thankless job, which is why I am saying thank you now.

Stand in the Box

Chapter 1

It was a moonless night and the glare from the oncoming headlights made driving even more difficult with the steady rain. The roads were slick with the fallen leaves and the car had skidded once already.

"Jeez, I hate these two-lane roads. They should straighten them out and make them less dangerous. I can barely see the double yellow line," Blake said through clenched teeth and with white-knuckled hands gripping the steering wheel.

"Damn it, slow down some more. There's not even a guardrail on the side of this road and all I see is black on my side of the car. Looks like it's all wooded, and I don't see any houses or lights," his wife Jackie replied.

Blake responded, "It was a great party, but I'm not sure it was worth this drive. We're not too far from 684. At least that's pretty straight, even if there aren't any lights."

Blake and Jackie's car headed up a large hill, and a tractor trailer, which had somehow gotten lost, headed down the hill toward them. The driver of the tractor trailer was also looking for the entrance to Interstate 684, but from the opposite direction. The grade of the hill, his speed and the wet leaves on the road all conspired against the driver of the tractor trailer and he lost control. The tractor trailer jackknifed, and the trailer slammed viciously into Jackie and Blake's car. There was a deafening sound as the metal exploded as the two vehicles collided.

The force of the trailer moving downhill, and the violent jackknifing flung Blake and Jackie's car over the embankment as if it were a child's Matchbox car into the blackness below. The last thing Blake heard was Jackie's scream and then he blacked out with the impact of the car hitting the ground several stories below the road. The tractor trailer followed the car over the abyss.

Behind the tractor trailer was a car being driven by Peter Boyd. His wife, Terry, was in the passenger seat. Peter saw the accident happen and his stomach lurched at the sight. He jammed on the brakes and veered dramatically to the right onto the shoulder. Terry hadn't been paying attention, but as the car lurched to the right, she got out about half a sentence. "What the hell...? Then she saw the tail end of what happened.

Peter yelled, "Call 911," as he undid his seatbelt and opened the car door in one motion. Terry sat there horrified for a few seconds as she watched her Good Samaritan husband bolt across the road toward the accident in the rain. She regained enough composure to call 911 and tell the operator approximately where they were. She got herself out of the car, but she could not force herself to cross the road to see what happened. She stood there in the rain, literally wringing her hands.

After what seemed like an eternity, Peter appeared and ran frantically back to their car, screaming at her to open the trunk. There was mud all over his clothes. Terry ran around the front of the car, leaned in, and hit the button to pop the trunk.

Before Terry could say anything, Peter screamed, "I can't get them out! There's a man and a woman in the car. The doors are locked. I need something to break the windows."

"What about the driver of the tractor trailer?"

"He's got a broken leg, but other than that, I don't think he's that badly hurt. He got himself out of the cab, but he fell. He can't stand up on that leg."

Terry stood frozen by the side of the car and watched as Peter threw things out of the trunk onto the wet ground. Finally, Terry regained enough presence of mind to say, "Robby's baseball bat is in the back seat." She reached in the back and yanked out Robby's metal bat, and shoved it into Peter's hand. He took off at a full gallop back across the road.

Terry could hear muffled sirens in the distance, but she didn't know how close they were. Were they muffled by distance or by the rain?

Peter prayed as he picked his way back down the embankment, sliding and tripping, that he was going to get them out and that they were still alive. He tripped, ripped his trousers and scraped the skin off his hand until he could stop his fall.

Both people were lifeless in the dark car and his first try banging on the window hadn't roused them. Peter couldn't tell if they were breathing or how badly they were hurt. He didn't know with all the safety features in cars if he could break the windows with a baseball bat, but he was certainly going to try. If he succeeded, he hoped they wouldn't be hurt by broken glass. Who even knows these things he asked himself?

Now Peter could hear the sirens and they sounded close. By now, he was praying out loud. " Hurry and get here, and help me get them out." Peter didn't know how many first responders there would be or what tools they would have to free the man and the woman. By now, he was frantic.

As Peter reached the place where the car rested, he could smell smoke. Some part of his brain acknowledged it, but his adrenaline was pumping so hard that he didn't take in the full implications of what that meant. Peter wound up and took as powerful a swing with the bat as he could against the passenger side window. This was where the woman was sitting. The window smashed, sending glass flying into the car. The window had partially cracked, but he would probably need to hit the window one or two more times to reach in.

As he hit what was left of the window a second time, the hood of the car went up in flames. Peter involuntarily jumped back. He ripped off his jacket and put it over his arm to reach in through the jagged glass. Before he could reach in, there was a tremendous boom, and flames engulfed the car. The noise, the explosion and the heat knocked him backwards, and he fell. Peter tried desperately to get closer to the car, but the heat and smoke kept him back.

As the first two police officers made their way down the embankment, they saw the flames shooting up into the night from the car. As they got closer to the scene, they saw a man on his hands and knees with only a shirt on in the rain. There was a baseball bat next to him on the ground and the man was sobbing profusely.

Chapter 2

One Week Later

The limousine pulled into the cemetery on a cold and rainy October day. The mourners stayed in their cars as long as possible since the chill was penetrating. The procession of cars following the two hearses extended all the way back to the entrance to the cemetery and snaked its way toward where the open graves were waiting. The funeral director had told the family to stay in the cars until he came for them, so that the pallbearers had a chance to get the two caskets to the grave, the minister was standing by the graves and the rest of the mourners gathered. Frankly, in all his years as a funeral director, he had never been so moved by the grief of a family. He had seen a lot of tragedy and grief in his almost forty years as a funeral director. It was almost never the right time for death, unless the person had been ill and suffering for a long time. But the deaths of children from cancer, or people from heart attacks, car accidents or murders always seemed to be brutal and senseless. Often the family was reeling, and the pain was so close to the surface. However, these two deaths seemed particularly cruel.

In the funeral business, you learned to harden yourself to the pain of the people you were dealing with, or the grief swallowed you up as well. It had seemed the natural thing for Ross to do. After all, his father and grandfather had both been in the funeral business, and Ross grew up living above the funeral home, so death had always been a part of his life for as long as he could remember. He hadn't ever seriously considered going into any other profession or doing any other job. Even if he had considered it, his father would never have approved. That was why when his eldest son said he wanted to be a CPA, Ross never fought or even questioned him about that decision. It was ironic that it was his daughter, Amanda, who expressed an interest in the family business and seemed to be quite good at her job. She was compassionate with the families; he could see that. She also made a conscious decision to live far away from the funeral home, something Ross wished he had done much earlier. He just hoped that the ever-present grief didn't eat her alive.

Ross roused himself from his reverie, even though he was still simultaneously doing what needed to be done at the cemetery. He realized that these two little girls sitting in the first limousine reminded him of his two granddaughters, who were about the same age. He couldn't even imagine what it must be like for these two girls sitting in a limo on a miserable day getting ready to walk to the graves of their parents. Telling them to stay in the limo for as long as possible wasn't only about keeping them warm and dry. Ross realized that in his heart he was trying to keep them away from the inevitable.

As he walked into the reception area of David Brennan's law firm four days after the funeral, Ross saw David sitting in the library typing away on his laptop like his hair was on fire and he had to finish whatever he was doing before the fire department came to douse his hair. "Hi, David, I have these for you," he said as he slapped the manila folder against his hand.

David looked up and said, "Thanks. Are those the death certificates?"

Ross answered, "Yeah, I thought I'd bring them to you rather than put them in the mail. I can't seem to get those two kids' faces out of my mind. I can just see them as I helped them out of the limo at the cemetery. They looked shell shocked. I hope they do okay. It's going to be a very hard road for them after losing both parents. What's the deal with the family? Who's going to be the Guardian and take care of them? There were a ton of friends there, but I only met two grandparents. Would you tell the family that I asked for them and I was particularly concerned about the girls?"

David watched as Ross seemed to be lost in his own thoughts. "I certainly will tell them you were asking for them. At a time like this, people appreciate any act of kindness, even a small one. People are so vulnerable that they need the support. Thanks again, Ross, for bringing these over, but I really need to finish these motion papers."

Chapter 3

The following day, David Brennan's secretary poked her head into David's office and said, "The family is here on the Estates. I put them in the large conference room, and I brought in some fresh coffee for them." David realized she didn't even need to say the name of the family. She had said it all by saying "the Estates." Plural. Thank God there weren't many instances when they were dealing with plural estates for the same family at the same time.

He walked around his desk, put on his suit jacket, and straightened his tie. He picked up the file and let out a huge sigh before he left his office for the conference room.

David walked into the conference room and looked around at a room heavy with silence and grief. David reintroduced himself to the three people sitting around the conference room table and shook all their hands. He had met them at the wake, but with all the people in the funeral home, he wasn't sure if they even remembered he had been there or what he looked like.

The elderly man sitting closest to the door was Edward Foxe. He was Jackie's father. David pegged him to be a man in his late seventies, or perhaps early eighties. The woman sitting across the table might have been older or younger than her husband, but it was hard to tell. The man looked to be in good health, but the woman looked frail, and her color was pasty. David knew her name from the Will. She had a cane next to her chair, and the conference room table propped it up. She was Jackie's mother and David could see the family resemblance. These were the parents of the wife killed in the car crash, and the grandparents of the two surviving little girls.

The third person in the room was Jake, Jackie's brother. He was sitting across the table from Eddie and Gloria, and he had a mug of coffee sitting in front of him.

David opened his file and pulled out a document with a blue back. It was Blake's Last Will and Testament. He looked around at the three people facing him and said, "This is Blake's Will, and I have copies here for each of you. Jackie's Will is what we call a mirror image Will, so her Will is the same as Blake's except that they made reciprocal provisions for each other. Would you like me to go over each Will paragraph by paragraph? I can answer your questions as we read each paragraph."

David handed out the copies of the two Wills to the three people sitting in front of him. There was no answer from any of them if he should go over the Wills paragraph by paragraph. Finally, David looked directly at Jake and said, "Is that how you want me to proceed?" Jake mumbled what seemed to David to be a "Yes," so he started summarizing each paragraph as he went along.

"You can see that Blake left his entire estate to Jackie and if she should predecease him, then to the girls." As he continued, he said Blake named Jackie as the Executrix of the Estate. "Since Jackie is deceased, Blake named his brother Tyler as the alternate executor of the Estate." Everyone nodded their assent.

"Since the girls are minors, meaning they haven't attained the age of eighteen years old, then there is a Trustee appointed by the Will to handle the finances for Kristin and Megan until the girls attain the ages for distribution as stated in this Will. So far, so good. Any questions?"

All three heads shook a "no" almost in unison, so David forged on. "Now, since both Jackie and Blake are deceased and the children are minors, they named Guardians for the girls." David knew he was about to drop a bombshell, so he took a second to compose himself and took a deep breath. "Blake and Jackie named Jake AND Tyler as the Co-Guardians." For what had been almost deadly quiet in the room as David read the Will, there was now an audible gasp. Tyler was Blake's brother, unmarried and somewhat of a free spirit. David did not know whether Tyler worked, and if he did, what he did. David had noticed him at the wake since Tyler stood out as the only man not wearing a jacket and tie, and in fact, looking like he was the handyman for the funeral home.

David figured he should drop the second bombshell sooner rather than later. "The Will specifically provides that the Co-Guardians are to live in the house with the girls.

"You can see that the language is very specific on this point. It says in the Ninth Paragraph, 'We have given this careful consideration and thought, and it is very important to us that our daughters, Kristin and Megan, stay connected to our families if we are not alive while they are growing up. That is why we have named Co-Guardians from each of our families. We named the two people whom we thought would comfort them in their loss, love them unconditionally, and provide them with a good life.

"It is very important to us that Kristin and Megan remain living in the only house they have ever known to provide them with stability. We have provided well for our daughters and there are more than enough assets for them to live comfortably in the house until they finish college. There will be no financial burden on either Co-Guardian. Therefore, it is my directive that the Co-Guardians both live in the house with Kristin and Megan until they each attain the age of twenty-one years old or twenty-two years old if they are full time matriculating students in a four-year college or university. Neither Co-Guardian shall pay rent or any other payment to my estate for living in the house. If either Co-Guardian fails or refuses to live in the house for a period of more than one month, excluding vacations or serious illness, then I direct that the Co-Guardian shall be removed as Co-Guardian and the remaining Co-Guardian shall become the sole Guardian.

"Since Megan is the younger, when she attains the age of twenty-two years old, she and Kristin can decide whether they wish to remain living in the house, or they can decide to sell it and divide the net proceeds equally between them."

As he finished reading those paragraphs from the Will, David looked up to see the reaction of the three people sitting in front of him. He was especially interested in Jake's reaction, since he was the one of the three people here whose life it would impact the most.

Jake was staring at the copy of the Will in his hand like it was some alien creature. He looked up slowly at David, and said, "Holy Cow! I don't know what to say. This is a tremendous responsibility. I wish they had spoken to me about this. Talk about a shot out of the blue. Does Tyler know about this?"

David shook his head no. "I don't think so, unless Jackie or Blake spoke to him before they died. They didn't speak to you, so chances are good they probably didn't speak to him either. Blake and Jackie had such definite ideas that I assumed they had spoken to each of you.

"Tyler didn't give me any indication at the wake when I spoke to him that he knew anything about it. I told him that perhaps he might want to come to my office when we discussed the Wills. He was kind of noncommittal about whether he'd come."

David said, "Do you want to call him, or do you want me to?"

Jake came up with a third alternative. "Why don't you send him an e-mail to him and to me and tell him the three of us need to get together and talk about the Estates?"

Chapter 4

Shortly after their meeting was over that afternoon, David sent an e-mail to Tyler and Jake and said that he'd like to have a meeting in his office with both men about the two Estates as soon as possible. That was on a Tuesday, and he had no return e-mail or call from Tyler the rest of Tuesday or on Wednesday. Just as he was about to send another e-mail on Thursday, there was a response from Tyler in David's in box.

"Dear David:

I'm agreeable to whatever you need me to sign on the Estate. Just e-mail it to me and I'll get it signed and back to you right away.

Best.

Tyler"

David read the e-mail and said "shit" out loud. "This guy isn't going to make this easy. If I had wanted a document signed, you moron, I would have sent it to you," David said to the computer screen.

David leaned back in his chair. He mused about what was the right thing to do and how to broach this with Tyler. Should he merely call him and blurt it out on the phone? He rejected that as being too punitive. He could send another e-mail, but he might very well get the same response from Tyler. He really thought it would be better if he, Tyler and Jake met in person—with no one else being present. David had picked up an undercurrent from the Foxes, Jackie's parents. He was pretty sure he was picking up on the fact that since Blake and Jackie hadn't named a married couple or someone more conventional as the Guardians for the girls, that wasn't sitting too well with the Foxes. Finally, David decided on a third alternative. He'd have his secretary call Tyler and tell him David was in Court and that she'd like to set up the appointment for them. She could say she was told it was important that they meet, but not have to give away the details.

Monday morning was the date set for the meeting, and David was glad the meeting was for 10 AM. So many things about these Estates were weighing on his mind that David wanted to get the meeting over with and get down to business about submitting the Wills to the Surrogate's Court. He knew that Eddie and Gloria were staying with Kristin and Megan at their own house to try not to disrupt the girls' lives any more than the deadly accident had already done. David really believed that they should all try to get on with the plan set up by Blake and Jackie, no matter how strange it seemed at first blush.

Jake arrived at the office about 9:55 for the 10AM appointment and about 10:15 Tyler called and said he was parking the car. David picked up the file and walked into the conference room to tell Jake that Tyler was outside parking the car. Jake rolled his eyes and then asked David a question about collecting on the insurance policies.

The door to the conference room opened and Tyler strolled in, not with any sense of urgency. "Sorry, I'm late. Can I get a latte?"

David coughed into his hand to suppress a laugh and motioned with his other hand toward a carafe of coffee sitting on a cabinet. "It's not a latte, but it's freshly made Dunkin' Donuts."

Jake surveyed Tyler and David watched Jake survey Tyler. Tyler had on a Polar Tec jacket, which looked as if it needed to be washed. He had on faded jeans, with a hole in the knee, and even though it was October and cold outside, he had on well -worn flip flops. He had not shaved, as was apparent from the stubble, and his blonde hair had the lived- in look of "bed head."

This was in sharp contrast to Jake, who had on a down vest, cashmere sweater, pants with a pressed pleat, and Gucci loafers.

David handed out copies of the two Wills, as he had done at the last meeting. "Tyler, Jake, Eddie and Gloria were here last week when we went over the two Wills. There are some very important provisions of the Wills that you need to hear, since they involve you directly. Should I cut to the chase, or do you want me to go over all the paragraphs of the Wills?"

Tyler slouched in his chair and looked up at David. "Whatever you want is fine."

David's first thought was to go across the table and choke him when Tyler said, "No, it's probably better that you explain things."

David explained the various provisions of the two Wills as he had done at the prior meeting. Tyler was reading along with David, and despite the body language which said, " I couldn't care less about this," he was paying attention. At one point, David thought Tyler was going to put his feet up on the conference room table.

When David got to Paragraph nine, he could see in his peripheral vision that Jake leaned forward in his chair to get a clear view of Tyler's reaction. Tyler looked up from the document and met David's gaze. He said nothing, he just stared at David. David met his gaze but didn't say anything. Tyler finally looked from David to Jake and then back to David. "Well, aren't you going to congratulate us? We just gave birth to a nine-year-old and a twelve-year-old."

Chapter 5

Gloria Foxe picked up the phone twice and twice put it down before she started dialing. "I can't do this, Eddie. I can't. I just don't think this is right. It totally ignores everything that Jackie and Blake wanted. Every time I read these paragraphs in the Wills, it seems that they thought this whole thing through. They knew exactly what they wanted, and they said that in the Wills. How is it our place to say we know better than they do what is best for their children?"

"For God's sake, Gloria, what the hell is the matter with you? This whole thing is absolutely crazy. I don't know what they were thinking. It's just a bunch of words that go on and on but make no sense. How can two girls be raised by two men? That is so stupid. How are two men going to talk to two girls about growing up? How are they going to talk to them about, uh, personal girl things?"

"Eddie, it's okay to say 'sex.' It is the twentieth-first century. I'm not sure about this because it goes against Jackie and Blake's wishes, but also, we've raised our children. I don't know if either of us has enough energy left to raise two kids. I certainly am not up to it. Do you really think you are?"

Eddie looked off to a spot in the distance over Gloria's left shoulder. "What about Sheryl? We need to talk to her about this." Sheryl was their oldest child.

"I don't think you can call her and tell her you think she should become the Guardian for Kristin and Megan. If she wanted to become the Guardian for her nieces, she would have said something by now. We spoke to her that same night we came back from the lawyer's office. You said that you thought she should become the Guardian. She certainly didn't seem to be too receptive to the idea. She said that she and Mike needed to discuss it fully. If Sheryl and Mike were to become the Guardians, then the girls would have to move to Florida, and that's not what Blake and Jackie wanted. They wanted them to stay in the house and not uproot them. Having them go live in Florida certainly qualifies as being uprooted. They'd have to leave their schools, their friends and everyone and everything they've known and are comfortable with. You can't tell me that you honestly think that is what Jackie and Blake really wanted. In fact, the Wills say the opposite of what you're proposing."

Eddie shook his head in dismay. "If you won't call the lawyer, then I will. Somebody has to step up and help these kids. These are our granddaughters, and I'm not just standing by for a disaster." Eddie walked over to the phone and dialed David Brennan.

"Maybe you should speak to Sheryl one more time before you talk to the lawyer, Eddie. You must be sure that Sheryl will do this. The whole thing will fall apart if Sheryl isn't willing to be the Guardian, plus I think she will have to move up here. That's two gigantic steps for her to take and we also don't know what Mike thinks about all of this."

When David Brennan returned from Court, he saw the phone message from Eddie Foxe. David made a face as he saw the phone message. His instincts about people were quite good. He knew as he read Paragraph nine out loud that Eddie and Gloria Foxe would not like it. If the truth be told, David wasn't so sure he liked it, but Jackie and Blake seemed so sure of what they wanted to do that he had only made a halfhearted attempt to raise some obstacles. However, they seemed comfortable with their decision. They wanted the girls to be raised by both sides of the family, as disparate as those viewpoints were.

Chapter 6

The doorbell rang and since Gloria was close to the door, she walked slowly to the front door using her cane and saw an attractive woman with long dark hair and a bright blue jacket on the porch. She looked somewhat familiar to Gloria, so she opened the door, but left the storm door locked.

As she opened the door, the woman smiled warmly and said to Gloria, "Hi, I'm Amanda Hunter. I don't know if you remember me, but my father and I own the funeral home in town."

Now Gloria realized why she didn't quite recognize her. At the funeral home, Amanda had on a black suit jacket, with a white silk blouse, black pants and black high heels. She had her hair pulled back in a ponytail with a small, dark bow. Not quite the woman in the bright blue jacket, yellow scarf and jeans standing before her.

"Oh, please come in, Ms. Hunter. For a minute, I didn't recognize you."

As Amanda stepped into the house, she said, "You probably didn't recognize me in any other color but black. Those are my work clothes, and they are always black. It's an occupational hazard. When I'm not working, I like color and lots of it. Please call me Amanda.

"I have been thinking of you and the girls. I brought a fully cooked dinner, courtesy of Boston Market. I thought maybe you could use an easy night with no cooking."

"Please come in and sit down, dear. That is so thoughtful of you. You just missed Eddie. He went to the gym. In the cold weather he likes to go to swimming. He'll be sorry he missed you."

"So, how are you all doing? This must be a very hard time for all of you."

"You're right. It hasn't been an easy time for any of us. There are days when I want to curl up and pull the covers over my head, but I can't. We all are trying to do the best we can for Megan and Kristin, but it's difficult. I'm not all that well, and I don't know how long I can keep up this pace of running a household and caring for two children. I lost my daughter and I feel I can't properly grieve for her, because if I break down, I'm afraid it will be worse for the girls. I feel like I'm holding on by my fingernails." The pain in her voice and on her face was heart wrenching.

"If I may, Mrs. Foxe, I would suggest two things. Perhaps you and your husband should take a break for a few days. Go home to your own house and settle in for a few days. That might give you the space you need. Is there some other family members or close friend who could relieve you?

"Second, are the girls seeing a counselor or therapist? While this has been awful for all of you, it has to be the absolute worst for them. Their parents are gone in a horrific accident. There was no warning and no time to get used to it, as it would have been if someone had been sick. If someone is sick and dying, then there's time to adjust. Kristin and Megan must be so traumatized. They need a professional to express their feelings, their grief and probably even terror. In the eyes of a child, parents are their rock. If their parents are gone in the blink of an eye, these kids are probably terrified that other important people in their lives will leave them as well."

Amanda couldn't quite read Gloria's expression. They were quiet for a few seconds and Amanda didn't know if she had overstepped. After what seemed like a very long time, Gloria finally spoke, and the tears were welling up in her eyes.

"I don't know if you have heard about the arrangement Jackie and Blake made as to who will be the Guardians for the girls?"

When Amanda shook her head no, Gloria explained the situation. "Eddie and I don't know what to do. We know Jackie and Blake loved those two girls more than anything else in the world, and probably thought they were doing the right thing, but having Jake and Tyler as the Co-Guardians seems like a big mistake. Both men are single and have never had their own kids. What do they know about raising two ready-made girls?

"Jake and Tyler aren't even related to each other by blood. I guess technically they aren't even related by marriage. I truly can't see how they are going to step in and raise two girls. I think it would have been a mess if it was just one of them being the Guardian, but two men." At that, Gloria's voice trailed off as she looked into the distance and tried to gather herself.

Amanda was a little taken aback by what she heard. She thought it was strange, but David Brennan had told her Jackie and Blake were solid citizens and not prone to doing strange or crazy things. Amanda thought she needed some time to think about this, and she didn't want to say something she would ultimately regret. The house was large and well kept on the outside and beautifully furnished on the inside. Jackie and Blake looked as if they had been prosperous and were probably well educated. They had consulted David Brennan about their estate planning. So, the whole situation gave Amanda pause.

Gloria picked up her tirade where she had left off a few minutes earlier, so Amanda didn't have to say anything. "My husband is very much against this whole thing. He thinks it's crazy. I just don't know what to think."

Amanda knew she might be treading on thin ice, so she tried to temper what she said. "Maybe if you and your husband were to go home for a few days with a definite plan to come back, you could let Jake and Tyler take care of the girls for the few days that you're gone and see how it goes. Give it a trial run."

Chapter 7

After her talk with Amanda, Gloria took the bull by the horns and take some action. The next day she called Amanda at the funeral home and fortunately, Amanda was in the office doing some paperwork. Gloria was afraid she would lose her nerve and be afraid to call back. She said since Amanda dealt with grieving people all the time, did she have any recommendations for a therapist? Amanda said she had two therapists in mind, but she didn't think either of them dealt with child and adolescent patients. She said she'd be happy to get the names of therapists who treated children and get back to Gloria. Gloria told her she'd like to get that squared away before she would consider going home and leaving the girls.

"Mrs. Foxe, I really think you are doing the right thing for the girls. Grief can be difficult to deal with for adults who have some coping mechanisms. It's just that much more difficult for young kids. They can just be overwhelmed. Have they opened up to you about this?"

"No, not really that much. I see flashes of anger or frustration over unimportant things, and some crying here and there, but not enough for the immensity of the loss. I think you are right that they need to talk to someone who knows how to get them to deal with this. God knows, I'm having a terrible time myself. I might ask for the names of those psychologists you know, for myself."

Amanda thought to herself that she might have opened the floodgates for the whole family with her conversation and that it was probably a good thing. There would be a lot of pain to work through this loss, and Amanda doubted that anyone in this family was going to do it alone.

"If you don't mind my asking, are the girls back in school full time?"

"Well, they sort of are. We kept them home for a few days after the funeral, because they were clingy, but now they seem to want to go to school and see their friends. We had a day or two when there were upset stomachs, real or imagined, so I didn't want to push too hard. I think that's the kind of issue we should get help on from the psychologist. Do we push them to go to school on those 'upset stomach days' or not?

"My husband is dead set against this idea of Tyler and Jake being the Co-Guardians. I'm liking your idea of letting Tyler and Jake stay with the girls for a few days and see what happens. Who knows what might happen? It could work out well and we all might be surprised, or it might be a disaster. If it is a disaster, then maybe that would give us some guidance what direction we should go in next."

"Mrs. Foxe, have Tyler and Jake said they'd like to move into the house and start acting as Guardians?"

"No, but in fairness to them, we haven't asked them either. I'm not sure if they are waiting for the official papers from the Court, or if they're waiting for us to say something to them. I just don't know. You said you think we should give it a trial run."

"I said that because if that's what Jackie and Blake wanted, maybe you should try to see if it works, even for a few days, with everyone knowing you and your husband are coming back. You told me you needed some time for yourself to grieve, and a few days off would probably give you a much-needed break as well. I think everyone is going to have to deal with the elephant in the room. You all know it's there, but are afraid to acknowledge it. In your case, there are two elephants in the room.

"Jake is your son. Why don't you broach the subject first with him? Was he surprised to have been named a Co-Guardian or did he know about it in advance?"

"No, I don't think either he or Tyler knew about it. Both seemed shocked when they saw what was in the Wills. It seems so unlike Jackie and Blake to do something so extraordinary without having said anything about it. To me, it seems so out of character for both of them. I'm baffled.

"Thanks, Amanda. I'm taking up a lot of your time. You've been wonderful. I like your idea. Now I just have to convince my husband. And please call me Gloria. Mrs. Foxe sounds so formal."

Amanda knew she was in a tough profession. Dealing with grief constantly was wearing. You had to keep some distance, or it would swallow you up in the family's grief. But this seemed like a special situation, even to a funeral director, who had to be somewhat hardened to tragedy.

Chapter 8

Kristin loved sports, but she especially loved tennis. There was a certain grace and rhythm to it, and the sound of the ball coming off the racquet was pleasing to anyone who played. The game could be frenetic and fast paced, and Kristin loved that even more. She got to run, hit the ball as hard as she could, and race back to be in position for the next shot. She had to think on her feet, react to a ball coming at her with spin or a slice, and hit it cleanly while deciding where she wanted it to go. For a young girl of twelve years old, she had a remarkable sense of the strategy of the game. Within the first year after taking up the game, she could beat her father. His ground stokes were not as smooth as hers and he mostly tried to muscle the ball. Kristin made great contact and great shots.

When her parents asked her if she would like to take private lessons, she jumped at the chance. Once she started taking private lessons, her game improved dramatically. Right after she started taking lessons, she begged her father to set up a backboard so she could hit balls in the back yard whenever she wanted to and without having to find a playing partner. Since she seemed so eager to learn the game and was doing great with her lessons, it wasn't a hard sell with Blake. Kristin never needed to be told to practice, and now she could practice whenever she wanted with the backboard right there in the yard.

Her coach started entering her in junior tournaments, and it took her a little time to get over her fear of playing better kids in competition, but then she started winning and she liked that even more. Her coach, known as Mr. Reece to his students, had a sense of humor. Mr. Reece got shortened down to "Mr. Ree," but pronounced "Mystery" with the stress on the second syllable. He was a man of about fifty years old, who has done remarkable things with aspiring tennis players who wanted to work on their game. Kristin loved him, and she blossomed under his coaching. There was encouragement and hard work, but no yelling or berating the kids.

Today Kristin was out in the back yard hitting balls. She was supposed to be practicing her serves before her next lesson, but she was lackluster. She was mostly just hitting easy forehands with every third shot being a backhand. She didn't have any concentration or purpose. It was just mindless hitting, and she didn't know why.

Mr. Reece was about at the end of a lesson with a young boy. Mr. Reece found himself distracted in the last ten minutes of the lesson. Then he realized why he was distracted. He was Kristin's tennis coach. He was thinking about Kristin and the impact her parents' death was going to have on her.

When the lesson was over, Mr. Reece called the house. He spoke to Gloria, introduced himself and asked if he could stop by to see Kristin since he had some free time between lessons. Gloria readily agreed and said to come over to the house whenever it was convenient for him.

Mr. Reece parked the car in the driveway and walked around to the back of the house when he knew Kristin would be. He stopped walking quite a way before Kristin could see him or know he was there. He watched some of the lackluster hitting before he finally made his presence known. This was unlike the Kristin who was eager to learn and was a feisty and determined player. Something was wrong, and Mr. Reece knew it didn't take a rocket scientist to spot an unhappy kid.

"Hey, kiddo, how's it going?"

"Fine," came the flat response.

"Yeah, really, fine? Doesn't look like that to me."

"No, I'm fine."

"Okay, so take a break and come over here and sit down with me and have some water."

Kristin shrugged the universal kid shrug of "Whatever." She came over and plopped down into the chair rather than sat down. This was so unlike the enthusiastic Kristin.

Mr. Reece was used to dealing with moody adolescents over everything from poor grades to losing a painful tournament to breaking up with the current love of their lives. But losing both parents was a whole different thing, and he wasn't sure how to approach it.

"Look, kiddo, one thing I always am is straight with you. You play well and I tell you. You play badly and I tell you that, too. But I tell you the truth. And the truth today is you look miserable to me. Your parents died, and that's the crappiest thing of all crappy things. It's okay to say you're sad or scared or really pissed off." He stopped for a minute to catch his breath and assess what impact his words were having on her.

In that heartbeat, and that's all it was, Kristin looked at him with the most soulful look he had ever seen. She didn't say one word in response. She just grabbed the sleeve of his jacket, buried her face in it and sobbed. He could feel the racking sobs. He put his arm around her and let her go.

Chapter 9

Gloria and Eddie Foxe came at the problem with two different approaches. Gloria took Amanda's words to heart about the trial run with Jake and Tyler staying with the girls to see how they all fared. Eddie instead of gearing up for a trial run, wanted to gear up for a trial.

He called David Brennan's office a second time before David could return his phone call. Eddie was very direct and firm that he wanted to make an appointment to see David again in person, and he wanted the appointment sooner rather than later.

When David returned from Court, his secretary handed him two message slips. She said four people left him messages in his voice mail and told him about the appointment with Eddie Foxe. David made a face and merely said, "When?"

"Wednesday morning at 10 AM. He sounded like he was all business. No small talk and wanted your first available appointment. I knew you would be tied up tomorrow at the Hansen closing, so I said Wednesday. I really don't think he was going to be put off or take no for an answer. I assume he's upset about the Estates."

"Apparently so. Eddie is an older man, and I don't think he liked the idea of Jake and Tyler being the Co-Guardians. I'm not sure if he doesn't like the idea of two men being the Co-Guardians or two men being the Co-Guardians for two little girls. I guess I'll see on Wednesday."

Shortly after Eddie got off the phone with David's office, he called his daughter, Sheryl. She was eight years older than Jackie. Jackie and Sheryl had been close growing up, but Sheryl went away to college and then took a job in Atlanta right out of college. Jackie had been ten when Sheryl went off to college, so the age difference had manifested itself. Sheryl never came home to live after college. Sheryl had moved around for work, but ultimately settled in Orlando, where she met Mike. They ran an employment agency that was quite successful because it recruited higher end jobs in medical research. The agency dealt with people nationally, so it didn't matter where Sheryl and Mike were located.

"Hi, Dad, how are you? How's everything going with the girls?"

"Well, I would say it's going as well as expected under these awful circumstances. Your Mom thinks the girls would do well to see a psychologist because she's afraid they are holding everything in. She got the idea from the funeral director who's going to get some names for us. But frankly, Sheryl, that's not the only problem.

"I don't know what the hell your sister was thinking naming Tyler and Jake as the Co-Guardians. Of all the crazy things I have ever heard, this is it. God, between Jackie and Blake I would have thought one of them would have had enough brains to see it's a bad idea. Two men, as the Guardians for two little girls, and these two men aren't even related to each other. Just a goddamn stupid idea!"

"When Mom told me after the funeral what Jackie and Blake had done, it seemed strange to me. She said that they hadn't even consulted Jake or Tyler about it in advance, so it came as an enormous shock to them too. I haven't spoken to Jake since I came home, so what is he saying?"

"That's the thing. He hasn't been around much and he's not really talking. I don't know what he thinks. And then there's that idiot, Tyler. I don't think that man has enough brains to come in out of the rain, so how is he going to care for two little girls?"

"How do Jake and Tyler get along?"

"Who the hell knows? I think they saw each other for some holidays, but I doubt they ever spent any time together other than that. Jake just broke up with Vicky after all those years together. I don't understand that either. What's the matter with him that he can't settle down? Vicky was very nice too. They would have made a great couple."

"Yes, Dad, I am well aware you disapprove. Can you just let Jake live his life without feeling your constant disapproval?"

"I would have been able to do that except for the fact that now he's the Guardian of Megan and Kristin. A fine kettle of fish.

"Sheryl, I want you to be the Guardian for the girls. You're their aunt and it's a much better fit than Jake and Tyler. You and Mike are a great couple, and you'd provide the girls with a much more normal home life. They'd have a real mother and father, like they're supposed to."

Sheryl was happy her father couldn't see her face at the other end of the phone, because she was rolling her eyes. Her father was the poster child for stereotypes.

"Dad, if Jackie had wanted Mike and me to be the Guardians for the girls, she could have named us. She didn't. I love Jackie and the girls, but the truth of the matter is that we haven't seen much of each other in the past few years. I very much regret that now. Megan and Kristin don't know us very well. They probably know Jake and Tyler a lot better and that's why she named them. Plus, I imagine that they wanted to have someone represent each side of the family. If you think about it that way, it makes a lot more sense."

Eddie couldn't contain himself any further. Even though Sheryl was presenting a rational argument, he was not in the mood for reason. He just didn't want his two granddaughters raised by two men. Period, end of argument. It was not the way the world was supposed to be. He lost his daughter in a tragic car crash, and that was not how the world was supposed to be. Now this insane choice.

He wanted to scream at Sheryl that she couldn't be this stupid, but he also realized that she was his best hope, and he didn't want to alienate her. He was going to scream, but somehow stopped himself.

"Will you at least call your brother and see what he says? That he's not saying much makes me suspicious that he doesn't like this idea very much. He gave your mother some bullshit excuse that he's waiting for the Court to appoint him as the Guardian before he takes over. She bought it. Well, I'm not buying it. I think he will be more forthcoming with you than with me."

Eddie's tone softened and Sheryl heard the pain in his voice. "Please, Sheryl, please call him."

"Okay, Dad, I'll call him, but just to see how he's doing and kind of get how he's seeing things. Don't forget, he lost Jackie, too. He's got to be feeling that loss as well. I'm not asking him about my becoming the Guardian."

She thought she heard Eddie take a breath at the other end of the phone as if he were going to say something, but then stopped. After a pause, she heard him say okay and nothing else.

When they hung up, Sheryl sat at her desk for a for a few minutes and mulled over the conversation in her head. She felt the guilt wash over her like a shower. She could have been a better sister to Jackie and a better aunt to Megan and Kristin. She could have made more of an effort. It wasn't as if she and Jackie fought or didn't get along. They simply drifted apart and let distance do the rest. For God's sake, she lived in Orlando, practically within spitting distance to Kissimmee, where Disney World was located. How come she never invited them to come? Or did they come to Disney World and never let her know they were coming? Sheryl thought she had a handle on her grief when the funeral was over, and she came home. But now sitting at her desk all by herself, she wept more than she had when she heard the news of Jackie's death and more than at the funeral.

Chapter 10

Megan was the younger of the two girls by three years. She was smaller in stature than Kristin, even considering their ages. Megan's hair was a sandy brown color, with green eyes. Kristin's hair was darker. Megan did not have the body of an athlete like her sister, and she was quieter and more introspective. Neither her parents, grandparents or aunts or uncles were artistic, so everyone was a little surprised when Megan expressed an interest in drawing and painting.

Jackie and Blake had given both girls music lessons. Kristin was indifferent to taking the lessons, and there had been more than a few nights of crying when she didn't want to practice the piano. She made half- hearted attempts to practice only because she was being forced to. One night Jackie was in the kitchen making dinner while Kristin was being forced to practice. Jackie thought that the piece sounded much better than normal. She was about to congratulate herself on having Kristin persevere and show how well she was doing, when she watched Kristin play. To Jackie's surprise, she found Megan playing the piano and the girls laughing hysterically thinking that they were fooling her.

That was the night the light bulb went on in Jackie's head that she had to stop trying to force the square peg into the round hole. The "piano caper" as Jackie fondly called it in her own mind,

32

cinched it that she could stop throwing away money on piano lessons for Kristin, and could save herself from the nightly battles around practicing. She had wanted to expose both girls to a broad array of experiences thinking that they could choose what they each liked. She didn't realize that it was going to be such an ordeal to get either of them to do the things they disliked.

Jackie started both girls with tennis within a few months of each other. Since Kristin had taken to it so well and loved it so much, Jackie thought she would let Megan try it at a younger age. Megan was all excited that she was going to take tennis lessons, because she kept hearing from Kristin how much she loved it. It thrilled Megan that she could pick out her own tennis racquet, which of course had to be shocking pink. She then could pick out two tennis outfits, since the pro shop was having a half-price sale. So far, so good.

Then came the day of the first tennis lesson. Jackie sat unobtrusively near the court with her tablet in hand, pretending to read it, but surreptitiously watching the lesson. The pro was a young woman with a bubbly personality who clearly was excited about the game and wanted to convey her love of tennis to the three little girls standing in front of her. She showed them the proper grip of the racquet, and the difference between the forehand and the backhand. She let them each bounce the bright yellow tennis ball to get the feel and then showed each one how to bounce the ball and hit it over the net. The two other girls got the hang of it quickly and could soon get the ball over the net from about mid-court. Megan whiffed at the ball several times, before she could even make contact with the ball and racquet. Getting the ball over the net seemed an obstacle too great for Megan, even though the other two girls could do it.

The pro didn't want to let Megan get frustrated, so she suggested that Megan just throw the ball over the net so that she could experience some sense of success. After about ten tosses, Megan could toss the ball over the net, to cheering from the pro, the two other girls and the people on the sidelines. Then the pro said that she would lob a few to each girl to hit back to her. Once again, Megan whiffed at the ball and never made contact. Since the other two girls were making contact standing still, then the pro hit the lobs to them so that they had to run a little to hit the ball. The other two girls adjusted and could return a few shots. Not Megan. She kept trying and missing.

As the lesson was nearing its conclusion, it was once again Megan's turn to hit the ball the pro lobbed to her. As she ran for the ball, no one was sure if she tripped over her own feet or her own shoelaces, but she went flying and landed on the court. The flying through the air was the most athletic thing that Megan had done all day, so once everyone ascertained that she wasn't hurt, they complimented her on the dive through the air.

When the lesson was over, and the girls went to get a drink, the pro suggested to Jackie that perhaps Megan should take an individual lesson, so that she could devote her full time to Megan. Two more private tennis lessons ensued with only marginal success. At the start of the first private lesson, it surprised the pro to see Kristin with Jackie and Megan. She was even more surprised that Megan and Kristin were sisters, since she didn't teach Kristin, but knew she was a good junior player. Apparently, there was a "tennis gene" that only one girl inherited.

The next sport which Megan tried when she gave up tennis was basketball. Jackie thought that a group sport might suit Megan better, since she had teammates who could help her out. Blake had suggested basketball in part because the ball was a lot bigger and harder to miss. The size of the ball seemed to have nothing to do with Megan's ability to miss. She was equally adept at missing no matter the size of the ball. She enjoyed bouncing the basketball and became okay with doing that, but not with dribbling the ball and running on the court. Megan's basketball career came to an even more abrupt end than her tennis career. She was playing at the weeklong summer basketball camp, and when jumping for a rebound, she missed it entirely and the basketball hit her squarely on the bridge of her nose. Poor Megan was stunned by the shot to the nose, and the blood. By the time Jackie arrived at the site of the basketball camp after the call from the director, Megan had an ice pack on her face and an ever increasingly swollen nose. When they got to the emergency room, she had the beginnings of two shiners under her eyes. Fortunately, not a broken nose, the ER doctor said.

The next day when Jackie went to do some shopping, she took Megan with her, since Megan was no longer going to basketball camp. They passed a store called A. I. Friedman's which had all kinds of painting and craft supplies. Megan wanted to go in, and that's when Jackie saw where Megan's talents were probably going to lie. Megan was already in awe of the craft supplies and the paints, and Jackie could see she had an eye for color. Despite herself and telling herself not to drop a bundle in this store, Jackie and Megan walked out of A. I. Friedman's with several hundred dollars' worth of art supplies. At first, Jackie thought she was just feeling guilty that Megan had a bulbous nose and two black eyes and wanted to make things up to her, but in a few days, she was impressed with what this little girl painted all by herself, and with no lessons.

Chapter 11

Sheryl didn't share the conversation she had with her father with Mike, but she kept turning it over and over in her own mind. She wanted to be certain what she wanted before she heard Mike's opinion. The two distressing questions in her mind were, why did Jackie and Blake name Jake and Tyler as the Guardians over her and Mike, who on the face of things certainly presented a much more stable and "normal" environment for the girls? The second question was did she have the right to try to override Jackie and Blake's wishes because she thought she and Mike were better suited to raising two little girls? Would that be better for them?

The following morning, after most of a sleepless night, when Mike went to play golf, she called Jake. Jake and Sheryl spoke occasionally, so it would not be that strange for her to call him, especially since the recent tragedy. Jake answered on the second ring, which Sheryl thought was a good thing. She surmised from her father's conversation, that Jake was probably avoiding calls from their parents.

"Hey, Jake, how are you? None of us is too good after all that's happened, so I wanted to check in with you."

"Not too good is a large understatement. I can't believe Jackie and Blake are gone. It doesn't seem real to me, no matter how many times I say it out loud or think it to myself."

"I know. It made me realize that our days here on this earth are really uncertain. I can't believe my little sister is dead. Dead is an awful word."

"You can say that again. They were both so full of life; it just doesn't seem possible that they're gone."

"What's happening with you and the girls? Did you and Tyler take care of them yet?"

There was a long pause on Jake's end of the conversation. Sheryl took that as a bad sign. She let the silence linger a few more seconds, even though she wanted to jump in and fill it.

"No, we haven't started doing anything yet. Mom and Dad are there, and I think it's for the best until we get appointed as the Guardians. Mom's good at taking care of things. And people."

"Why is that for the best? They named you and Tyler as the Guardians. That's what Jackie and Blake wanted, right?"

"Yeah, it's what they wanted, but I'm not sure it's what I want. I wish Jackie and Blake had spoken to us about this before they named us as Guardians. Maybe they never expected to die."

"Would you have refused if they had asked you in advance?"

"I dunno. But at least I would have had time to think about it. What the hell do I know about being a parent? Nothing, nada, zippo."

"Jake, look, none of us knows anything about being a parent until we are parents for the first time. Do you think Mike and I knew what we were doing with Brian? No, of course not. I'm sure we made many mistakes, but look, he survived and even thrived. He's a great young man now. I can't believe he's graduated from college."

"Yeah, but at least you got Brian as a baby. These are two girls, not babies. They'll know if I'm making a mess of things. And to make matters worse, I have to deal with that flake, Tyler. I swear I don't know if he's stoned half the time." The agitation in his voice was palpable.

Sheryl was about to say something when Jake continued. "I really don't know what Jackie was thinking naming us and I'm not sure either of us, or both of us together, is suitable for this job. I don't know if I can do this. Jackie must have had some friends who were better suited to this than Tyler and I. Shit, why didn't she name you and Mike, for God's sake?"

"Jake, I hear you, but we have our two nieces to think about and what is best for them. Jackie and Blake made a very specific plan in their Wills, so it seems that they didn't just shoot from the hip. That wouldn't be like Jackie in any instance, but especially so where the girls are concerned.

"I'm asking you something and I haven't even discussed this with Mike yet. You need to level with me. Would you want to resign as the Guardian and have Mike and me take over? I'm not trying to insult you, but I'm hearing a lot of negative talk from you."

Again, another pregnant pause from Jake. Sheryl waited on her end of the phone. Maybe she had insulted him.

"I feel bad. I feel I'm letting Jackie down, but I don't think I can do this."

"So do you want me to speak to Mike about this and tell him what you just said to me?"

"Yeah, I think you guys should do this, not me."

"Okay, I will speak to him and let you know. What about Tyler?"

"What about Tyler?"

Despite herself, Sheryl let out a sigh. Jake couldn't be this dense. "Tyler is the Co-Guardian with you. What do you think he will want to do about this? He certainly will have a say."

Chapter 12

After Sheryl's conversation with Jake, she poured herself a very large glass of iced tea and sat down to consider the situation. Maybe she should have poured herself a big glass of wine or scotch instead, but certainly not this early in the morning. If Jake really didn't want to be the Guardian, then maybe it was incumbent on her to step up and become the Guardian. She tried to think back to when Brian was a little boy and what would have happened to him if she and Mike had been killed in a car or plane crash. She was virtually certain that she would not have named Jake as Brian's guardian. It would have been a close call whether they would have named Mike's sister or Jackie. As she thought about it, she realized that they would have had two good choices between those two people, but she thought that maybe Jake would have been the third choice, if at all.

Another problem was that she hadn't spent much time with Kristin and Megan. The distance between New York and Florida had contributed to that. By the same token, she didn't think that Tyler or Jake had spent any considerable amount of time with the girls either. Maybe some holidays, but she was certain that neither man had ever taken the girls anywhere on their own.

Then there was the problem of having to move to New York. Apparently, the two Wills had said explicitly that they wanted the girls to remain living in their current house. Brian was out of college and was about to take a job in Atlanta, so he wouldn't be living home anymore. They could conduct their business anywhere, and in fact, they often never met their clients in person. They could work from New York without damaging their business.

Sheryl also believed that she would probably spend more time in New York and Mike could go back and forth to Florida if he wanted to. They could take the girls to Florida during vacations and get them to like Florida for an eventual move there. She even thought they could bribe the girls a bit by Disney World, Sea World, water skiing, parasailing and a host of other warm weather activities. She knew Kristin was very athletic and Mike would love to teach yet another kid how to play golf. She also knew that Westchester County had some of the best golf courses in the country, so this might be another inducement for Mike, if they had to move to New York. She hadn't even mentioned any of this to Mike, so she might get way ahead of herself.

Mike returned from playing golf to find Sheryl in front of her computer ostensibly working. What he didn't know was that Sheryl had been looking at private country clubs in Westchester which were renown for having outstanding golf courses. Just a little extra ammunition if she needed it.

"Hey, honey, anything going on?" Sheryl mentally rolled her eyes but was careful actually not to roll her eyes. In her mind, she answered, "You should only know, and shortly you will."

"How did you play today?"

"Pretty well. Shot an 85. I won a whole five dollars. Not about the money; it's about the bragging rights. It really was muggy hot on the course today. How about I take a shower and we grab some food and go out on the boat for a few hours later?"

"Good idea. I'll get the cooler. I made chicken salad and egg salad this morning. I can't think of eating anything heavy in this heat."

"Anybody get in touch with us on the York deal? Any movement from anyone?"

"Nope, not yet, but he's asking for a lot of money and that gave the employer pause. We might have to talk to him to lower his expectations if he wants to get this job. He may have to compromise." She had hoped to get a lot of work done this morning while Mike was playing golf, but every time she tried to tackle something on the computer, she was distracted and stared at the computer screen without comprehending what she was reading.

Sheryl wasn't sure if she should broach the guardianship idea while they were on the boat together. On the one hand, she would have Mike's uninterrupted attention, but if he didn't like the idea, they were trapped together in close quarters. She made sure they also had lots of beer. Enough beer and winning five dollars from his friends would put him in a good mood.

Sheryl had decided about ninety-five percent that becoming the Guardian was the right thing to do. There were a few lingering doubts in her mind, but she thought that was to be expected on a decision this important. She didn't want to call her parents to tell them until she spoke to Mike. She wasn't sure what she would do if Mike really opposed the idea, but usually she could bring him around to any decision with a little time and persuasion. Mike was also very family conscious, and she thought that might well be the trump card. She would tell him that there were two little orphaned girls who needed parents.

The more Sheryl thought about it, the more she felt an old familiar ache. She had always wanted a daughter. After Brian was born, they waited a few years to try again. Somehow, she could never become pregnant again and she sort of suppressed her feelings. But now she knew she still wanted a daughter. And now maybe she might have two.

Chapter 13

Megan had seemed out of sorts all day. She picked at dinner and Gloria did not feel any need to force Megan to eat if she didn't want to. Megan said she felt fine, but just wasn't hungry. Eddie was about to say something about eating, but Gloria gave him an "I'm going to turn you to stone" look that shut him up. Gloria asked Megan if she would like her to make some scrambled eggs or perhaps some of her famous chicken soup, but again Megan refused. Gloria just let it go.

"Why don't you go inside and watch something on TV, and we'll be in shortly. There isn't much to clean up from dinner. Kristin, you can go too, when you're finished eating and then Grandpa and I will be in. Maybe we can play cards or another game in a few minutes."

Megan nodded, got up from the table and silently walked off to the den. Her body language said it all. She looked so unhappy. Tonight, Kristin seemed in better spirits, but they alternated about which one was miserable on any given day.

When Kristin left the room, Gloria shook her head and said in a hushed voice, "I hope Amanda Hunter gets back to me quickly with the names of the psychologists, because I think we have a real problem on our hands. It's sinking in that their parents are gone, and they're having a hard time adjusting. One day one girl is okay, and the next day she's not. We haven't yet had a day when they both are upset. I'm really dreading that one. My heart breaks thinking we lost Jackie, but for these two sweet girls, I can't fathom what the loss of both parents feels like."

At first, Eddie had been hesitant to say that the girls should see a psychologist, but he couldn't deny what he was seeing, and things were getting worse. Just as he was about to answer Gloria, his cell phone rang, and it was Sheryl. Gloria knew he had been lobbying Sheryl to consider becoming the Guardian, but neither Eddie nor Gloria had any idea if Sheryl had spoken to Jake. Jake had been avoiding his calls, so Eddie wasn't sure if Sheryl had fared any better. Both Eddie and Gloria thought Jake certainly hadn't been around or acting like he was interested in taking the reins.

Eddie got up from the table and walked into the kitchen which was farther away from the family room where the girls were, and therefore almost impossible to hear what was being said in the phone conversation. The conversation lasted a few minutes, and Gloria said a few silent prayers that Sheryl would say yes. At first, when she heard what was in the two Wills, Gloria was very surprised and skeptical, but she was also somewhat hopeful that it could work out. But as the days passed, Gloria just couldn't see Jake and Tyler handling this cauldron of boiling emotions with the girls. Sheryl and Mike had done a good job with Brian, and Gloria was proud of her only grandson. Sheryl and Mike's influence and values had a good deal to do with how well Brian had turned out.

When Eddie returned to the dining room, Gloria couldn't read the expression on Eddie's face. Eddie picked up a few plates off the table and nodded to Gloria to follow him into the kitchen. When they got into the kitchen, Eddie closed the door and told Gloria that Sheryl said she had spoken to Jake and that he didn't want to be the Guardian, didn't think he was equipped to do it, nor had he ever been consulted by Jackie and Blake. Mike was not wholeheartedly in favor of it but understood that there really wasn't anyone else who was suitable. Sheryl wanted to fly to New York and meet with David Brennan in person about the situation and she didn't want her parents to mention anything to the girls until she had a better handle on the legal situation. Sheryl correctly assessed the situation in that she didn't want to put any more uncertainty in the girls' lives and upset them more. She wanted Eddie to change the appointment with David Brennan so that she would come up and meet with him as well.

Eddie clearly was happy with Sheryl's decision, because it was what he had been pushing for. When he told Gloria, it surprised her with how relieved she felt. She felt a weight come off her shoulders. That relief was a little short lived because Eddie told her that Jake hadn't spoken to Tyler about their both resigning and didn't have any idea what Tyler thought. Tyler was the wild card in many senses, and no one really had their finger on his pulse for this situation.

Eddie and Gloria finished cleaning up and went into the family room to find Megan and Kristin watching Wheel of Fortune. Gloria purposely sat next to Megan on the couch and put her arm around her. After a few more spins on the wheel, Gloria looked down at Megan who had snuggled up to her and found the tears running down Megan's face. No sobs, just pathetic looking tears.

Chapter 14

Later that night, when the girls were in bed, Megan got up and went into Kristin's room. Megan got into the bed with Kristin and hugged her. Normally, Kristin was a heavy sleeper, but lately she had been waking up several times each night. Usually, playing tennis exhausted her and slept soundly, but that had not been the case since her parents' deaths. When Megan got into bed with her, it woke Kristin up.

"What are you doing here?"

"I'm scared," came the miserable response.

"Scared of what?"

"Everything. Scared that Mom and Dad are not here. Scared that Grandma will go away. Will she die, too?"

Kristin normally could shrug off a lot of things, but Megan hit a nerve when she asked about Grandma dying. Before Jackie's death, Kristin had overheard Jackie talking to Blake about Gloria's health. Kristin could tell from her mother's tone of voice that her mother was worried. Kristin didn't get all the details, nor did she understand all of what she heard. Her mother said that Grammy had congestive heart failure. Those terms didn't really have a meaning for Kristin, so she looked up the words. By the time she looked up the word congestive, she had forgotten what it was. When she looked up the word, she saw the word "conjugal," which sort of sounded like the word Jackie had used. When she read the definition of the word "conjugal," it didn't make any sense to Kristin. Since that time, she thought that perhaps "conjugal heart failure" meant that Grandma didn't like Grandpa anymore and perhaps headed for a divorce. Now it was even scarier that Grandma was sick -and they might get divorced. Could two more important people leave them?

"Yeah, I guess it is pretty scary. Grammy really loves us, so I don't think she'll go away. Plus, I heard her tell someone she was really sad about Mom's dying and that she was so glad she had us."

"If Grammy goes away, who will take care of us?" Now Megan was on the verge of tears and her voice trembled.

"Well, it can't be Grandpa. He can't do anything for us except drive us places. He can microwave stuff, but that's about it. He told Grammy that he would do the laundry the other day when she went to rest, but he called me in to the laundry room to show him how to do it. He didn't want me to tell Grammy that he needed help. The washing machine isn't very hard. You put in the laundry detergent and push a button. That's it.

"You and I gotta stick together on this. We have to listen to everything the grown-ups say and pay attention. Sometimes they're talking really quietly or even whispering and they sort of stop when one of us comes into the room."

"Well, what are they talking about that they don't want us to know?"

"That's just it, stupid. We have to find out, because it probably has to do with us."

Now Megan was crying. "So is Grammy gonna die or are they sending us away to an orphanage?"

"How do you know about orphanages?"

"I saw Oprah on TV. She opened an orphanage for kids whose parents had died in Africa."

"Yeah, well that's in Africa and they used to have them in England. I read a kid's version of this book called Oliver Twist and he was an orphan, but that was hundreds of years ago. I don't think they have orphanages in the United States anymore."

Despite her bravado with Megan, Kristin now wasn't so sure of herself that there weren't orphanages in the United States. Tomorrow she would have to Google it to be sure. She thought she might try to find some way to ask Mr. Reece. He was a great source of information, and he always told her the truth. But suppose she was wrong and there were orphanages? Would her Grandparents send them to an orphanage? Now Kristin was upset, too.

Kristin overheard Eddie talking on the phone and making an appointment for him and Aunt Sheryl. That meant that Aunt Sheryl was coming to New York. Kristin didn't know why Aunt Sheryl was coming up from Florida. The only time in a long time that she had seen Aunt Sheryl and Uncle Mike was at the wake and funeral.

She especially liked Uncle Mike because he knew about sports, and it wasn't only a little knowledge. When he talked to her, he wasn't just asking questions of a kid to be polite. He asked questions with knowledge of tennis, and he said Brian had played tennis in high school on the varsity. Then after the funeral, he brought Brian over to talk to her about playing on the team. Kristin thought that was very cool. She was still two years away from high school, but the thought of playing on the junior varsity and the varsity made her want to work even harder at tennis. It was just that since her parents died, ` she found she had little concentration and energy.

She hoped he was coming with Aunt Sheryl. Kristin didn't know what questions she could and couldn't ask her grandparents. She could see that they were upset too, but it was very scary for her not to know what they were talking about. She decided not to tell Megan about Aunt Sheryl, because she didn't know if this was going to make Megan more upset. Megan would have more questions than Kristin had answers.

Chapter 15

Sheryl stepped out of the terminal and the cold and damp hit her in the face. She had lived in the south, and most recently in Florida for a long time now, so that she had forgotten how cold it could be in New York, even in the fall. It was penetrating cold, in a way not the same as in central Florida which could occasionally experience frost in the winter.

She hadn't expected to come back to Westchester County Airport so soon. In fact, she hadn't expected to come back to this airport at all. It was a refreshing change from the airport in Orlando, which had now become crowded at virtually all times of the year.

The limo driver pulled right up to the curb in front of her, and he bounced out of the car to take her suitcase and put it in the trunk. Sheryl was originally going to stay in a hotel, but her parents had insisted that there was plenty of room in the house, and that it would give them a chance to see her, since the wake and funeral had been one big blur. It would also give her a chance to see the girls in their own home away from the stress of the funeral home. Gloria and Eddie thought that it was best, for the time being, if they only told the girls that Sheryl was here for business, and not tell them yet the true nature of her visit.

It was mid-afternoon when she arrived at the house and the girls were in school. In the few weeks since the funeral, Sheryl thought her parents had aged, especially her mother. Gloria's color looked bad, and Eddie looked tired with dark circles under his eyes. Sheryl surmised it was a combination of grief over Jackie's death and trying to manage a household with two active kids, which was a task too large for people of their age. Sheryl had a flash of anger over Jackie and Blake's decision about guardianship and a much larger flash of anger at Jake who had made himself conspicuously absent. To Sheryl it was total bullshit that he wanted to wait until the Surrogate's Court appointed him as the Guardian before he would step in. He should have been there helping with the girls in whatever way he could, getting to know their schedules, and taking some burden off her parents. Had her parents always given Jake a free pass on the things he didn't want to do? She didn't know much about Tyler, but the press on him was not good either.

Gloria and Eddie had waited for her for lunch and so she stowed her suitcase and raincoat in a bedroom upstairs, washed her hands and put on a cheerful face before she came back into the kitchen. They made some small talk about her flight and the weather. Gloria wanted to know about Brian's new job and how he was doing. Sheryl guessed Gloria had told Eddie to cool it about anything serious until after lunch, because otherwise she thought that would have been the first thing out of his mouth.

When they had finished lunch and were lingering over a second cup of coffee, Eddie broached the subject. "We have an appointment with David Brennan tomorrow morning. I gave him a heads up about what we want to discuss."

Sheryl nodded in agreement. "Are Jake and Tyler coming, too?"

"I know Jake is coming, but I don't know about Tyler."

Sheryl let out an exasperated sigh. "Well then I think you or Jake needs to make sure he is coming. This entire plan will fall apart if Tyler isn't on board with it. I told the same thing to Jake when I discussed this with him on the phone. What's the problem? Why is everyone pussyfooting around Tyler?"

"No one seems to know what Tyler wants."

"Then how the hell are you going to know what he's thinking if you don't ask him? We need to know one way or the other. This will be a vastly different scenario if he says he agrees to resign than if he wants to stay on as a Co-Guardian. Hasn't this crossed anyone's mind?" Now the annoyance in Sheryl's voice was very apparent.

Eddie just sat there looking unhappy, when Gloria spoke up. "You're right, Sheryl. Just as we haven't seen much of Jake since the funerals, we have seen nothing of Tyler. If he wanted to be a part of the girls' lives, he could have come around."

"Now don't take this as a criticism, but did anyone ever tell him he's welcome to come by?"

Gloria and Eddie looked at each other and shrugged. Then they looked back at Sheryl.

"Then I suggest you tell Jake to get off his lazy ass and make a phone call to Tyler. Right now! We need to know before tomorrow morning when we see David Brennan."

Sheryl stood up to clear the table and walked over to the sink with the dirty dishes. Her back was to the door. As if on cue, the back door opened and Megan and Kristin tumbled through the door with backpacks and coats, a jumble of arms and legs. Megan came through the door first. Sheryl had the same build, height and hair color as Jackie.

Megan took one fast look at Sheryl and screamed, "Mommy!" When Sheryl turned around and Megan saw it was not her mother, her lip quivered, and she dissolved into tears. Sheryl was so shocked by the reaction, but she ran forward and scooped up Megan in her arms.

Chapter 16

The following morning Sheryl and Eddie arrived at David Brennan's office to find Jake sitting in the conference room texting away on his phone. Jake got up and walked around the conference room table to hug Sheryl. Sheryl could feel her mixed emotions toward her brother. While Jake was usually responsible, sometimes Sheryl thought he acted like an adolescent. This was one of them. Instead of stepping up, he had retreated under the two excuses that Jackie and Blake had never formally spoken to him about the guardianship, and second that he didn't want to take control until the Court had formally appointed him as the Guardian.

Sheryl felt that these were two bullshit excuses, yet it nagged at her that Jackie and Blake saw something in Jake and in Tyler which made them name the two men as Co-Guardians. What was it that Jackie and Blake saw in them that perhaps was being missed by everyone now? Jackie and Blake were hardly reckless, and certainly not with the girls.

Sheryl was not in the mood for double-talk this morning, so she asked, "Is Tyler coming?"

Jake said he had left a message on Tyler's cell phone, and he had texted him. "Yeah, but is he coming?" Sheryl persisted in an attempt not to let Jake wriggle out of a difficult situation yet again.

"He texted me back a yes, so I assume he will be here. He's not exactly known for his punctuality."

"Okay, so let's give him a few more minutes and then call him to see where he is. I'm really not in the mood for games."

David Brennan walked into the conference room holding a file which had increased in size substantially in the last few weeks. His expression was grim, and he introduced himself to Sheryl and extended his hand. He already knew Jake and Eddie and shook their hands as well. He put the file down on the table and poured himself half a cup of coffee from the carafe in the center of the table.

"Well, folks, I just got an e-mail from Tyler which said he's not coming to the office this morning. He said that if Jake wants to resign as the Co-Guardian that he will act as the sole Guardian. Kind of amazing to me that he doesn't want to meet Sheryl or hear what she has to say on the subject."

There was a kind of collective groan from the three other people in the room, as the words David uttered sank in.

"So where does this leave us?" Sheryl asked.

David responded with a shrug and a more muted response. "There are several permutations depending on what you want to do, Jake. Do you want to stay on as the Co-Guardian, or do you want to withdraw that part of the Petition to the Court?"

Jake didn't answer right away and looked down at the table and then at Sheryl. "I dunno, this changes everything."

Before anyone could say anything else, David jumped in. "Before we go any further with this, I think I should give you time to talk about this among yourselves. Second, I think I may be in a potential conflict of interest situation here. I am the attorney for the Estate, and if there is going to be litigation between Jake and Tyler, I may have to recuse myself.

"Once I got this e-mail from Tyler this morning, I took the liberty of calling a colleague of mine who does a lot of litigation. His name is Matt Westfield, and he's an excellent attorney. He will come over to the office this morning, if you want to talk to him. You obviously don't have to meet with him if you prefer to find someone else. I just thought you might want a recommendation. Or you can meet with him and decide if you like him and want to retain him. Why don't I go back to my office, and you can discuss this and let me know what you want to do. Take your time. No one needs this conference room, so it's all yours."

When David left the room, Jake said, "That's too bad, because I really like David."

"What do you want to do, Jake? Do you want to stay on as the Co-Guardian?"

"I'd rather you were the Guardian. That was the entire plan. But Tyler is throwing a monkey wrench into this whole thing."

Sheryl asked, "What do you make of the fact that he said he would come to the meeting and then just e-mails David that he's not coming, but would stay as the sole Guardian?"

Jake responded, "It seems kind of erratic to me, but then again, he seemed genuinely surprised, but also happy to be named as the Co-Guardian. "

"Have you two actually talked to each other about what you are going to do or how you are going to take care of the girls since you first learned what was in the Wills?"

"No, we haven't talked."

Now Eddie, who had been quiet, interjected. "Jake, I think you better get together in person with Tyler and try to talk some sense into him about this. I don't think the two of you can take care of two little girls, and I sure as hell don't want my two granddaughters raised by that guy alone. You gotta step up to the plate, son, and get him to agree. This is vitally important."

Jake was nodding in agreement. "I'll try, I'll really try. Maybe I should just go over to his house unannounced and talk to him."

Sheryl said, "In case you don't have success with Tyler, I think we should tell David to have this Matt Westfield come to the office now to talk to us."

"Maybe I should try him now on the phone asking why he didn't show up, while we're asking for Matt to come to meet us."

Chapter 17

While they were waiting for Matt to come to the office, Jake walked out of the conference room and into a second smaller conference room. He dialed Tyler's cell phone number fully expecting it to go to voice mail. It surprised Jake when Tyler answered the call on the second ring.

"Hey, Tyler, it's Jake. It surprised me to hear from David Brennan that you weren't coming to the meeting this morning. What happened?"

"Nothing happened. I told David that if you don't want to be the Co-Guardian, that's okay with me. But I'm going to stay on. It's what Jackie and Blake wanted, and I plan to honor what they wanted. It's okay with me if you want to bail, man, but I'm staying on."

"Look, Tyler, my sister Sheryl is willing to be the Guardian. She's willing to move up here from Florida with her husband. They have a son who just graduated from college. They know how to raise kids. We don't know a thing about doing it."

"There are millions of people who raise kids. They all can't be that much smarter than us. Anyway, how hard can it be? You can resign if you want, but I'm staying on."

Jake was silent at the other end of the phone for a moment. "Okay, I'll tell my sister. I'll be in touch. Bye."

Jake slumped down into one of the conference room chairs and let out a low whistle. It was one thing to hear from David that he received an e-mail from Tyler, but quite another to hear the words directly from Tyler's mouth. Jake walked back slowly to the large conference room where Sheryl and Eddie were sitting.

"Did you get him on the phone?"

"Yeah. He says that I can do what I want, but he's staying on. He says millions of people raise kids and it can't be that hard."

There was another collective groan from Eddie and Sheryl. They sat there in stunned silence each lost in their own thoughts.

Sheryl got up to go the Ladies room. She knocked and went into David's office to ask him to call Matt Westfield to come to the office and meet them. She also called Mike to tell him of the latest developments. Mike had very little to say in response. Sheryl wasn't expecting much of a response from him. She was stunned, and she relayed the new facts to Mike. She told him she would call him back after their meeting with Matt Westfield.

Within a few minutes after she returned to the conference room, the door opened, and David led a tall thin man into the conference room. The impeccably dressed Matt Westfield arrived in a dark blue suit with a light blue shirt and bright blue tie. He was nice looking, but not stunningly so until he smiled, and then his whole countenance lit up. That was the winning smile that was flashed to a jury and made him seem to be Mr. Sincere.

After the introductions, David excused himself and left the conference room. Matt opened the conversation and said David had filled him in on the phone, but that he wanted to hear from Jake and Sheryl personally. Jake told Matt about the latest conversation with Tyler. Matt took out a legal pad from his briefcase and took notes as he asked his own questions.

After Matt finished with his questions, then Sheryl, Eddie and Jake asked all their questions. An hour had flown by since Matt's arrival, and then he explained what he thought was the best plan. Jake and Sheryl agreed to sign a Retainer Agreement with Matt, and he told them he would call them in a few days to come to his office to review the documents to be submitted to the Surrogate's Court.

Chapter 18

Three days after their initial meeting with Matt, Sheryl and Jake met in his office. Matt had explained the options to them and that it was a long shot. Matt had prepared a motion to the Court using an Order to Show Cause. By using this vehicle, Matt could get the case into Court quickly and get a quick read from the Surrogate if he viewed favorably Sheryl's chance of becoming the Co-Guardian.

The supporting documents to the Court said that Jake would resign as the Co-Guardian if the Court would appoint Sheryl as the Co-Guardian instead. Matt also wanted to get some indication whether the Court would ultimately entertain the idea of letting Sheryl become the sole Guardian and get rid of Tyler. Matt pointed out the enormous problem was that Jackie and Blake had not named Sheryl in any capacity in their Wills. She might well appear as an interloper in the eyes of the Court.

Matt hoped that a conservative Surrogate Court judge might be skeptical of naming two unrelated men as the Co-Guardians of two little girls, especially if one man was willing to resign in favor of his sister who was an aunt to the girls and presented a more stable home life with her husband. From the description of Tyler presented to Matt, he hoped Tyler would show up in Court wearing rumpled and dirty clothes as he had done at the wake and funeral and at the meeting at David Brennan's office.

Matt also hoped he could convince the Surrogate to appoint a psychiatrist to evaluate what was in the girls' best interest by interviewing not only the girls but also Jake, Tyler and Sheryl. Matt felt that the longer he could keep the case before the Surrogate's Court, the more traction he could get with the Court and make the Court more sympathetic to his clients' view.

Matt hand delivered the papers to the Court and then waited for a date to appear in Court.

The Court set the return date on Tuesday of the following week at 9:30 AM., just one week after the Court received the papers. Matt saw this as a good thing that the Surrogate's Court viewed this as an important issue to be dealt with quickly concerning the welfare of the two girls. They were all hoping that Tyler would get cold feet when confronted with a definite Court date in the very near future. Matt was also hoping that the prospect of having to retain an attorney would also be a deterrent.

Chapter 19

Tuesday started out as a chilly morning. Matt, Jake, Sheryl and Eddie emerged from the stairs of the parking garage and took the walk across the plaza to the Westchester County Courthouse where the Surrogate's Court was located. No matter how beautiful the day, the plaza was a wind tunnel and more than one unsuspecting person who didn't have their papers secured in a briefcase or folder, had their papers blown across the plaza when a gust of wind came up.

Matt went through security in the Courthouse using his Secure Pass, which allowed attorneys to bypass the line and the metal detection. He waited on the other side of the metal detection station for Jake, Sheryl and Eddie to be cleared and then they proceeded to the bank of elevators to the eighteenth floor where the Surrogate's Courtroom was located. Gloria had declined to come to Court saying the walking was too much for her, and she didn't feel she was up to the stress of the situation in Court, especially if the decision might be an unfavorable one.

Since this was not a normal calendar day for the court, there was only one other case on before the Court. When they arrived, there were two groups of people sitting on opposite sides of the courtroom, presumably the two opponents and their attorneys on the other case. When Matt and company arrived in the courtroom,

Tyler was not there. None of them knew quite what to expect from him. Would he show up? Would he show up with an attorney? Matt told his assembled group that he thought perhaps he would get a call the day before the court appearance from an attorney saying he was representing Tyler, but that had not happened.

The door in the back of the courtroom opened and David Brennan came in carrying a hefty looking folder. He came over to the assembled group and shook everyone's hand, but then sat in a bench on the opposite side of the room. Jake was concerned by David's appearance and thought that David had somehow double crossed them and was representing Tyler. Matt quickly explained that David was solely representing the Estate and none of the litigants concerning the Co-Guardianship. The Court had also ordered his appearance as the attorney for the Estate.

At about 9:25 AM, another man came through the doors to the courtroom. He was wearing a dark suit, carried a briefcase and looked every inch the part of an attorney. Matt hesitated a moment about getting up and introducing himself to this gentleman, but then thought better of it. If this was Tyler's attorney, it was not someone that Matt was familiar with as an attorney in Westchester, nor was he a regular in the Surrogate's Court. Matt decided to wait him out, but if this man was Tyler's attorney, where was Tyler?

Chapter 20

At 9:30 AM, there was activity in the front of the courtroom as the court stenographer, and Chief Clerk came into the courtroom and took their seats near the bench where the Surrogate would sit. About two minutes later, the bailiff banged on the door near the bench and said in a booming voice, "All rise. The Surrogate's Court of the State of New York, County of Westchester, is now in session. The Honorable James Brevard presiding."

Everyone in the courtroom rose and Surrogate Brevard marched up the three steps to the bench and sat down. He then said, "Please be seated. Good morning. We only have two cases on this morning. The first is the Estate of Rheims."

With that, two of the attorneys on opposite sides of the aisle, jumped up and walked forward to the counsel tables. After each attorney had stated their name and who they represented, the Surrogate said, "Counselors, I have read the petition, the answer and the supporting affidavits. No need for you to repeat everything here, but I have some questions."

That case went on for about fifteen minutes with each attorney arguing the points of the case to the Surrogate, answering questions, and arguing with each other. Not quite a free for all, but close. Finally, the Surrogate was satisfied that he had the answers to his questions.

"Counselors, you will have my written decision on this matter. Thank you."

The attorneys gathered up their papers, exhibits, legal pads and briefcases and left the counsel tables. They walked to the back of the courtroom with their respective clients in tow. The Surrogate waited until they and all the commotion surrounding them left the courtroom before he called the next and only other case on for that morning.

"Next case is the Estates of Peterson." Matt Westfield, David Brennan and the mystery other attorney approached the bench and the same ritual ensued about putting appearances on the record as had happened on the prior case.

The Surrogate started by saying, "Counselors, this is a particularly tragic case. Both parents killed in a horrific car accident leaving behind two young children.

"Mr. Westfield, your client, who is an uncle to the two children, is willing to resign as the Co-Guardian and have his sister, who is the aunt of the children become the Guardian, if Mr. Peterson, who is also an uncle to the children on the decedent's father's side of the family, will resign as Co-Guardian as well. You have suggested both alternatives to the court. In one scenario, both uncles resign as Co-Guardians, and the aunt becomes the sole Guardian, and in the other, one uncle resigns and his sister replaces him as Co-Guardian. Is that a correct summary, Mr. Westfield?"

"Yes, Your Honor. We would obviously like Ms. Avery to be the sole Guardian. She is married and she and her husband would provide a stable home environment for the girls. Mr. and Mrs. Avery have raised a son, who recently graduated from Florida State University, cum laude. Mr. and Mrs. Avery will move back to Westchester if she is the Guardian, and she grew up in Westchester.

"Your Honor, we would also request that the Court order that the girls be examined by a psychiatrist to find out their preferences as to the Guardians, and we ask that all three candidates for Co-Guardians be examined as well."

Now Tyler's attorney jumped in. "Your Honor, I vehemently object to this."

"What, in particular are you objecting to, Mr. Markport?"

"Well, for starters, there is absolutely no reason not to honor the wishes of the decedents in naming their preferences in Co-Guardians as stated in their Last Wills and Testaments. The Petitioner has not offered one shred of evidence that either testator did not have testamentary capacity. If I am not mistaken, Mr. Brennan, who is standing right next to me prepared both Wills. You can ask him now about the testamentary capacity of the two decedents."

Mr. Markport almost didn't even take a breath before plowing on. "The two children are twelve and nine years old. It would be highly unusual to ask children that young about their preferences. Naming Guardians was a decision their parents made. In addition, a Court will usually not consult a child younger than fourteen years old.

"I also object to my client having to be interviewed by a psychiatrist. There are no allegations that my client has done anything untoward and should submit to a psychiatric exam. I would like to remind the Court that the decedents chose my client as one of the Co-Guardians. Ms. Avery is not even mentioned one time in the Wills in any capacity."

Matt Westfield knew his request for psychiatric evaluations was unusual. He was hoping to drag this matter out and hopefully Tyler would lose interest or run out of money. He was prepared for this argument. "Your Honor, Kristin is twelve and a half, and she's quite an articulate and bright young woman. Certainly, a child psychiatrist would know the right way to approach this to get Kristin's thoughts. There's no law that says a child can't be interviewed at twelve and a half. I don't think we should stand on ceremony and not do the right thing for these girls.

"As to Megan, maybe we should let the child psychiatrist decide about whether Megan understands enough about this to have input. This is just too important a matter for these two girls not to avail ourselves of every tool to do right by them."

The Surrogate seemed to nod in agreement with Matt's argument. Matt had a burst of hope that he had convinced the Surrogate of his position. But then the Surrogate veered off in a different direction.

"Mr. Westfield, you have not responded to the issue of testamentary capacity. I have directed Mr. Brennan to be here today, as the draftsman of the two Wills. I would like to take a brief recess and then come back and put Mr. Brennan on the witness stand. I would like to hear him testify as to his clients' capacity and if the testamentary formalities were observed when the Petersons executed their Wills. You will each have the opportunity to question him, and his answers will be under oath and preserved on the record. We will recess now for fifteen minutes and then come back."

Apparently, Tyler had slipped into the courtroom late as usual. He came in unnoticed while the oral arguments were at their hottest and everyone was focused on the front of the courtroom where the two attorneys were arguing.

Matt led his entourage out into the hallway at the recess and told them to stay put. He walked over to David Brennan and asked him if he had advance notice that he would be called upon to testify. David said he didn't know.

Matt then walked back to his group and said, "This is bad for us that David is going to testify. He's going to say that Jackie and Blake had capacity to execute their Wills, which they most probably did. For him to say that they didn't have testamentary capacity, would mean that he committed malpractice to let them sign the Wills.

"You see where this is going. If they had testamentary capacity, then they knew what they were doing in naming Tyler and Jake as the Co-Guardians. There's no reason for the Court not to honor that. Jake, you're going to have to decide if you want to stay on as a Co-Guardian. If you don't stay on as a Co-Guardian, I don't think the Court is going to go for the idea of Sheryl. If you resign, you are most probably leaving Tyler as the sole Guardian. "

That last sentence of Matt's seemed to land with a resounding thud, as everyone in the small-assembled group realized the implications of Matt's words.

"We can go back in and have the hearing with David on the witness stand, but it will not go well for us. I need to know what you want to do, Jake. If you want to stay on as the Co-Guardian, then I should say that to the Surrogate at the end of the testimony and before this matter concludes today. At least we will have a fallback position that you can live with."

Jake looked sick. Sheryl touched Jake on the arm and said, "Look, Jake, you need to stay on as the Co-Guardian. We'll all help you, but you have to do this."

Jake shook his head yes.

Chapter 21

Matt Westfield and his clients knew at the close of the hearing that they were going to lose. There was nothing amiss in the execution of the two Wills, and David Brennan testified he had met with Blake and Jackie twice about their estate plan before they came into the office to sign the Wills. Eddie was the most upset over how things had gone. Following the court proceeding, Sheryl, Jake and Gloria spoke to Eddie multiple times to try to calm him down and to get him to accept the inevitable.

Sheryl took the most realistic approach. "There has to be some smooth transition for the girls. You and Mom are going to have to get Jake and Tyler in the house while you are still here. They need to see the girls' routines and for the girls to get used to having Tyler and Jake around a lot. You and Dad can't just disappear without the girls freaking out. Jake and Tyler should ease into this. Why not start with having them come for dinner a few nights, help with homework and play some games?

"Perhaps Jake and I can meet with Tyler and propose some alternatives for getting both of them here regularly."

Eddie remained adamantly opposed to this. Finally, Sheryl asked Matt if she and Eddie could stop by his office to go over the Court's decision, which they all had received and read multiple times. Matt offered to stop by the house about 9:30 the following morning.

Eddie was reading the newspaper when Matt arrived, and they ushered him into the family room. Sheryl, Gloria and Eddie were all there to hear Matt out. Matt had a clear sense of what he was up against in Eddie and so he took the lead.

"Eddie, I understand that you're upset over the Court's decision, but you were in Court and heard everything for yourself. Once David Brennan took the witness stand, we were sunk. He testified he met with Jackie and Blake twice about the estate plan. They knew what they were doing. They weren't coerced or forced, and this is what they wanted."

Eddie was like a dog with a bone. "That lying son of a bitch, David. I liked him originally. I thought we could trust him."

Matt countered, "Ironically, you could trust him. He told the truth. He said what Jackie and Blake wanted in plain English. Now you know exactly what they were thinking and what they wanted. I'm not sure it's what David thought was the right thing, but ultimately it wasn't his decision to make, and it's not yours."

Eddie acted as if he hadn't heard what Matt just said, and maybe with his mindset, he truly hadn't heard Matt at all.

"Maybe we should appeal the decision. A different judge, a different result."

Sheryl and Gloria both groaned.

Matt had taken a somewhat conciliatory tone with Eddie, but now his tone changed. "You're wasting your time. We knew this was a long shot. We've taken that shot and we didn't get anywhere. You're going to spend a lot more money on legal fees with nothing to show for it. Your daughter and son-in-law were intelligent people. Maybe you have to have some faith in them and their decision. I personally will not move forward with the appeal, because I honestly think it's frivolous. You'll have to get another attorney to handle the appeal.

"Look, Eddie, if you really cannot stomach this, maybe you should go home for a while and let Gloria, Sheryl and Jake work this out with Tyler. The worst thing would be for Megan and Kristin to feel your upset and disapproval. This transition is going to be a hard enough task, without your sabotaging it. This may not be my place, but if you think you can't do this, maybe Gloria should stay, and you should go home."

"Matt, whose side are you on, anyway?" Eddie's tone was now one of contempt.

"Eddie, get it that there are no 'sides' anymore. The Court has decided this, and it's what your daughter wanted. You have to let it go. Let it go for Kristin and Megan's sake. Think about what's best for them."

With that, Matt stood up, and picked up his folder with the decision in it. "I can let myself out."

Chapter 22

After Matt left, they sat there in stony silence and then Sheryl got up and poured herself a mug of coffee. As she came back to the kitchen table, she said, "Dad, you've read this decision from the Court multiple times and now you've heard from Matt. Remember the old saying that you're part of the problem or part of the solution. Well, now we need you to be part of the solution. You need to do this for the girls' sake.

"I'm going to stay on for a few more days to help with this transition. I called Jake to have him come over here this morning, and I told him to see if he could get Tyler to come over too. We need to talk about how to get Jake and Tyler into this house and have them take over slowly but taking over nonetheless."

Eddie was listening intently to Sheryl's every word, but his expression didn't soften. Finally, he said, "Maybe Matt was right. I can't be a part of this, when I think it's so wrong. I'm going home." With that, he got up from the chair and walked out of the room.

Sheryl expected her mother to follow him and try to talk him out of leaving. However, her mother stayed put and didn't say a word. Sheryl looked expectantly at her mother. Gloria took a long sip of her coffee and put the mug back down on the table.

Gloria said, "There's no talking to him. He's always been so stubborn. I have been talking to him, and nothing. There's no reasoning with him. I wasn't sure the whole Court thing was the right thing to do. That was completely his idea. He thinks he knows best, and he forgets you aren't kids any more.

"Jackie and Blake loved those girls. They wouldn't have done anything to hurt them. I certainly think you and Mike would have been the better choice to be the Guardians, but that's not what Jackie and Blake did. The Court apparently agreed with them. I think it's time that we do what Jackie and Blake wanted. It's good that you'll stay for a few more days, because I'm not really sure where or how to start."

The doorbell rang and Sheryl answered it. Jake came in and kissed his mother and sister hello. Gloria and Sheryl explained what had gone on so far this morning and that they believed Eddie was upstairs packing to go home.

"Okay, if he doesn't want to help, maybe it's better that he goes, rather than upset the girls. They will definitely pick up on his negativity. I'm not convinced that he could keep his mouth shut either. That would just make things harder. Mom, are you going to stay for a while?"

Sheryl asked, "What about Tyler? Is he coming?"

"He said yes, but the guy can't seem to get anywhere on time. How the hell are we going to get kids off to school if he can't do anything on time like normal people?"

Gloria said, "Maybe we should start off going over the girls' routine. What days they have after-school activities and how they get home. Then we should go over what they like for lunch.

"Then I'll tell you about what they eat and won't eat for dinner, so you know what to buy when you do the shopping. Also, Megan has contact dermatitis, so they are only two laundry detergents you can use when you do the laundry.

"Then there's their homework."

Before Gloria could continue any further, Sheryl interjected and stopped her because Jake's expression was grim.

"It's okay, Jake. We'll make some lists and Mom and I are going to stay for a while and ease you into this."

Chapter 23

"Why don't we start with the girls' schedules? What days they have after-school activities and where they have to be and how they get from school to the activities," Sheryl said as she started the list and looked at her mother for the answers.

Gloria rattled off the activities and the carpools that transported the girls, and which days they handled as Sheryl took notes. Then they moved to lunches and which girl would and would not eat certain things. Jake nodded but said almost nothing.

Then the doorbell rang, and Jake opened the door and Tyler strolled in. The thought flashed through Sheryl's mind that Jake wanted to answer the door so that he could keep on walking and leave. Tyler walked into the kitchen looking as disheveled as before, but made a gesture that Sheryl realized was a favorable sign from Tyler and probably was an immense effort for him.

"Morning, everyone. I brought doughnuts and coffee. Hope everyone likes coffee. I never know how to order tea. Whether you're supposed to put milk in it or sugar or what." Tyler shrugged his shoulders in a sheepish gesture.

"Why, that's very nice of you to think of us," Gloria was quick to respond. "Please sit down. We were just going over the schedule for the girls."

Now Sheryl chimed in to make Tyler comfortable. "We all love coffee and doughnuts in this family. Let me get some mugs, some milk and a few napkins." In her mind, Sheryl was congratulating Tyler. He was making a conscious gesture to break the ice. Maybe the guy wasn't as clueless as they all thought.

They moved from the schedules to the lunches to the favorite dinners. "Maybe you two would like to come back later and stay for dinner. I was planning on making baked ziti, which is a favorite. No complaints about that, the Caesar salad or the garlic bread. Everyone eats everything and no complaints about not liking what's for dinner," Gloria continued.

Both men nodded yes. Now Sheryl picked up the ball and ran with it. "I've been helping the girls with their homework while I've been here, but Kristin has math that's getting beyond me. Can you give her a hand with the math, Tyler?"

"Maybe. It seems like a long time since I've done any math. First, there were calculators and now my phone does math for me."

"Well, what time do you want us back here tonight? I need to get into the office now." This was the first Jake had spoken.

"You could get here about five so you can spend some time with the girls, maybe help us with dinner and you then stay for dinner." Sheryl continued. "You also better hone your video games skills, because they have both been destroying me."

Chapter 24

"So how do you like the idea that your uncles are staying with you for the weekend?" Dr. Moran asked Kristin.

"It's okay" came the answer from Kristin.

"Okay, good or okay bad?" Dr. Moran prompted. She waited for an answer hoping for more than one word.

"I like it when Grammy is there, and I liked it best when Aunt Sheryl was at our house. She's so much fun because she can do a lot of things that Grammy can't do because she doesn't feel well. Grammy has some trouble breathing. Aunt Sheryl promised she would come back in a month to see us. I've also been talking to her on the phone and texting her. She PROMISED." She said that with real emphasis in her voice.

"I'm sure she'll keep that promise, but do you think it will be fun with your uncles? Can they play with you?"

"I guess."

"What do you like to do that you could do with your uncles this weekend?"

"I like to play tennis. Neither of them is very good."

"Do you think you could coach them a little so they could get better?"

"Maybe Uncle Jake. Uncle Tyler says he doesn't like to sweat. How can you possibly play tennis if you don't run for the ball? Then you sweat."

"Well, maybe there's something that Uncle Tyler does like to do. Have you ever asked him?"

"And another thing. He smokes. He doesn't think that we know it, but we do. He makes up an excuse to go outside, but it's just so that he can smoke."

"Does he smoke in the house?"

"No."

"Is there anything else that your Grandma and Aunt Sheryl do your Uncles don't do?"

There was a long hesitation on Kristin's part and Dr. Moran waited. She was a Board-Certified Child Psychiatrist and most of her practice was young adolescents. The key was to probe and wait for an answer, and then probe some more.

"I'm scared."

"Okay, scared of what?"

"What happens if we don't like it with our Uncles? What happens if we want Grammy to come back?"

"Well, I know your Grammy will come back after the weekend. She's going to be back and forth between her house and your house. Your Grammy is going to be there with you. I want you to understand that no one is abandoning you and Megan."

Kristin thought about that statement for a few moments. "Mommy and Daddy left us." She said it in words just above a whisper.

Now Dr. Moran knew they were getting to the heart of the matter, even if it was going to be a painful trip for Kristin.

"Kristin, your Mom and Dad didn't leave you because they wanted to. They died in the car crash. Leaving you would have been the absolute last thing they would have wanted. They certainly didn't want it to happen, but unfortunately it happened. The good thing for you and Megan is how many of your relatives love you and want to step in and be there for you. No one else is leaving you.

"Our time is up now, but we'll talk about this some more when you come back to see me next week. Is that okay? Now I want to speak to your Uncle for a few minutes."

Chapter 25

The plan was for the first week, Tyler and Jake would come to the house about 5 pm and help the girls with their homework, and they would have dinner with the girls and Gloria. Eddie had made a conscious decision that he wanted no part of this situation, so he stayed at their own house and made himself scarce while the initial part of the plan was taking place. When the girls questioned where Grandpa was and why he was not there for dinner, Gloria said Grandpa had some business to take care of which he hadn't had time to do while he and Grammy were staying with the girls. The adults and Dr. Moran all agreed that it was better for Eddie to stay away if he would not be on board with the transition, and especially if he was going to sabotage it.

For the second week, the plan was for Gloria to "visit" with a few friends for dinner and let Tyler and Jake take over making dinner, helping with homework and play some games with the girls after dinner. Gloria would come back after dinner and sleep at the house and mostly oversee that things were going smoothly, if in fact, they were going smoothly. On Monday of the second week, Megan got off the bus and Tyler was there to meet her. Kristin had tennis practice and a teammate's mother was picking up both girls and dropping off Kristin at the house after practice. Jake would try to leave work a little early and come to the house as soon as he could.

Megan got off the bus and walked into the house. Her expression said it all before she even said a word. She looked around the kitchen, saw Tyler, but clearly was looking for someone else- Grammy.

"Hi, Megs, how was school today?"

Megan acted as if she hadn't heard the sentence directed to her. "Where's Grammy?"

"She out visiting a friend of hers. She'll be back later. So how was school today, Megs?"

Megan stopped in her tracks and spun on Tyler. "My name is Megan. Megan," she said with even more emphasis. "I hate that name, Megs. Don't call me that!"

"Okay, okay, don't get upset. Your name is Megan. Got it. Sometimes people use a shorter version of the name, as a nickname. Like your Grandfather's full name is Edward, but people call him Eddie or Ed."

"Well, I don't like it."

"Okay, my mistake. Sorry, I won't use that name again. I'll only call you Megan."

To himself, Tyler was thinking, that he could also call her a pain in the ass. He tempered that thought that this was all new to her and that her parents had been violently ripped from her. But this wasn't going to be easy.

"So how about a snack? We have apples, oranges and yogurt."

Megan shook her head no. "I want chocolate chip cookies."

"That's not what your Grandmother said was for snacks."

Megan shrugged her shoulders as if to say his comment didn't matter, and apparently it didn't to her. She marched over to the cabinet and pulled out the package of chocolate chip cookies. Tyler really didn't know what to do. He could say no, or he could walk over to her and take the package of chocolate chip cookies out of her hand. Tyler was panic stricken. He was pretty sure that if he tried either of those remedies, that there would be a major confrontation, a melt down by Megan, and probably tears. These thoughts were all going through his brain in a nanosecond, but he didn't know what to do. So he capitulated.

"Just for today, you can have cookies. But only two. How about some milk with that?"

With that Tyler walked toward the refrigerator to pull out the milk. As he was opening the kitchen cabinets looking for a glass, Megan wolfed down two cookies and had the third one stuffed in her mouth, with the fourth one on the way.

"Hold on a second, Megan. That's too many cookies. Take a breath and have some milk." Tyler felt that was a completely lame thing to say, but suddenly he didn't know what to say. This adorable nine-year-old had been completely defiant, and he had been completely ineffective as the adult.

Another thought flashed through his brain. Megan two and Tyler zero.

Chapter 26

Jake was a " youngish" accountant in a twenty-person accounting firm in White Plains, and his last client had cancelled, so he slipped out early. This was Tuesday of the plan in the second week. He texted Tyler that he was going to get to the house in time to meet the bus, so if Tyler wanted to come to the house a little later, that would be fine.

Although most of the time Tyler appeared to be laid back, the skirmish with Megan the day before left him shaken. He didn't say it, but he was glad there was going to be reinforcement in the person of Jake. Tyler hadn't yet talked to anyone about the incident with Megan, nor was he sure that he wanted anyone to know about it. Did it make him look like a jerk? Tyler knew from the Court case that Jackie's family didn't want him to be the Guardian or Co-Guardian, so he was reluctant to tell them that in his first encounter with Megan, she had won. Maybe this wasn't going to be as easy a job raising two kids as he thought.

Jake made sure he had plenty of time to get to the house before the bus arrived. The last thing he wanted was for the girls to come home to an empty house. He had packed a gym bag with sweatpants, sneakers and a tee shirt in case he had time for a quick work out on the treadmill while the girls were doing homework.

He really didn't know how long homework would take or how much help was going to be needed.

The psychiatrist had suggested that maybe he should try to play tennis with Kristin, to bond with her doing something she loved. Jake liked to work out, but he wasn't great at sports that required hand/eye coordination. Jake also wanted to have time to change his clothes, because he didn't want to get his suit dirty. Jake was a meticulous dresser. Although the house was clean, Jake noticed that there were a lot of sticky surfaces in the house right after the girls had touched things. Jake wasn't sure if he would ever get used to that, or if he even wanted to get used to that. Although Jackie and Blake had a cleaning woman, Jake was considering having his own cleaning woman come in and clean a second day during the week.

After he changed his clothes and checked the time on the clock in the kitchen with his cell phone, and decided it was time to walk to the front of the house to meet the bus. Jake was mentally shaking his head that here he was, going to meet a school bus like some suburban parent, which was the last thing he ever thought he would be. Life had some weird twists and turns. Even as he was thinking about it, he had a pang of guilt that he was here, and his sister was dead.

He saw the bus turn onto the street and move toward him. For a second, he had another pang, but this one was close to anxiety. What was he supposed to do when the girls got off the bus? Was he supposed to kiss them hello? What would the other kids think if he kissed them? What would they think if he didn't kiss them? As the bus crawled down the street, fortunately, he saw it stop at two other houses. Kids got off the bus with mothers or nannies standing there. Jake noticed that there was just a wave to the bus driver and then everyone turned to go toward the house. No kissing required. Okay, just do what everybody else did and fit in.

Jake barely got to say hello as the girls made a beeline for the door. They abandoned backpacks just inside the door and Jake almost went flying across the room as he tripped over one. "Damn it! Can't you at least bring the backpacks into the room so we don't fall?" Jake instantly regretted his words and his tone. He was supposed to have patience with the kids, and yet on the very first thing that happened, he lost his cool. The psychiatrist had warned him.

"Sorry!" came the automatic chorus, but no one made a move to pick up or move the backpacks.

"So would you guys like a snack?" Kristin has already pulled a container of yogurt and a bottle of water out of the refrigerator. Megan felt emboldened after her skirmish the previous day with Tyler. She said, "I want cookies." After all, this ploy of merely going into the cabinet and grabbing the cookies had worked quite well yesterday. No one knew about the skirmish yesterday because Tyler was too embarrassed to tell anyone. Fortunately, for Jake, there was not a repeat of the previous day because Kristin answered immediately, "You know you can't have cookies as a snack." Jake didn't realize he had just dodged a bullet.

As an accountant, Jake liked the rules and followed the rules. The psychiatrist had said he should try to do things the kids liked, so as they were having their snacks, Jake asked Kristin if she would like to show him how to hit some tennis balls and improve his game. Kristin readily agreed. However, no one ever told him about the fiascos with Megan and sports. Jake assumed wrongly that all three of them would go hit tennis balls against the backboard in the yard. Both girls went upstairs to change their clothes and Kristin was back in a flash with balls and racquets. Kristin and Jake went outside, and Jake was absorbed in what Kristin was showing him. He assumed, and assumed wrongly again, that Megan would be along shortly.

Some time elapsed, and suddenly Jake heard screams and the piercing sound of the smoke alarm coming from the kitchen. Jake dropped his racquet and took off at a gallop. As he rushed into the kitchen, he heard rather than saw, Megan plastered up against the wall screaming, and flames coming from the microwave. Jake cursed that had no idea if there was a fire extinguisher in the kitchen, so in one motion, he hit the off button, opened the microwave and with a towel he had grabbed, threw the offending pot into the sink and turned on the water to put out the fire.

"What the hell happened here?" Jake screamed. As Jake turned his attention to Megan, the scare from the fire and Jake's screams, made her hysterical. Megan decided she wanted a hot chocolate and couldn't reach the mugs. Instead, she used a pot which had metal in it and Megan left the kitchen. When she returned, the microwave was on fire.

Jake's hands were shaking, and the sweat was pouring down his face, but he walked over to Megan and gathered her in his arms. At least now the smoke alarm had stopped screeching, since that sound was unnerving. He originally wanted to throttle her, but she was so pathetic looking and crying, that he wanted to comfort her. As he looked over Megan's shoulder, he noticed that the glass door on the microwave was black and hanging at a peculiar angle.

"How am I going to explain this?" he mumbled to himself. "God, I haven't been here twenty-four hours and we're wrecking the place."

Chapter 27

It took quite a while to get Megan calmed down and then Jake opened a few windows to get the acrid smell of smoke out of the kitchen. Megan settled for a glass of orange juice instead of her original choice of hot chocolate. Jake realized he had no idea of where Kristin was. He left Megan in the kitchen with the admonition that she stay put in the chair until he came back into the kitchen.

Jake found Kristin outside hitting tennis balls against the backboard as if nothing at all had happened.

"Kristin, you okay?"

"Yup," came the answer.

"Did you see what happened with Megan in the kitchen?"

"Yup," came the answer again. Kristin never missed a beat as she continued to hit ball after ball.

"The microwave was on fire." This time Jake's voice was louder and more exasperated.

"Yup."

"Kristin, I'm talking to you."

"Yup, and I'm answering you."

Finally, Jake's exasperation got the better of him and he walked over and caught the ball before she could hit it again.

"Hey, what are you doing? I'm practicing," came the annoyed response.

"Damn it, there was a FIRE in the microwave! The house could have burned down; Megan could have been hurt."

"I know. Megan is pretty klutzy. These things seem to happen to her a lot," came the matter-of-fact response.

"You mean she's set the microwave on fire before?" Now Jake's tone was moving from upset to extremely upset, and maybe even hysterical.

"No, she never set the microwave on fire before, but she has broken a lot of stuff and she's been in the emergency room a bunch of times. You sort of get used to it."

"You what?"

"You sort of get used to it because it's happened so many times before." With that Kristin picked up another ball and started her volleying again.

Jake raised his arms above his head in a gesture of "What the hell!" He turned and headed back toward the house to take an Aleve for his now pounding headache. He was muttering to himself and thinking that no one had ever mentioned anything like this before to him.

Jake walked back into the kitchen to find Megan up on the top step of the stepstool. "Megan, what the hell are you doing? Didn't I tell you to stay put in the chair until I came back?"

"Yeah, but you went outside, and I could still hear the tennis ball hitting the backboard, so I figured that you were playing with Kristin again."

Jake took Megan by the hand and helped her back to terra firma. Jake didn't even want to know what she was doing on the top step.

"Don't you have some homework to do? I think it's time to do your homework. Go start your homework."

This time Megan picked up on Jake's tone of voice and went to find her backpack.

Jake rummaged through the kitchen cabinets for the Aleve.

Chapter 28

Jake made himself a cup of coffee, and as he waited for it to brew, he surveyed the scene in the kitchen. He walked over to the microwave. The door was hanging askew being held by only the bottom bolt and the window in the door was completely black. Jake touched the door with his finger to see if the soot would rub off on his finger, but it appeared the fire had singed the window.

To say that Jake was not handy with tools, was the understatement of the year, so he didn't think he could fix the door. He also didn't like to cook very much either. When he was growing up, his mother had cooked. In his prior relationships, he had been fortunate that his girlfriends liked to cook. So now without a microwave, Jake felt helpless. Jake was mulling this over in his mind. "If I use the oven, I have no goddamn idea of how hot the oven should be to bake things and how long to keep the chicken in the oven," he said out loud.

He was thinking to himself that he could cook the veggies on the stove and make a salad, but he also didn't know how to cook the sweet potatoes in the oven. "We're back to the stone age," he said with a loud sigh.

Jake decided to bite the bullet and call his mother rather than try to Google the answers. Fortunately, Gloria answered her cell phone on the second ring. "Mom, it's me. I need a little help with making dinner."

Gloria was very glad that Jake couldn't see her at the other end of the phone. While she was concerned that Megan had set the microwave on fire, she also had to contain her laughter. She could visualize the microwave door hanging on for dear life, but she also knew that these were the situations and skirmishes anyone raising kids learned to deal with. If the microwave was the only casualty and not either of the girls or Jake, Gloria could chuckle a little to herself. She also felt that it was fine that while Jake wasn't happy, he wasn't freaking out either.

A few minutes after Jake got off the phone with Gloria, Tyler breezed into the kitchen. "Crap, it smells bad in here. It smells like charcoal or fire. Did something get burned?"

Just as Tyler was about to add to the commentary about the smell, he saw the microwave door. "What the hell happened?"

Jake gave Tyler the blow by blow of what had happened. Jake didn't expect much sympathy from Tyler and when he finished, he figured that Tyler was going to make some sarcastic comment. There was a pregnant pause as Tyler considered whether he should tell Jake about his chocolate chip cookie situation yesterday with Megan.

"Jeez, for a little girl, she's like a walking disaster area. And she's stubborn as hell. Let me tell you what she did with me yesterday."

Before Tyler could tell Jake his story, Kristin came into the kitchen. "Boy, it smells bad in here."

To which, Tyler and Jake replied in unison, "We know."

The dinner was a semi-disaster. The chicken was dried out and burnt in a few places, the veggies were only lukewarm, and Tyler burned his hand taking the sweet potatoes out of the oven.

Jake told Tyler that he would buy a new microwave tomorrow.

Chapter 29

Since there were four people involved in this new situation, Dr. Moran felt she needed to see Megan and Kristin individually and that she also needed to see Jake and Tyler individually. She wanted each of the two men to speak freely not only about the girls but also about his Co-Guardian. As to each of the girls, she wanted to see how each one was handling the untimely death of their parents and then getting used to having two uncles with whom they hadn't had much interaction as their new Guardians.

They decided they would switch each week, with one week Tyler taking Megan and Kristin to see Dr. Moran and the next week Jake would bring them.

This week it was Megan's turn to go first. Being a nine-year-old and losing your parents was beyond difficult and Dr. Moran wanted to see how Megan was processing this. Kristin acted like she was dealing with everything better, but Dr. Moran thought Kristin was holding a lot in, and that the dam was going to break, and the deluge was going to drown Kristin.

Dr. Moran came around from her normal psychiatrist chair and sat at a smaller table and chair on the other side of the office. This was where she sat with the younger children to make things seem more informal. She had a jigsaw puzzle on the table.

Dr. Moran opened the door to the outer office, said hello to Jake and Megan and ushered Megan into the office. They sat together at the small table. Dr. Moran fiddled with a few puzzle pieces on the table and as Megan looked at and picked up a piece, Dr. Moran started the conversation.

"So, Megan, you told me last time you were here that you liked to draw, and I hear you are pretty good. You said you were going to bring me a few of your pictures. Did you bring any?"

"Yeah, I did." Megan felt Kristin got all the attention with her tennis, especially when she won tournaments, so Megan was happy that someone was asking about her artwork.

Megan pulled a pad out of her backpack. She then took two pictures carefully out of the sketchpad. The first picture was of a rose, and it was good work for a nine-year-old but was fairly unremarkable. The second picture was of an ocean scene with dark and angry waves in the background and two figures in the foreground. One on the figures was an adult with an arm around a child.

Dr. Moran started asking about the picture of the rose. Megan said she saw it in their backyard, and she liked pink. It seemed uncomplicated, because in fact, it was.

The second drawing was impressive, no matter what the age of the artist. Considering the death of Megan's parents, the symbolism was fairly screaming at them.

"This is really a wonderful picture. Do you remember when you drew it?"

"Last week."

"Did you go to the beach and see the ocean and that's why you drew the picture?"

"No, we didn't go to the beach."

"What made you think to draw this picture?"

Megan shrugged, but no verbal response.

"Who are the people in the picture?"

"I dunno."

"Well, it looks like it might be a mother and child. Is that you and your mom?"

"I dunno."

"The mother and child have their arms around each other. Do you miss hugging your mother?"

Megan never looked up, never answered, but her lip quivered.

Dr. Moran waited, but still no answer.

"What things did you do with your mother that you miss now?" Based on the look on Megan's face, she had struck pay dirt.

This time Megan didn't hesitate at all. "I miss that we used to go to the art store together, we used to go shopping together, we made cookies together, she would do my hair, she would sit with me every night and we'd read together." As Megan stopped for a breath, her emotions got the best of her, and she put her head down on the table and sobbed.

While this was pathetic and extremely difficult for Megan, Dr. Moran knew that this was the first breakthrough, and she hoped the first of many. She also knew that she had yet to make any significant breakthroughs with Kristin.

Chapter 30

The bumps in the road continued to come. Some of them were small and as time passed, some bumps were much larger. One of the first skirmishes between Jake and Tyler involved what would normally have been minor issues about the running of a household.

Jake and Tyler were practically opposites. Jake was neat to a fault. His closet could have been an ad on TV for California Closets. Every pair of pants hung neatly on a hangar facing the same way. His dress shirts came back from the dry cleaners on hangers in plastic bags. He didn't like them boxed because often there were wrinkles on the sleeves when the shirts came out of the boxes. His ties were on three separate tie racks. One tie rack held ties which matched blue, gray or black suits. The second rack held ties which matched the brown suits. The third tie rack held the "fun ties." Those were the ones suitable for Christmas, Easter, Halloween, Thanksgiving, etc. His shoes lined up neatly on the floor of the closet, again by color.

Tyler, on the other hand, was the epitome of the saying, "a place for everything and nothing in its place." Tyler's shirts lay in a heap on the chair in his bedroom. He owned one dress shirt which was hanging in his closet because he couldn't remember the last time he wore it. He had golf shirts, turtlenecks and long sleeve collarless shirts, which were stuffed into several drawers in his bedroom.

The tee shirts were also stuffed into different drawers by themselves, because he wore those the most. Some of the tee shirts, both clean and dirty were in a pile on the floor. He had four pair of sneakers scattered around the room, and he had two pair of work boots. Tyler could only find three of the boots. He knew he needed to make a search for the fourth boot somewhere in his room, but for now it was not imperative that he find it. He never made his bed, and the comforter lay askew, half on the floor and half on the bed. He stripped the bed the morning he knew the cleaning ladies were coming, but he didn't bring the sheets down to the laundry room; he just left the sheets on the floor.

It didn't take a rocket scientist to realize that these two sartorial lifestyles were going to clash quickly in the new house with the girls. Jake told the girls that they had to make their beds every morning and put their dirty clothes in the hampers he bought for each room. They were not to leave the clothes on the floor. The cleaning ladies were two sisters, and they came to the house together. They would do the laundry and leave it neatly in each girl's room to be put away.

The edict was sent from on high, but the peasants were going to ignore it. Three days after he told the girls about the new rule, Jake knocked on Kristin's door. When she said to come in, Jake was just checking to see that the rule was being mostly followed. He was not expecting what he saw. Kristin's bed was made, sort of. The comforter was mostly pulled up to the top of the bed, but it was listing badly to the left side so that the sheets were sticking out prominently on the right side of the bed. As to the second part of the edict that clothes not be on the floor and put in the hamper, that was a fair to middling success. Technically, the clothes were not on the floor. However, they appeared to be everywhere else. They were on the bed, the desk chair and the window seat. A number were draped over the hamper.

"Are these dirty or clean clothes?" Jake asked gesturing around the whole room. Kristin shrugged.

"I guess some of both," came the honest answer.

"Well, how do you tell which are dirty so you don't wear them again?"

"The stuff lying on the hamper is dirty. Those are my workout clothes. They get pretty sweaty."

He switched to a different tack and tried again. "Okay, but what about the rest of the clothes?"

"I just remember what I wore and don't wear those clothes again."

"Kristin, the cleaning ladies don't know which you've worn and which they should wash. How about we just throw the dirty clothes in the hamper now so they can wash them tomorrow?" With that Jake grabbed a handful of clothes draped over the desk chair and held them up to Kristin. "Clean or dirty?"

Kristin gave him a signal to dump them in the hamper.

"All of them?"

"Yup" came the response.

Jake heaved a sigh of relief and moved to the next pile of clothes and got the same reply. In the last pile, he saw two wet towels and a soggy washcloth. Jake, the neat freak, didn't even want to touch the towels and washcloth, but forced himself to pick them up by his fingertips.

And so it went in Kristin's room. When Jake finished in Kristin's room, needed to go downstairs and make himself a cup of coffee. He couldn't bring himself to go look in Megan's room.

Chapter 31

Jake was toying with the idea of having the cleaning ladies come a second day each week, so things didn't get out of hand. The other thing which was driving Jake crazy was the fact that the sports equipment and toys were never put away and lying on the floors everywhere. The only pieces of sports equipment not lying around were Kristin's two tennis racquets.

Jake realized he was going to have to enlist Tyler's support in the battle. However, Tyler was smart enough to realize that since he couldn't care less about this rule and ultimately the ensuing battle Jake was waging, that he was going to stay away from the subject with Jake and keep the door to his bedroom closed.

Shortly after the clean-up in Kristin's room, but before Jake was even willing to tackle Megan's room, Jake knocked on Tyler's bedroom door and poked his head in. In the split second it took Jake to take in the mess that was Tyler's room, he took a step backward and gave a slight gasp.

"Holy shit, it looks like a tornado went through here! How can you live like this?"

Jake's comments or his attitude did not surprise Tyler. "Look, man, do what you want in your room. This is my room, and I can do what I want in here. I don't criticize you, so don't criticize me."

"Tyler, you can't do this, even though this is your room. How can we get Kristin and Megan to clean up their rooms when your room is a pigsty?"

"Jake, this clean freak thing was your idea. You never asked me about it or discussed it with me. You just made a statement, like you were some sort of dictator. I'm not buying into this because it's too much. It's over the top and I'm just not doing this."

Jake surveyed the room again, sighed, and gave himself time to choose his words. He felt he would choose the same tone he would use to address an idiot. "First, we have an obligation to teach the girls the right things. You saw this house after Blake and Jackie died. The house was immaculate. It sure as hell didn't look like this," he said, waving his hand across the width of the room. Do you think they would want their kids growing up in a pigsty?"

"Oh, my God, this house is hardly a pigsty! But you want to turn this place into a museum, where you can only look at things, but not really live here. You're so obsessive about everything. Only a crazy person can live like this. You are a lunatic!"

"You're the crazy person. You don't act like an adult. You act like an adolescent yourself and not a very mature one at that. Half the time I think Kristin is more mature than you. She has the right to be a kid because she is a kid. You have no excuse."

"You would have done great as a drill sergeant because all you want to do is give orders. Putting clothes in a hamper and making your bed are not the most important things in the world, yet you make it like they're up there with world peace."

"You have adult responsibilities now, so you better act like an adult. Jackie and Blake thought you could handle this responsibility. Can you really handle this or not?"

Jake really didn't feel like waiting around for another adolescent response from Tyler, so he basically turned on his heel, walked out of Tyler's room and slammed the door. In the back of Jake's mind, he knew walking out and slamming the door was also an adolescent thing to do, but at this point he was so aggravated that he didn't care. Maybe an adolescent response would get through to an adolescent.

As Jake walked down the hall, he decided that tomorrow he would call Dr. Moran and discuss this situation with her. Maybe she needed to tell Tyler that she wanted to see them together because Jake didn't think he would get through to Tyler without help. Jake felt he was right. He always felt he was right.

In his anger and preoccupation with the problem, Jake wasn't really paying any attention to his surroundings. Before he went into Kristin's room, he had taken off his shoes to polish them, so he was in his slippers with the soft soles. As he was now walking down the hall, he stepped on something plastic which not only crunched and broke under foot but also jabbed him through the soft sole of the slipper.

"Shit, what the hell was that?" he yelled. As he hopped in the air from the pain, he came down and tripped on something else on the floor in the hallway. During his second hop in the air, he came down awkwardly and twisted his ankle. If he was mimicking a scene from a movie, it couldn't have played out any more perfectly. In his attempt not to fall down the flight of stairs, he reached out and grabbed whatever was closest to steady himself. This was a table with a heavy glass top, and he banged his face into the glass. He then fell forward onto his wrist. The force of his body coming down against the glass, cut a deep gash in his forehead and next to his eye. The sound of the glass shattering was incredibly loud. Jake sat there stunned on the floor in the hall. The sound of the glass had Tyler and Kristin out of their bedrooms in a flash.

Kristin surveyed the situation, saw Jake on the floor and the blood pouring from his face. She backed herself up against the wall and started to cry. Tyler took in the same sight and ran toward Jake.

"Shit, man, are you okay?" He knew Jake was not okay because besides the broken glass all around Jake on the floor, there was blood all over his face. "I'll call 911," he yelled at Jake.

Tyler's yelling brought Kristin out of her shock. As Tyler ran into his room for his phone, Kristin ran back into her room, and grabbed the wet towels out of her hamper. She ran to Jake and applied pressure with the towels. Tyler then reappeared and grabbed towels out of the linen closet and went to Jake to apply more pressure to his face.

"Kristin, go downstairs and open the front door. Turn on the porch light and when you hear the sirens, go outside on the porch so the police see where we are."

Kristin nodded and jumped over Jake and ran down the stairs. Megan heard the commotion, but she had been downstairs in the family room when Jake fell. She came to the bottom of the stairs but remained frozen in fear there. As Kristin came flying down the stairs, she pushed Megan out of the way and opened the front door.

Chapter 32

About two hours later Jake and Tyler returned from the Emergency Room. Tyler pulled his truck into the garage and went around to the passenger side of the truck. He helped Jake get out of the truck. The door to the kitchen opened and Beverly Layton stood there. Right behind her were Kristin and Megan. Both girls looked terrified. Beverly's daughter Shelby played tennis with Kristin. After the ambulance left with Jake inside and Tyler followed in his truck, Kristin called Shelby crying and so Shelby and Beverly came over to be with the girls.

Jake looked like something out of a horror movie. He had a huge bandage on the right side of his face, and he had a black eye. His forehead was also swollen and black and blue. His right arm was in a sling, and he appeared somewhat unsteady on his feet as Tyler helped him into the house. He had an air cast on his leg as well.

Tyler's expression showed he had a question about why Beverly was in the house, so she jumped in. "Kristin called Shelby and was upset about Jake, so Shelby and I came over to stay with the girls, since we didn't know how long you would be in the ER."

Megan was wide eyed about how Jake looked and backed out of the kitchen. Since Jake and Kristin had barely finished their conversation about picking up things off the floor, Kristin was not at all sure how Jake was going to react. Was he going to be furious?

Kristin wasn't even sure what Jake had fallen on, but she was sure he was going to be upset. It was going to be a question of degree.

Beverly took control of the conversation since she understood Kristin's upset after the conversation Kristin had described with Jake before his fall. "How are you feeling, Jake?"

"Right now, in pain," came the answer through clenched teeth.

"Did they give you anything for the pain?"

"Yeah, they gave me a shot in the hospital and a couple of pills for the pain for tonight and tomorrow."

"Do you have to go back to see the doctor?"

"I have to go back in a week for him to look at the wound. My wrist isn't broken, but they want it immobilized for the sprain. Right now, it's pretty swollen. The air cast is for the sprained ankle."

Tyler said, "Do you want me to help you get upstairs to bed?"

"No, right now I need to sit down for a few minutes. I'm not sure I can make it up the stairs now."

Beverly asked, "Would you like a cup of tea or some water?"

"Yeah, a cup of decaf tea would be great."

Kristin hadn't said a word. She had moved to the far end of the kitchen as far away from Jake as possible.

Beverly moved to get a mug out of the cabinet and Tyler pulled two boxes of tea out of the cabinet. As Beverly filled the mug and put it in the microwave, she sensed the tension in the room. She did what she thought was the best thing in the situation. "While you were gone, I cleaned up the glass upstairs, and I ran the washing machine with the towels. They're in the dryer right now.

"I thought that maybe for tonight until things settle down, Kristin and Megan might want to come back to our house and spend the night with Shelby. What do you think?" She looked from Kristin to Jake and Tyler.

Tyler, who was often clueless, was the first to speak up and this time he got it. "Yeah, that's a good idea. That way Jake can get a good night's sleep. You wanna go to Shelby's house, Kristin?"

Kristin nodded yes.

"Will Megan want to go too?"

Kristin nodded again.

Beverly jumped in again and said, "Why don't you girls go upstairs and get your things." As she said this, she walked out of the kitchen into the family room and found Megan curled up on the couch under a blanket. Beverly bent over Megan and touched her gently the shoulder.

Beverly said in a quiet voice, "You girls are going to come spend the night with Shelby. Can you go upstairs and get your pajamas and toothbrush and some clothes for tomorrow? Do you want me to come up and help you?"

Megan got up off the couch and took Beverly's hand and they walked upstairs together.

Chapter 33

Beverly and the three girls tumbled into her kitchen with backpacks, tennis racquets, jackets and other important "stuff." Beverly's husband, Frank, came into the kitchen from the family room as he heard the garage door open. It surprised him to see the troop of kids who followed Beverly into the kitchen.

Frank caught Beverly's eye as she walked into the kitchen and saw her roll her eyes. "Hey, girls, do you need help with all your things?" He grabbed a backpack and a pillow which Megan was clutching and shot another glance at Beverly, who shrugged.

"Let's get everyone settled upstairs in Shelby's room and then maybe we should have some ice cream," Beverly said. "Frank, we have a few different flavors in the freezer in the garage, so please get them and bring them in here. They're probably hard as a rock, so they might need a few minutes to defrost a little."

Frank handed the backpack to Shelby and the pillow back to Megan and he walked toward the garage. Beverly led the group up to Shelby's room. There were twin beds in the room and Beverly said, "We have an air mattress and a sleeping bag. Which one do you want to use, Shelby? Our guests can take the twin beds."

Shelby did a double take when her mother said that, but her mother's expression told her not to protest. "I'll take the air mattress," came the not too cheerful response.

"Okay, Dad will get it out of the closet in the other bedroom. You girls get settled and Dad will bring in the air mattress. Then come on down and we can have some ice cream."

When Beverly got back downstairs to the kitchen, Frank was sitting there with a concerned look on his face. "What happened? I was a little surprised to see you come home with Kristin and Megan in tow. Is Jake in the hospital?"

"No, he and Tyler came back from the ER, but Jake is pretty banged up. His face is all swollen, and he's got a huge shiner. He's in an air cast with a sprained ankle. He was in a good amount of pain.

"But Jake's injuries are the least of the problems over there. He's pissed off that he fell on something left in the hallway and he almost fell down the stairs. Everyone in that house is on edge. You could cut the tension with a knife. I just thought it would be better to get Kristin and Megan out of there for tonight. Both girls were wide eyed at how Jake looked, and I think they were afraid of what his reaction was going to be when he came home from the hospital."

"Why, what did his getting hurt have to do with the girls?"

"Apparently, Jake had just laid down the law about cleaning up their rooms and not leaving things all over the floor. It was the worst possible time, because he fell right after her came out of Kristin's room. Then Kristin was terrified by all the blood. She told me that Tyler went to get his phone to call 911, and she ran into her room and grabbed towels to help stop the bleeding.

"Kristin didn't know what it was called, but she got the irony of the situation that it was the damp towels he had just yelled at her about that she used on him."

"This sounds like a royal mess. Are they afraid he's going to hurt them?"

"No, I don't think it's that, but from what I'm gathering from Kristin, this arrangement of having the two uncles as the Guardians is not working out too well. Tyler and Jake are two completely different people and neither of them ever spent any significant time with the girls. Now they're expected to step in and be parents to these two girls, when neither of them has ever had a child before. I'm gathering that neither of them has much of an idea what the hell they're doing. I'm really surprised that Jackie and Blake came up with this arrangement."

Chapter 34

The following morning Jake hobbled to the stairs and then gingerly lowered himself step by step down the flight of stairs to the main floor of the house. Tyler had suggested last night that perhaps Jake might want to sleep downstairs on the couch in the family room instead of trying to negotiate the stairs. Jake had considered that possibility, but when he looked closely at the couch, he declined. The couch looked dusty to him in places, and he saw two things which he could not identify stuck to the couch. In Jake's mind it was a Petrie dish of bacteria to which he did not want to subject his body.

As he hobbled into the kitchen, Tyler was sitting at the kitchen table with a big mug of coffee in front of him and reading something on his iPad.

"Morning, how do you feel?"

"About as bad as I look."

"Want some coffee?"

"Yes, thanks."

As Tyler got up to get the coffee he asked, "How's the pain? Did you take the pain pills last night and get some sleep?"

"I took them, but I don't know which hurts worse, my face or my ankle. It made it almost impossible to sleep, because I couldn't find a comfortable place in the bed."

Tyler nodded and brought the mug to Jake. He really didn't know how he was supposed to respond to him. "Want something to eat?"

"Yes, there's yogurt and bananas in the refrigerator. Please bring me a container of yogurt and a banana?"

Tyler obliged and put the yogurt and the banana on the table. He went to get a bowl for the yogurt, a spoon and a knife to cut the banana. Tyler was afraid of the explosion he was sure was coming from Jake. Jake's accident had certainly fueled his demands about the condition of the house, but Tyler still felt they were unreasonable. Even more than that, he really didn't want to be a part of rules. He had assiduously spent his life avoiding them as much as possible and now Jake wanted to impose arbitrary rules that seemed pointless to Tyler.

Tyler sat back down at the table and picked up his iPad again. He was pretending to read, but out of the corner of his eye he could see Jake meticulously scooping out the yogurt and slicing the banana onto the yogurt. He could just as easily have gotten up and walked into the other room, but he knew a volcano was about to erupt and he wanted to gauge the force of it. Jake ate in silence for a few moments and then put down his spoon.

"Well?" was how Jake started the conversation.

"Well, what? If you have something to say, say it."

"You know goddamn well what I'm gonna say. I almost got killed last night. I could just have easily fallen down the stairs. If it wasn't me, it could have been you or the girls. It's ironic that it was me who took the brunt of it, when I was the one saying that the house must be cleaned up and crap not left everywhere. So what are we going to do about this?"

Tyler shrugged, but still didn't answer.

"You would feel differently if you were the one sitting here with and a black and blue face and an air cast."

Tyler had to admit to himself, even if he didn't want to say it out loud, that Jake looked worse this morning than he had last night. The discoloration on his face was more pronounced and the side of his face looked more swollen.

"What are we going to do about this situation?"

"Look, Jake, I'm sorry you fell and got hurt, but you're blowing this up way out of proportion. Every house with kids gets messy. That's the way kids are, and every parent fights this battle with the kids being slobs.

"It got so bad in my house when I was growing up, that every week my mother would make my father go into our rooms with her and strip the beds. Then she'd wash the sheets, which must have been pretty ripe. She describes having to climb over shit on the floor just to get to the bed. Blake's room was as bad as mine. She'd yell at us to clean our rooms and we'd yes her to death. But we all grew up and somehow we got through it.

"It's been the perpetual battle with kids and their parents. The parents demanding the kids clean their rooms and the kids ignoring them. I don't know why you think this is so unusual. The girls' rooms don't even look that bad to me."

Jake had been listening to Tyler, but his body language was bad. He had his arms crossed over his chest in a defiant mode.

Tyler thought he had one more chance to plead his case, and he took it. "Jake, you can't seriously tell me you grew up and your room was clean and that the bed was always made, and your clothes always hung up and put away."

When Jake spoke, it was if he had not heard Tyler at all.

Chapter 35

The following morning unbeknownst to each other, Jake and Tyler each called Dr. Moran and left her a message. Much to her surprise, each of them had called her. Neither had been very specific about what they wanted to discuss with her, but it was highly unusual to hear from each of them on the same day. From the tone of each message, she knew that something had happened, and almost certainly nothing good. She felt that Jake and Tyler came to the sessions begrudgingly, but many other times she felt that Jake and Tyler hated coming for their sessions with her.

Two days later Dr. Moran sat in her office with the two men staring at her. She hadn't told them that each of them had called. If they thought she spoke only to each of them to confirm the appointment, that was fine. She wanted to get the unvarnished view from each of them. Even though she had met with them several times before, she was still somewhat amazed at the physical contrast between the two men. Both were roughly about the same age, but how they carried themselves and how they dressed were light years apart.

"Okay, I've spoken to both of you briefly on the phone about what happened in the house. So obviously this was a big problem for each of you and most probably for the girls. I haven't had the session with the girls yet, but I'm sure this shook them up too.

"I can see the remains of what happened on your face, Jake, and the boot you're wearing, so do you want to go first?"

Jake's body language had been bad from the moment he limped into the office and his seating posture wasn't good either. She could see that Jake was seething.

"Well, I think it's apparent what the problem is. Just look at me. I could have fallen down the stairs or lost my eye hitting the edge of the table. If it wasn't me who got hurt, it could just as easily have been the girls, or it could even have been you, Tyler. If something had happened to the girls, we would never have forgiven ourselves, because it's our job to protect them. Think of the criticism coming our way if something happened to the girls. People would say that their two uncles are incompetent and unable to take care of them."

Tyler jumped in, but Dr. Moran stopped him. "Let him finish what he wants to say and then we can hear from you."

Jake almost snickered when Dr. Moran stopped Tyler as if to say, 'What I have to say is important, and you can shut up.'

"It's ironic that I got hurt just a few moments after I had the discussion with Kristin about cleaning up her room and not leaving stuff all over the floor for people to trip on. I was just on my way downstairs to talk to Megan when I fell. My falling and getting hurt only proved my point very dramatically."

"Okay Jake, I hear you and now, Tyler, I'd like to hear from you."

"Look, we're all sorry that Jake got hurt, and I'm not just saying that. But if he hadn't gotten hurt, all this would be is a fight over housekeeping."

"Are you crazy?" Jake yelled.

Dr. Moran again stepped in. "Jake, we let you speak, now let Tyler speak."

"There's the problem right there. Jake blows up every little thing into a huge deal in the house. This is just an issue of kids being told to clean their rooms. A problem every family with growing kids faces. No different in our house. No different just because we're the uncles and not the parents. We had this problem in my house growing up with Blake and me with our parents.

"The other problem is that Jake thinks he can just make these decisions and impose them on the kids and without talking to me. He doesn't ask for input from me, and he doesn't listen to what the kids have to say or what they want."

"Oh, yeah, we should consult with the kids about whether they want to clean their rooms or whether they even want to go to school. No kid wants to do either of those things, but they have to be done."

"Well, you've both raised issues. Jake, you are unhappy with the condition of the house, but you also mentioned that you think people are, or will criticize you, in how you are handling raising the girls. Tyler, you're raising the issue about cleaning the house, but you are also raising not being consulted in decisions by Jake about the girls. I think it's good that we get these issues on the table because they have been festering just below the surface."

Chapter 36

Jake left his boss' office pleased with his new assignment. He and one of the other associates had been told that they were going to Boston to meet with one of their important clients at their headquarters. Jake had been told he was going to take the lead with the client meetings. This was great for his career. It was a big client and Jake had been working with one of the partners, Ron Davis, on the account. However, Ron Davis had just had back surgery and wasn't going to Boston or anywhere else in the near future. Since Jake had been primarily interacting with the client in Ron's absence, the client told Ron that they were fine if Jake came to the office without Ron. It was a great way for Jake to shine and show the partners once again that he was partner material. This meeting was slightly more than two weeks after Jake's accident and the black and blue and swelling on his face had gone down and he was out of the boot, and he no longer needed the sling for his wrist.

As Jake walked back to his office and looked at the calendar, since the client wanted them to come to Boston next Monday, Tuesday and Wednesday, he would have to move one meeting. As he sat down at his desk, he reveled in the thought that his career was really taking off. He decided they should probably leave Sunday afternoon so they could be in Boston first thing Monday morning for the meetings. Then he thought that this would give him four days without Tyler and the girls, and he really liked that idea. Jake didn't think that Tyler pulled his weight with all the tasks with the house and the kids, so now let Tyler try to cope with everything that needed to be done without him. "Good luck with that, Tyler," Jake said out loud.

I'll give him the dates this evening and let him figure out how he's going to handle everything - all by himself, Jake thought to himself. Tyler apparently did some carpentry work, when the spirit moved him. It seemed to Jake from some conversations he overheard when Tyler was on his cell phone that he was in demand, but Tyler seemed to pick what jobs he wanted to do. There were a few general contractors who called Tyler frequently, so his work must be good, but it seemed to Jake that Tyler took a job, earned some money and then took a break.

Jake thought that it was probably a godsend for Tyler financially that he moved into the house with the girls, since all his daily household expenses were being paid for. When Jake was being cynical, he thought that Tyler just wanted to be the Guardian, for the free food and housing. It sometimes seemed impossible for Jake to believe that Tyler and Blake had been brothers since Blake had been a go getter and a no-nonsense person. Everything about Blake seemed as if he had his life together.

Considering all that Jake had seen with Blake, his life had a purpose and made sense. Except for the decision to make Tyler the Co-Guardian for the girls. Maybe Blake was the one smoking some marijuana. But this decision would not have been made without Jackie's approval. David Brennan had confirmed his several meetings about estate planning with Jackie and Blake. David had also testified about those meetings, and he had said nothing about dissension about the choices for the Co-Guardians when David spoke with Blake and Jackie. If Tyler had been born earlier, he would have been a perfect hippy in the nineteen sixties. His hair was not quite long enough, and he needed a few peace symbols on his truck to complete the hippy scenario. As far as Jake could see Tyler did not do drugs, but Jake could smell cigarette smoke on Tyler's clothes. At least Tyler was smart enough not to smoke in the house. That would have set off another major battle.

Chapter 37

Jake was running late getting home, but the traffic mercifully cooperated, and he was home before Megan came home from her art class. He had to admit that for a little girl she was quite talented, and she liked the art classes more than anything else she did. She certainly was stubborn, but art was the one thing they agreed on and it was an easy afternoon activity. Jake had only recently heard the stories going back to before Jackie died about trying to get Megan to play a sport. Jake wanted no part of that battle. If it hadn't worked with Jackie at the helm, it certainly would not be a cause he wanted to take up. Every day some hurdle large or small presented itself.

He put his briefcase onto a chair in the kitchen as he came in and threw his keys on the counter. He filled the pot with water and put it on the stove to start it boiling. He put the boxes of rigatoni on the counter and then went upstairs to change his clothes. He didn't want to get grease or meat sauce on his suit. Once he changed his clothes, he would come back downstairs and make the salad and the garlic bread.

As he was about to leave the kitchen, the door opened, and Megan came in. According to the schedule, Kristin was going to be late because they were playing a match away.

"Hi, Megan, how was school today?"

"Okay, tomorrow they're going to bring in service dogs who help people. Some of them are puppies, but when they get to be a year old, then they can start training. You should see the pictures. They are so cute! Can we get a dog? Please, please, please!"

Jake had learned that sometimes it was best not to fight the battle. If he could find the right way to change the subject, then he had dodged a bullet. Since Megan had just come in from art class and this was clearly the favorite activity, maybe, just maybe, art would be the key.

"So how was art class today? Can you show me any of the pictures you did today?"

"Yeah, I can show you what I did today, but it's not finished."

"That's okay, even if it's not finished, what you do is good. It will be even better when it's finished. I kind of like seeing it in varying stages as it moves along to being finished." That was an accurate statement on Jake's part, but he was also praying that the distraction would work.

"Let me go get changed first. I'll be right back. Then you can show me the picture. Go bring your backpack upstairs and wash your hands. Looks like you have paint on your hands. Might even be a good idea to use a little soap and not just rinse your hands under the water." Jake smirked. He didn't know if Megan got the sarcasm.

Megan walked up the stairs ahead of Jake. As he was getting changed, his cell phone rang. It was one of his important clients. Jake knew he had to take this call, and he hoped it wouldn't be that long a call. Since Jake had been leaving work early when it was his turn to be home for the girls, he felt that he had to take these calls, because under normal circumstances, he would still be at work.

When the call ended, Jake bolted down the stairs to work on dinner preparation. After a few minutes, Kristin came home looking happy. "So how was the match?"

"Great, the team won, and I won my match."

"Good going, Kristin. You work hard on your game and it's really paying off."

"I've been working on my serve and today it was great. I could move the ball and mix it up. My opponent had a hard time with it."

"Okay, why don't you go get cleaned up. We're close to getting ready to eat and you can tell me more."

Just as Kristin headed out of the kitchen, the phone rang, and Kristin grabbed it. "Hello, yes, I can get my uncle."

Kristin held out the phone to Jake, but from the pained expression on her face, he knew something was wrong immediately. "It's, it's the police and they want to talk to you." Kristin's lip was trembling. For anyone, a call from the police was a bad sign. For this family, with the tragic loss of Jackie and Blake, any call from the police was devastating.

Jake grabbed the phone. "Yes, this is the Peterson residence. Yes, I'm Jake Foxe. I'm Megan's uncle. She WHAT?

"Where are you? Are you with her now? Is she hurt? Okay, I'll be right there."

Kristin was afraid to ask, but still couldn't contain herself. "What happened?" The fear was evident in her voice as it trembled a little.

Jake felt through the pockets of his jeans as he answered, looking for his car keys. "Apparently, Megan took my car for a joy ride. The police found her because she drove the car up onto the sidewalk and then onto someone's lawn. She was trying to back the car up but couldn't get the car off the lawn. The more she tried to back the car off the lawn, she more she spun the tires and dug the car in. The homeowner saw the end result of what happened and called the police. I guess everyone was really surprised to find a nine-year-old behind the wheel.

"But how did she get my car keys? They're not in my pockets, so where did I leave them?"

As Jake looked around the room, his eye caught his briefcase and then he remembered. "Oh, God, I threw my briefcase on the chair and my keys on the counter when I first came in. I guess she took the keys off the counter. This is crazy! A nine-year-old driving a car. She could have been killed, or she could have killed someone.

"I have to go upstairs and find my other set of keys."

Kristin said, "I don't want to stay here alone. I want to come with you." Jake was so upset that he didn't recognize the obvious problem, but Kristin recognized it.

"How are we going to get there? Megan has your car."

"Oh crap, you're right. Let me call Tyler. I hope I can get him. He wasn't going to come home for dinner."

Jake called Tyler on his cell. Tyler saw Jake's name come up on his cell. Tyler was on his way to a pickup basketball game. Jake didn't normally call him, so while Tyler didn't feel like hearing from Jake, he picked up anyway figuring this couldn't be good news. He was happy that Megan wasn't hurt and said he'd be right there.

Once Tyler hung up the phone, he turned to his friend, Grant, and told him what happened and that he had to go. Tyler couldn't get the story out to his friend, because he was laughing so hard. "I gotta get all the details of this. Imagine this kid driving a car. I'm not sure how she could even see over the steering wheel. What the hell ever gave her the idea to do this? And funnier still, she used Jake's car! He's got to be apoplectic over that alone."

Chapter 38

Tyler, Jake and Kristin arrived at the "crime scene" not too long after the call from the police. By this point, a small crowd had gathered and when it became known that the driver was a nine-year-old girl, social media spread the word like wildfire. The crowd was a mixture of people who lived on the block and surrounding blocks, as well as teens who had tweeted and re-tweeted the story. There were cell phone pictures of the car on the lawn, but surprisingly no pictures of the little girl.

Jake and Tyler bounded out of Tyler's truck. They were so preoccupied with the situation that they never told Kristin to stay in the truck, so she followed closely behind them. There was an officer keeping the ever-increasing crowd back, and an ambulance was parked near the curb where Jake's car was marooned on the lawn. Jake and Tyler pushed through to speak to the officer and explained who they were. They were let through and the sergeant in charge was standing near the ambulance. From the determined pace of these two men, the sergeant presumed these were the father and a friend, or the father and uncle.

The sergeant walked a few yards from the ambulance to meet them. The sergeant had been on the police force for almost thirty years, and he had seen more than his fair share of death, mayhem and violence. While he knew that as the senior officer at the scene he was supposed to take this seriously, he was trying to keep a poker face and not smirk, once he found out that it had been a nine-year-old driving and that she really wasn't hurt.

After some brief introductions, the sergeant told them that Megan was not seriously hurt, but she had a good- sized egg on her forehead, and the EMTs wanted to transport her to the hospital so that she could be checked out further for a concussion. The air bags hadn't deployed, so they thought she hit her head on the steering wheel. Megan was tucked into the ambulance with the EMTs, but Megan was in there wailing, apparently not from injury but from upset.

The sergeant said, "The first officer on the scene expected this to be a DWI based on where the car came to rest, and that the driver couldn't get the car off the lawn. It really surprised him when he saw who was at the wheel. She was still pretty determined to back the car up until the officer reached in and took the keys. I think then the gravity of the situation dawned on her then and she got upset and started to cry.

"He called the EMTs and once they arrived, we tucked her in the ambulance since a crowd was growing. You can go in and talk to her, but I'm not sure if that's going to calm her down or not. She knows she's in trouble."

Jake responded, "She sure as hell is in trouble. Megan is a kid, but she's also very stubborn once she gets an idea in her head."

Tyler tried to intervene and diffuse Jake's anger. "Look, she's just a little kid. Kids do stupid things and never think about the consequences of their actions. Nobody got hurt, there was no damage to the car, and the lawn took the worst of it."

Tyler looked to the sergeant for some help. "You must have seen a lot worse, Sergeant."

The sergeant replied, "I spoke to the homeowner, and he says it's not that big a deal with the lawn. He says the gardener can fix it. He's not even looking for you to pay for it. He says he has kids of his own who did hair-brained things when they were young, and they were lucky nothing terrible happened to them or anybody else."

Jake wasn't buying any of this and was still seething. "That's very nice of the homeowner, but it does not excuse her behavior. Don't try to make light of this, Tyler."

Tyler shrugged and said, "I'm not making light of this, but it's not like she murdered anyone either. Don't blow this up out of all proportion. I'm going to see how Megan is now." With that he walked away and toward the ambulance.

The Sergeant asked a few questions like how she got the car keys, was Megan home alone and had she ever done anything like this before. He took notes on the answers.

"I think the D.A. is going to charge her with something, so I'm going to give you an appearance ticket. She was driving without a license, and she is underage. This is going to get transferred to Family Court because of her age. You may need an attorney."

Jake thanked the Sergeant and turned to go into the ambulance. He turned back to the Sergeant, and said "Will you thank the homeowner for me, or should I go speak to him myself?"

"No, go see the kid. I'll tell him you thanked him.

"By the way, how far away do you live from here?"

"About two miles."

"Two miles, huh? The kid did pretty well to get this far." With that he turned and walked off.

Chapter 39

As her plane began its descent into Westchester County Airport, Sheryl looked out the window to see if she could identify any landmarks. It was cloudy, and she couldn't see anything, so her thoughts drifted. For what seemed like the fiftieth time, Sheryl went over the events of recent months in her head.

She had promised Kristin and Megan that she would come up and visit regularly, yet five months had gone by, and she had yet to visit. She was coming up now to visit primarily because what seemed like an innocent enough prank by Megan driving Jake's car had now turned into a major deal with Court appearances. Jake seeming to be enraged over the incident and the fallout.

Sheryl tried again to examine her own motives honestly with no input or influence from anyone else. She had offered to become the Guardian, but that idea failed when Tyler said he would not step aside as the Guardian and if Jake wanted to step aside, so be it. Tyler said he act as the Guardian alone.

In hindsight and only in her own mind, Sheryl wasn't sure if she was relieved with the way things turned out in Court. If she had become the Guardian for the girls, she would have had to uproot everything in her life and move to New York. She really loved living in Florida. It would have meant taking on tremendous responsibility for the two girls at a time when their lives were in severe turmoil since Jackie and Blake's deaths. Sheryl was also at a time in her life when she was mostly free from child responsibility since Brian was now out of college and starting his career. Mike said he would be okay with the move to New York, but again Sheryl was not sure how that was going to work out when push came to shove. Was Mike really going to want to move to New York after all the years in Florida?

Once the Guardianship issue was settled, why then was she reticent to come to New York and visit? Deep down, did she feel bad that her own sister had not chosen her to be the Guardian and had instead chosen Jake and Tyler, which seemed a questionable choice at best?

Then there was the other issue of not wanting to step on Jake and Tyler's new attempts at parenting. Was she giving them time and space to work out their own style or was she giving them enough rope to hang themselves? Sheryl also wasn't sure how Tyler would feel about having her in the house after her bid to be the Guardian and displace him? However, after the "car caper," it seemed Tyler was grateful for anyone who could help to diffuse the situation and bring the tension level down in the house.

For right now, Sheryl tamped down all these thoughts and deal with the situation at hand. From what she had heard so far, it seemed Jake was melting down, and that Tyler was negotiating it better. There was an incredible twist of fate. Tyler managing the situation better than Jake? Who would have thought it?

For right now, she said she was going to try to be a help without being too judgmental. Maybe the perspective of another adult would help. She was hoping not to have to be the referee. Since she could work remotely from the house while the girls were in school, she was also hoping to take some of the burden of the household duties off Jake and Tyler. Sheryl sensed that even the simple household tasks were causing stress. She could be home when the girls came home from school, so neither Jake nor Tyler had to leave work early.

Sheryl had promised her parents that she would come up and stay at least while the court case was pending. It was only because of that promise that Gloria and Eddie had gone to Virginia to visit Gloria's sister- and brother-in-law. Sheryl was happy that they felt they could stay in Virginia for a while since Gloria wasn't feeling all that well. It gave her parents, but her mother especially, a chance to take it easy and finally to grieve over Jackie's death. Sheryl felt that it was too much for her mother with her health problems to try to take care of the girls and run the household.

Sheryl wasn't sure, but maybe the girls missed having a woman around. "God, what a mess."

Chapter 40

Sheryl wandered through the main floor of the house after she put her things away in the guest room. The house still looked to be in good shape largely, Sheryl presumed, because of Jake. Jake had told her he had the cleaning women come to the house twice a week, because he couldn't stand the mess. Jake was fastidious about everything and looking back she could remember that when they were growing up, his room was always much neater than hers or Jackie's. It amazed her as a kid that having his room so neat was very important to him.

The family room looked a little worse for the wear and she noticed some stains on the rug and the furniture. There was a ping-pong table, and an easel set up, presumably catering to both girls' interests. There was a large flat screen TV and video game boxes. Sheryl noticed that the easel did not have paints anywhere near it, just some colored pencils and some charcoal. It surprised Sheryl that Jake could tolerate charcoal. Paints would probably push Jake over the edge.

Considering what she saw in the family room, Sheryl decided to brave it and see what the bedrooms looked like on the second floor. As she climbed the stairs, she now remembered that all the bedroom doors were closed. "Oh, God, what is behind those doors?"

The first door on the right on the second floor had a picture of Raphael Nadal in mid-air serving a tennis ball, so presumably this was Kristin's room. As Sheryl opened the door and looked around, the room didn't look too bad. There were posters of tennis players and boy bands on the walls. There were two tennis racquets and two carry bags for racquets and equipment leaning up against the desk. The bed was made, sort of. The comforter had been pulled up to cover the sheets, but it was lumpy, as if the sheets underneath it hadn't been pulled up or smoothed out. There were two pair of sneakers near the bed with dirty socks stuffed in them. There was a hamper which looked to be about half full, and there were clothes draped over the desk chair. Not too bad for a twelve-year-old. Sheryl closed the door and proceeded to the next bedroom.

The next door had a small wooden nameplate which said "Megan." Sheryl took a deep breath and pressed on. She was afraid what she was going to find, and with good cause. As she opened the door and stepped into the room, she tripped over a sweater on the floor and went flying. As she caught herself, she then tripped over a shoe and stumbled again. As she surveyed the room, it was hard to find a place to walk where there wasn't some article of clothing on the floor. The bed wasn't made, and the comforter was mostly on the floor. As Sheryl tried to put it back on the bed, she found more clothes lying on the floor under the comforter.

Sheryl clearly remembered the phone conversation where Jake said he had the cleaning women come in twice a week. If that was true, then how could this room possibly look like this? Did the cleaning women ever come into this room, or had they merely given up?

Sheryl picked her way much more carefully as she retreated out of the room. She had yet to see either Jake or Tyler's rooms. She was pretty sure what she was going to find in Jake's room. He had the master bedroom. As she opened the door, Sheryl was not the least bit surprised with what she saw. Jake's room looked like something out of the show, Open House, on Channel 4. The bed was perfectly made without a wrinkle showing. Although there was a nice spread on the bed which was much nicer than anything in the military, the way the bed was made would have made a drill sergeant proud. Sheryl opened the closet and, of course, everything was perfectly in order with the shirts, ties and suits all hanging neatly. In the master bathroom, there was nothing sitting on the vanity, and the sink was sparkling and looking as if it had never been used. Not a trace of shaving cream or toothpaste in sight.

Sheryl walked out of Jake's bedroom and walked to Tyler's room. Sheryl hesitated to go in for several reasons. It somehow seemed like a breach of Tyler's privacy to walk into his bedroom uninvited. The second reason was that based on her conversations with Jake, she was pretty sure what she was going to see. As she opened Tyler's door, it was as bad as she imagined. Tyler's room had clothes everywhere, including hanging out of dresser drawers. Tyler's bed looked as bad as Megan's, and Sheryl wasn't sure if Megan's bedroom was a mirror image of Tyler's or if Tyler's was a mirror image of Megan's. No matter which was which, Sheryl knew the battle lines were clear. Now that the incident of Megan's driving was also brewing and taking on consequences not seen by anyone the day it happened, Sheryl was thinking that this visit was going to be very trying. Sheryl didn't come to New York to take sides, so she hoped that maybe she could be a force for compromise, without getting herself singed in the process. At the end of this trip, she still wanted to have a relationship with her brother and her nieces.

Chapter 41

Sheryl had called Jake and told him she was at the house and that if he wanted to take a night off that she would make dinner, help the girls with their homework and get them settled for bed. Jake said it was his night to take care of the girls, and he would be very glad for the night off. His relief was almost palpable. He said he was going to call some friends and meet them for dinner. He said he would text Tyler and tell him Sheryl was there. She asked him what was happening with Megan and the "car caper." Jake said it was a long story, and he'd tell her when he got home. He said what looked like an innocent prank had now turned into a big deal involving the Court.

Jake told her both girls were coming home on the bus today and if she wanted to meet the bus, what time to be outside. At the appointed time, Sheryl put on her jacket and went out to meet the bus. As she stood there shivering, she remembered why she hated New York as she felt the wind was whipping against her skin.

Kristin and Megan were clearly delighted to see Aunt Sheryl, and the feeling was mutual. They knew she was coming, but they still both hugged her tightly as they jumped off the bus. "I am so glad to see you, but it's freezing out here. Let's take the hug into the house."

The three of them sat at the kitchen table for a long time drinking hot chocolate as the girls vied for her attention to tell her about school and birthday parties, and even some cute boys. Sheryl wondered if Blake or Tyler even knew to do this with the girls, and if not, they didn't know what they were missing. During the conversation, Sheryl dropped her napkin on the floor and as she sat down in the chair after retrieving it, she found Megan out of her seat and next to her giving her a hug. Megan then went to sit on Sheryl's lap and continued the hug. Kristin never missed a beat as she continued her story about her last tennis match.

After close to an hour of their talking, Sheryl said, "Okay, I think it's time for you both to do some homework and I am going to make dinner. I can help with your homework if you get stuck, I hope. I was never too terrific in math, but I can try. If you get your homework done before dinner, maybe we can play video games or a board game after dinner."

About ten minutes after the girls went upstairs, Kristin startled Sheryl having come back into the kitchen in her socks, so Sheryl didn't hear her. "Wow, Kristin, you scared me. I didn't hear you come back in. Get stuck on something with your homework?"

"No, I wanted to talk to you without Megan being here. I overheard Uncle Jake talking to Uncle Tyler and saying that he had spoken to an attorney about the thing with Megan driving the car. She must really be in trouble if they're talking to an attorney. The treat us like we're little kids and don't tell us anything. I'm practically grown up. I'm twelve, you know."

Sheryl had to suppress a grin about Kristin's comment being twelve and practically a grown up. "To be honest, Kristin, I don't know everything about this yet myself. Uncle Jake wanted to wait until he could talk to me in person while I'm here. I know that this is not some prank which can be taken care of just by punishing Megan here in the house. The authorities are now involved and your Uncles thought that they needed to get an attorney. I don't think they wanted to worry you about this. Worrying and handling this problem are the jobs of the actual grownups.

"How about this? Let me talk to your Uncles about it and then we'll sit down and explain more to you. What you can understand and what Megan can understand are two different things since you are older and practically a grown up. Does that sound okay?"

Kristin said yes and turned to walk out of the kitchen, but then did an about face. "Is Megan going to jail?" Kristin's lip trembled and then the tears brimmed in her eyes.

Sheryl walked over to Kristin and pulled Kristin to her in an embrace. "No, sweetheart, I definitely don't think Megan is going to jail. You don't have to worry about that."

While still in Sheryl's embrace, Kristin mumbled into Sheryl's shoulder, "Good, because a lot of bad things have happened to us. We can't let Megan go to jail."

"She won't, honey, she won't. All of us are here to protect you and Megan."

Chapter 42

Kristin's comments about a lot of bad things happening to them weighed heavily on Sheryl. She couldn't even really imagine what it must be like to lose your parents in a violent car crash when you are twelve and nine years old. She knew the girls were seeing a child psychiatrist, and now Sheryl wanted to talk to her herself. She wanted to make sure that the psychiatrist knew how Kristin was feeling and she also wanted to know how much was appropriate to tell Kristin. The car incident was weighing on Kristin apparently more than she was letting on.

She also couldn't wait for Jake to get home to get all the facts about what was going on with Megan. She knew a case was pending in Family Court about the car incident and that's why Jake and Tyler had engaged an attorney, but she didn't know what Megan was being charged with at nine-years-old, or why a nine-year-old was even being charged with anything. Sheryl could understand why Jake and Tyler didn't want to burden Kristin with all of this, but she had overheard at least one conversation which was making her upset.

Sheryl had no idea of what Megan thought about the whole car incident. Was she ignoring it and going about her merry way? Did she understand why a nine-year-old driving a car was a bad thing? Did she just think it was a prank or did she get the idea into her head that she'd like to take the car for a ride and then just did it? After all, in Megan's mind, she may have thought she had seen the adults driving cars a million times, and it didn't look all that hard. Sheryl suspected that there was more going on in Megan's world than she was letting on. Were all these little skirmishes in the house culminating in the joy ride, a cry for help from a little girl who was hurting much more than anyone was seeing?

Sheryl and the girls were alone for dinner and the stories about their activities and their friends continued throughout dinner. Apparently, chicken cutlets, sweet potatoes, salad and sting beans almondine were good choices, because no one complained about hating anything and no one refused to eat anything.

Clean up was relatively easy and everything was put away and the dishwasher started. "Let's go play some video games," came the plea from Megan.

"Is all your homework done? Let me see your assignments so we can make sure everything is done." Megan groaned. "It's all done. I'm finished. Let's play."

"Megan, I learned something very valuable from your cousin Brian when he was in school and that was to check the homework against the assignments before it got too late and before he could play video games. Sometimes he conveniently 'forgot' to do his Social Studies assignment because he thought it was boring. He also hated Spanish when he was in middle school, so that was another subject that he often 'forgot' to do.

"Do you have your assignments on a piece of paper or on the computer?"

Kristin answered for both of them. In Megan's grade they have it on paper and on the computer. In my grade, it's just on the computer."

"Okay, Megan get your backpack and let's look at everything. Kristin, let me see your assignments on the computer. This applies to both of you."

Kristin was more diligent about getting her homework done for two reasons. Some nights she came home from practice, or a match and she was just too tired to do a lot of homework, so she often knew what nights she was going to be late and did a little more the preceding night.

The school was adamant that if your grades slipped, you couldn't play on the teams, and Kristin didn't want anything to jeopardize tennis.

Megan, on the other hand, had no such sense of discipline. She hated sports, and she thought sports hated her based on her prior encounters with tennis and basketball. Plus, she really hated being sweaty. She was content to slide by in school. If she missed an assignment, it was "who cares?" She had somehow picked up on her radar that since her parents died, the teachers were more inclined to let things go with her. She didn't know it was called milking the situation, but that was precisely what she was doing.

She had done about half her math homework tonight, and that seemed like more than enough for her. Who needed math anyway? It was a big fat annoyance. She would never use math once she got out of school and that was what calculators were for. She wanted to draw and paint, not do stupid equations. She had never seen an equation on any painting or drawing.

Sheryl looked at the assignments and then at Megan's work. "Megan, it looks like you did about half your math homework. You have to finish the rest of it."

"Nope, that's enough for tonight. I'm tired."

"Look, based on the list, you have to finish these two pages to hand in tomorrow. If you get stuck, I'll help you, but this has to get done."

"I can do it tomorrow morning before school. I'm really, really exhausted tonight."

"Megan, I know all the tricks from your cousin Brian. He was often too tired to do his homework, but he wasn't too tired to play games with his friends. There won't be enough time tomorrow morning before school to finish this. Kristin's homework is done, and she and I are going to play games in about fifteen minutes. That's about how long it will take you to finish your math homework. So finish it if you want to play with us or if you want to watch TV. You decide."

"But this isn't fair, and it isn't any fun."

"You are correct on both accounts. You can decide, but the clock is ticking."

Chapter 43

They ushered Jake and Tyler into a conference room while waiting for Harris Mayfield to meet them there. Someone who worked with Jake had recommended Harris to them, and Harris apparently did a good deal of Family Court work. Harris was a man of about forty years old with a head of curly red hair.

Jake brought the Court papers for Harris to review and explained what had gone on with Megan and the now infamous "car caper" as the adults referred to it. Jake also explained the guardianship situation as the result of Jackie and Blake's deaths.

"How old is Megan?"

"She's nine."

"That's a pretty gutsy thing for a little girl to do. Has she ever done anything else like this in the past?"

"Well, if you mean, has she ever driven a car before, the answer is no." Jake's tone had a bit of sarcasm to it.

"Look, gentlemen, don't get defensive about this. I have to ask these questions so that I understand what kinds of things go on with Megan, both before and after you became her Guardians. I need to know everything. You need to be completely honest with me. If you feel you can't tell me everything, then you should probably get another attorney. I can't do my job and represent you and Megan effectively if I don't know everything, good or bad."

Jake started to interrupt, but Harris held up his hand to stop him.

"I want to finish and then you can ask me whatever you want to. Let me also tell you that I'm sure Child Protective Services is going to get involved and interview all of you. I don't want to be surprised by anything they find out. If there's something bad, I need to know it and then we can figure out how to deal with it and hopefully diffuse it.

"So, is there anything else that Megan has done that I need to know about? Was she ever suspended from school, or did she ever have any other brush with the law? Ever hit another kid, and the family pressed charges? Anything like that?"

Now Tyler spoke up. "Okay, Harris, we get it, but as far as I know, she's done nothing, even when my brother- and sister-in-law were still alive. But I need to ask you, isn't this thing being blown out of all proportion? She's a nine-year-old kid, and she did a stupid thing. I'm sure she never thought this through and none of us expected that she would end up in Family Court. She's being charged with driving without a license, like some guy who's had his license revoked or something."

"I understand, but it's not up to us. We're being presented with charges against her and because she is a minor, we'll be in Family Court. We have to defend her as best we can."

Tyler spoke again. "She didn't hurt anyone, or damage anyone's car. All she did was go up on the guy's lawn and he didn't even care about that. Not even looking for us to pay for the damage to the lawn. Said he'd take care of it himself."

"Look, I agree with you that it seems excessive. We never quite know what goes into these decisions to prosecute someone. Especially something like this, which on the face of things, doesn't seem like much. The fact of a kid driving a car seems to have struck a nerve somewhere.

"The other thing that this might be about is lack of supervision. You said that Jake was home when she took the car. Or it might be about something else. It might be about your somewhat unusual living situation. It remains to be seen and I will try to get a feel for that as we get further into the case."

"Oh, crap, this is about some narrow-minded view of what makes up a family?" said Jake.

"It might be. I'll try to see.

"I want to meet Megan before we go to Court. I want to talk to her to see what she says about what happened. I will also want to talk to her again before Child Protective Services talks to her.

"You said she is seeing a psychiatrist. I will want to talk to her as well. We still have a few weeks before the first Court appearance. If you should get a call from CPS, let me know and I will speak to them first. If you retain me, I will get the name of the case worker and speak to that person to see what they are thinking.

"It goes without saying, that you are not to speak to any reporters or any parents of the girls' friends. No one. Any inquiries should come to me.

"Let me know by the end of the week if you intend to retain me. I will send you a Retainer Letter for you both to sign and you can return it with your check.

"I want both of you at the first Court appearance with me, and Megan must be there. Tyler, don't take offense. You need to come to Court, preferably in a suit. If you don't own a suit, you need to wear a dark sport jacket, and pants, not jeans. You need a dress shirt and shoes, not flip flops like that you have on now, or sneakers. Oh, and a matching tie. If you have questions about what you can wear, or what matches, come by the office and I'll check it out and let you know."

Tyler rolled his eyes. "I'm serious, Tyler. This is important. Every time you come to Court, you need to make a good impression."

Tyler mumbled okay and Jake smirked.

Chapter 44

Jake, Tyler, Sheryl and Megan walked across the plaza from the parking lot toward the Courthouse. It was a vast open space and the wind blowing could take anyone's breath away. Inside the lobby of the Courthouse, the line snaked toward the security checkpoint. Once through security, they walked toward and got into the elevator, which made all the local stops on each floor until they reached the floor with the Family Court. They checked in at the desk with the Court officer. Since the case was scheduled for 2pm, the bulk of the calendar had been called in the morning. The waiting room for the litigants was mercifully not too filled, because it was small and windowless.

About five minutes after they sat down in the waiting room, Harris Mayfield showed up in a dark suit with a shockingly white shirt and a red tie. He motioned them out into the hallway to speak to them.

"You look good today, Tyler. You should wear a jacket and tie more often." With that Harris winked and turned toward Megan.

There were benches lining the walls, and Harris knelt down to speak to Megan as she sat on one bench. It was obvious that Megan was terrified, and she was white as a sheet. She was clinging to Sheryl.

The tone of Harris' voice was the gentlest and calmest that Jake and Tyler had ever heard come out of him. "Hi, Megan, how are you doing today? Do you remember meeting me in my office?"

Megan nodded yes, but no words came out of her mouth.

"Okay, so remember that we talked about that when we go into the Courtroom, it's going to be you and I and your two uncles sitting at the counsel table. Your aunt can sit in the Courtroom, but she will not sit at the counsel table with us." Harris waited and Megan nodded again.

"The Judge is going to be sitting up high on the bench, just like we talked about. And then remember I told you that there is going to be an attorney sitting at the other counsel table. The Judge is going to be talking to me and to the other attorney and we are going to be talking to her. I'm going to be telling the Judge your side of the story.

"Remember I told you that the Judge may want to talk to you. If she does, she may ask you a few questions. She may ask if you have any questions about what's going on and if you know that driving a car without a license is wrong because you're a kid.

"What would you answer her?"

Megan's lip quivered, but she answered the question. "Yeah, it's wrong, " came the almost imperceptible answer.

"If the Judge asks you why you drove the car, what would you say?"

A long pause and one big tear ran down Megan's cheek. Jake took a step forward, but Harris put his hand on Jake's sleeve to stop him.

Megan answered, "My mommy and daddy were killed in a car crash, and I wanted to know what it was like when they were driving the car that night." Then the tears flowed and Megan sat down and buried her face in Sheryl's arm.

Harris swallowed hard and said, "That's a great answer, Megan. Just like what we talked about in my office." Then Harris turned away quickly and brushed a tear from his eye.

Chapter 45

Jennifer Rockford taught one of the fourth grades in Davis Elementary School. Her class was an exuberant bunch who got excited over every new project. Jennifer just had to explain this new subject as a fun concept that they had never tackled before. The curriculum called for teaching how to write business and personal letters. Considering that they had recently worked on penmanship, Jennifer presumed that learning to write letters was supposed to build on that skill. However, the curriculum glossed over the fact that most people now simply sent e-mails or texts. Jennifer really puzzled over how to explain this to make it seem like an adventure. There were a few skeptics in her class about various assignments and Megan was often one of them.

Finally, Jennifer thought she had figured out the way to make this fun for the kids and given some of the quirky personalities in the class, she thought it might actually work. So, on Wednesday morning, she broached the subject.

"Today you are going to learn how to write two kinds of letters. Business letters and personal letters. Business letters might be something you would use to complain to a company about something and personal letters would be what you would use to write to a celebrity, movie star, or professional athlete to tell them how great you think they are in a movie or how well they did in a football game or baseball game, for example."

Jennifer was well aware of whose picture were on the backpacks of her students and what movies they talked about, so she gave them some ideas of who they could write to.

"These are just some examples, but you are free to write to anyone you want. Now let me explain to you that there are five parts to a letter. Look at page 43 of your books and we'll go over them. As you see in the book, the first part is called the heading.

"The second part is called the salutation, the third is the body, the fourth is the complimentary close, and the fifth is the signature." As she pointed out each part of the letter in the book, she explained each part.

"Okay, by next Wednesday, I will expect to see two letters from each of you. One a personal letter and one a business letter. Remember that each letter should be on a separate piece of paper when you hand them in. You can ask for help to find the right address for whomever you are writing to. So be creative. I'm looking forward to reading your letters."

Jennifer would have no idea the effect that this assignment would have on her students and the ensuing consequences. She especially would have no idea of what would happen when Megan wrote a third letter not called for by the assignment.

Chapter 46

"All rise, the Family Court of the State of New York, County of Westchester, is now in session. The Honorable Ann Waverly presiding," intoned the bailiff.

Judge Waverly ascended the three steps to the bench. "Good afternoon, please be seated. Counsel, please place your appearances on the record and tell the Court who is present with you in Court today at the counsel table."

The County Attorney stated his name and office address, and Harris stated his name, office address and that he was representing Megan Peterson. He also stated that Megan was present and stated Jake and Tyler's full names and that they were the legal Guardians for Megan. Harris thought he saw a slight smile on the Judge's face as he motioned toward Megan who looked positively small sitting at the counsel table in her little pink dress. Her hair was in a ponytail held by a pink bow. Sheryl had done an excellent job with the outfit and Megan looked even younger than her nine years. Megan's legs were swinging under the counsel table because her feet didn't touch the floor.

"Mr. Blaize, your office is moving forward with a Vehicle and Traffic offense under Section 509 (1), which is driving a motor vehicle without a license and as an underage driver, as well as a Vehicle and Traffic offense Section 511 (1), which is aggravated unlicensed operation of a motor vehicle. Is there any other charge?"

"No, Your Honor."

"Mr. Mayfield, your position on these charges?"

"Thank you, Your Honor. We don't dispute that Megan drove a car at nine- years- old, for which she is very sorry, and she has been punished at home. We believe that these charges have been blown out of all proportion. No one was hurt, there was no damage to the car or any other vehicle, and there was minimal damage to a neighbor's lawn, who didn't even want any reimbursement because there was such minor damage to his lawn.

"There are some extenuating circumstances since Megan's parents were both recently killed in a car crash. Megan is seeing a child psychiatrist about that terrible tragedy and the car issue is also being addressed with her. Megan's uncle, Jake Foxe, was home with her at the time she took the car, so there was no question of supervision. Mr. Foxe merely went upstairs to change his clothes."

Harris was just warming to the task. "Frankly, Your Honor, we don't understand why these charges are even being brought. Section 511 is a misdemeanor and carries a fine of $75 to $300 and/ or up to fifteen days in jail."

With that, Steven Blaize jumped in. "Mr. Mayfield doesn't understand why these charges are being brought? That's unbelievable. What this child did fits every element of the statute."

Before Mr. Blaize could take another breath, Harris Mayfield jumped back in with both guns blazing. "Oh, give me a break! This statute was meant for adults who don't take having a driver's license seriously or who have had their licenses revoked or suspended for other offenses, yet drive anyway. This situation is about a little girl who made a mistake. This isn't repeated behavior on Megan's part; she has never done this before. She's never been in trouble in school. In fact, she's quite talented in painting. For some bizarre reason, the D.A. and now the County Attorney are making a big deal out of nothing. That we are here today wasting the Court's time, especially considering the severity of the charges, is absolutely preposterous."

Both attorneys wanted another round of argument, but the Judge cut them off.

"All right, gentlemen, that will be enough for now. Mr. Mayfield, do you have an objection if I ask a few questions of your client right now? Normally, I might ask to see the child in chambers with counsel, but I think considering the circumstances, that would be more intimidating."

"No objection, Your Honor. I appreciate the fact that you recognize that Megan is nine."

That was a great answer on Harris' part. He agreed to the Judge's request and also reminded her in the same short sentence that Megan was a nine-year-old. The Judge nodded.

Judge Waverly began, "Megan, would you mind if I talk to you here for a minute?"

Megan jumped in her chair when the Judge spoke directly to her. "Okay," came the answer.

"Megan, you drove a car for about two miles, is that right?"

Megan nodded, but the Court said, "You have to answer out loud so the court reporter can take down everything that anybody says in the Courtroom. She pointed to the court reporter as she was speaking.

"Yes," came the one -word answer.

"Have you ever driven a car before?"

"No."

"Do you know that it was wrong for you to drive a car?"

"Yes."

"Do you know why it's wrong?"

"Yes, because I'm too young. And I had a little trouble seeing over the wheel."

The Judge was about to speak, when Megan interjected again, much to the Judge's surprise.

"I forgot to say that I never had driving lessons."

With that, a slight chuckle broke out in the courtroom.

"All right, then Counsel, I do not intend to hold a hearing with a nine-year-old as the witness. I want each of you to submit affidavits and briefs in support of your position by two weeks from today. The total number of pages for the affidavits shall not exceed ten pages and the briefs shall not exceed seven pages. If you can make your case in fewer pages, the Court would appreciate it. Right now, everything will be on submission. Let's set a date for three weeks from today in case the Court wants oral argument. My Clerk will notify you if the Court wants oral argument.

"If there are no further questions, then we are adjourned."

As they walked out of the Courtroom, Harris explained to them what had just happened. "There are a lot of good things which happened in there. First of all, the Judge could have ordered that Child Protective Services visit your house and talk to you two gentlemen and Megan and Kristin and give a report to the Court. She didn't do that. Second, she could have ordered a hearing on this matter, during which the Court would have heard testimony under oath. She didn't do that either and that's huge.

"She ordered the two attorneys to submit Affidavits as to what happened and briefs about any points of law we want the Court to consider. I think based on that, there's a good chance that the Court is going to dismiss the charges or reduce them because the D.A. and the County Attorney made too big a deal about this, and the charges they picked were excessive."

Chapter 47

Jennifer Rockford thoroughly enjoyed reading the letters. A few letters were boring, and a few letters were routine, but some of the letters had her in stitches.

She read a few out loud to her colleagues in the faculty room.

Senator Bernie Sanders
United States Capitol Building
Washington, D. C.
Dear Senator Sanders,
I know that you are running for President. You look a lot like my grandfather. His hair is white, and he wears glasses like you. I am scared of you because you yell a lot. My grandfather doesn't yell, so I like him better than you.
Are you related to Colonel Sanders from Kentucky Fried Chicken? I like his ads and his chicken.
Your friend,
Tommy Reilly

Jennifer read the second to her colleagues.

President Donald Trump
The White House

1600 Pennsylvania Avenue
Washington, D. C.
Dear President Trump,
    My name is Betsy Romano and I am ten years old. I am in the fourth grade at Davis Elementary School. I am just learning how to play golf and I shot 105 the other day when I played with my dad. I think if I practice hard, I can break 100 and maybe even break 90. I really like golf a lot. My putting is very good.
    I heard that you are a good golfer. Do you think that I could come play with you at your golf course in New Jersey or in Florida?
    My Dad says that if I can come play with you, that we should be polite and take you out for dinner afterwards. He will have to pay, because I don't have that much money. Maybe you can even ask him to buy me a new 5 Wood before we play.
    I will wait to hear from you.
    Yours truly,
    Betsy Romano

The third letter was from John Morgan

Green Giant Corporation
Le Sueur, Minnesota
Dear Green Giant,
    My mother made me eat your frozen cauliflower two nights ago. I hated it. Then last night she made me eat your frozen broccoli. That tasted even worse than the cauliflower. If that's all you make, I don't think people are going to buy your stuff and you will probably go out of business.
    Don't bother to send us any free samples either.
    Why can't you make something good like ice cream or Hershey Bars or M&Ms?
    Yours truly,
    John Morgan

The fourth letter was from Megan

Ms. Serena Williams
Ballin Isle Country Club
Jupiter, Florida

Dear Serena:
My name is Megan and I live in Rye Brook, New York. I went with my parents and my sister to see you play tennis at the U. S. Open last year. You are really a great tennis player and I like how strong you are and how hard you hit the ball. I also like your tennis outfits. I have a good sense of color. Maybe I could help you design your tennis outfits.
My sister's name is Kristin. She is a good tennis player but not as good as you. She would like to meet you. Can we meet you when you come to New York for the U. S. Open this year?
My parents were killed in a car crash so they won't come to meet you. I am living with my uncles so they will come with me and Kristin.
Yours friend,
Megan Peterson

The fifth letter was to Derek Jeter

Mr. Derek Jeter
St. Petersburg, Florida
Dear Derek:
I saw that they voted you into the Baseball Hall of Fame. I wish that I had been old enough to see you when you played at Yankee Stadium. My Mom and Dad are big fans of yours. We watch some of your old games on YES. You were a terrific player.
I would like to be the shortstop for the Yankees when I am older and since you retired, I wouldn't be taking your job. I would really like to be the first woman shortstop for the Yankees. My Mom says I

can do it. My Dad shrugs his shoulders and is not sure. What do you think?

    I hope you will answer me.
    Your friend,
    Debbie Johnson

Chapter 48

Megan walked into Jake's bedroom and saw the Court papers sitting in a neat pile on his desk. She really was scared the day she went to Court, even though her two Uncles and Aunt Sheryl went with her. The Judge was sitting way up high on a bench and looking down at all of them. The attorney did a lot of the talking, but she didn't like sitting at the counsel table with her two Uncles. Until they called the case, and they went into the courtroom, Megan sat on the bench with Aunt Sheryl and remembered being terrified.

She saw Aunt Sheryl motion to Uncle Tyler who was standing closer to her in the hallway. When he bent over to her, even though Aunt Sheryl whispered it, Megan heard Aunt Sheryl say to Tyler, "Megan is clutching my arm, and she's trembling. When they call the case, make sure you take Megan's hand and walk her into the Courtroom. I can come into the Courtroom, but I can't come to sit at the counsel table."

As Megan looked at the papers, she recognized the name of the Judge from when they had been in Court last week. The whole time she was in the Courtroom, she was terrified because everything in the Courtroom was new, scary and large. She didn't really understand what was going on and the two lawyers were talking very fast. She understood that her lawyer didn't like the other attorney because he was yelling at him. She guessed that was good.

Megan had a piece of paper with her, and she wrote the name and address of the Judge. She also knew that Uncle Jake had a roll of stamps in the kitchen. She went back to her room and put on paper the five parts of the letter she had just learned.

Judge Ann Waverly
Family Court
111 Dr. Martin Luther King
White Plains, N.Y. 10601
Dear Judge Waverly,
My name is Megan Peterson and I am 9 years old. I met you two weeks ago when I went to court with my two uncles. I was in court because I took my uncle's car and drove for a while. I didn't drive very far with the car and it was pretty easy to drive because I saw my parents and a bunch of other grown- ups drive cars. My parents were killed in a car crash and I wanted to see what happened to them. I miss them very much. One night they went out, and it was raining and they never came back. My uncles have been taking care of us. That means me and my sister Kristin. I don't like living with my uncles and I don't know why I have to do that. Sometimes they are mean to me. I know my parents aren't coming back to live with us because they are dead. I miss them more each day. I want you to fix this so that we can live with my Aunt Sheryl. I heard when we were in court that you decide a lot of things, so please decide this. I think we have to come back and see you soon. So tell all the grown- ups that we can live with Aunt Sheryl when we see you. I really don't like living with my uncles because they are mean to me.
Your friend,
Megan

Three days later, Judge Waverly's Clerk brought this letter to the Judge's Law Secretary. A Law Secretary is a full-time paid attorney of the Court who works for the Judge. Among other things, the Law Secretary usually reads all the motion papers and gives the

Judge some suggestions about deciding the case, researches the law, and conferences the case with the attorneys to try to settle the cases.

"Frank, you need to read this letter. It's written in pencil from a nine-year-old girl who was before the Court about ten days ago. Here's the file number. She was the kid who drove the car a couple of miles and ended up on someone's lawn. No one got hurt and not even any damage to the car."

Frank looked up from his computer. "Yeah, so what? I wasn't in the Courtroom, but I think the Judge thought the D. A. and the County Attorney were making a big deal out of nothing."

"The kid wrote a letter? Does it look like the attorney wrote the letter for the kid to gain sympathy from the Court?"

"This little girl wrote the letter, but it's really not about the case with her driving the car. She says her parents were killed in a car crash and she's living with her uncles, and they're mean to her." She held out the letter to Frank. "Maybe the Judge should see this."

Frank got up from his desk, took the letter and read it. "Yeah, I think the Judge has to see this. It looks as if the kid wrote it herself and not the attorney ghosting it. It opens a whole new set of problems that no one saw coming here. No attorney in their right mind would have drawn up this letter and pretended that the kid wrote it."

Chapter 49

Harris Mayfield sat back in his chair and considered what he had heard. He had just hung up the phone with Judge Waverly's clerk who said the Judge asked that Harris Mayfield and the County Attorney appear in Court on Wednesday afternoon, even though the date that they were supposed to appear in Court again, wasn't for another two and a half weeks, and then only if the Court wanted to hear oral argument. When he tried to press the clerk about why the Judge wanted to see them in two days, the clerk was not forthcoming. All she would say was that the Judge wanted to see the two attorneys without the clients.

Now Harris wasn't sure what to do. He felt he had an obligation to tell the clients about the call and his Court appearance. He knew this would make them very upset, and he could certainly understand why. Harris really had no idea of what the Court wanted, but it was very unusual. Harris couldn't comfort them because he was puzzled at best and worried at worst.

Harris called Tyler and Jake on a conference call and explained what he knew, which wasn't much. "I couldn't get any info out of the Clerk about what the Judge wants, and she only wants the attorneys to appear."

Tyler asked if this was unusual. Harris said yes, but he knew nothing more. Tyler and Jake were upset, and Harris had nothing to say to calm their nerves.

When Wednesday afternoon arrived, Harris was antsy, and he watched as the minutes crawled by on the clock on his desk. He wasn't getting much work done, so finally he took a walk around the block and maybe get some soup for lunch.

Finally, it was time to leave for Court and Harris was sitting outside the Courtroom at 1:50 pm. Steve Blaize walked off the elevator and walked over to say hello to Harris. "Hey, Harris, do you have any idea why we're here?"

"Nope," came the response. "I'll tell the bailiff we're here."

In a few minutes, both attorneys were in the Courtroom and at the counsel tables. Shortly thereafter, the bailiff recited the same sentence about the Court being in session, and the Judge walked in and took her seat on the bench. The Clerk announced the name of the case for the Court reporter.

Judge Waverly started. "Good afternoon, gentlemen. As you know, I am going to decide this case about the child driving the car on submission, and I may ask for oral argument, but that is not why you are here today.

"The Family Court is always charged with doing what is in the best interest of minors, in this case Megan. After you appeared here last time, I received a letter, which is troubling. The letter is handwritten, and it's from Megan. The letter was written to me. When you see the contents of the letter, I am sure that Mr. Mayfield didn't of its contents, nor did he prompt the writing of the letter. I'm asking the bailiff to give each of you a copy of this letter now."

The bailiff handed the letter to the two attorneys, and it only took them a minute to read it. When they finished, the Judge said, "Since the Court's mandate is to do what is in the best interest of the child, I am going to appoint a Court Evaluator for Megan. The Court Evaluator will interview Megan and her sister, the two Uncles who are her Guardians, and the Child Psychiatrist and anyone else she feels is appropriate. Your clients are to cooperate. The Court Evaluator will set up a schedule.

"Am I correct, Mr. Mayfield, that you had no knowledge of this letter or its contents until now?"

"Your Honor, I had no knowledge of this letter. This is certainly not what we were expecting. We were only expecting to deal with the Vehicle and Traffic offenses."

"Mr. Mayfield, I realize that this is highly unusual for the Court to hear directly from a nine-year-old. Yet here we are. She wasn't exactly specific what was going on. It could be the complaint of a child who doesn't want to be told to go to bed at a specific time, or it could be something much more serious. In any case, I can't take this complaint lightly until we know what it really is. I can't and won't brush this under the rug.

"Please also tell the Guardians that I don't want to hear that the child is in trouble or is being punished for making a complaint. I'm going to tell the Court Evaluator to make that point with the child, the Guardians and the Child Psychiatrist. Are we clear?"

"Yes, Your Honor."

"I am still going to rule on the V and T case, but that seems now to have taken on a much less important role. Anything further?"

"No, Your Honor."

"Then we are adjourned."

Chapter 50

As Harris sat in his car outside the office, he read the letter twice more. He truly didn't know what to think. His interactions with Megan had been brief, and the prospect of having to go to Court frightened her. That probably masked her true personality somewhat. He had to prompt her to tell him the story about driving the car. She wasn't too forthcoming with the details, and he had to probe to get all the details, but that didn't seem unusual to him. After all, she was a nine-year-old in trouble, and very few nine-year-olds must deal with a strange man who is an attorney or deal with going to Court. He remembered her clinging to her Aunt and not to either of her Uncles, while they were waiting to go into the Courtroom. Again, that didn't seem unusual to him at the time.

When he finally arrived at the office, he decided to get this call over with sooner rather than later. He called Tyler and Jake and put them on a conference call. Harris read them the letter. There was dead silence on the other end of the phone. Harris waited for a reaction, and for a good ten seconds, there was none. At first, he thought maybe someone disconnected the call by mistake. When he said, "Are you there?" they both answered yes.

Then Tyler started laughing. This set Jake off into a rant. "Are you goddamned crazy, Tyler? Don't you ever take anything seriously? The Judge probably thinks we're child molesters. She could think that's code from Megan that we're molesting her or that we're running a child porn ring out of the house. We could have charges brought against us and go to jail. You are a fucking idiot if you're laughing.

"This is the thanks we get for upending our lives to move in with the kids. My gut was telling me that this was a bad idea from the beginning. I should have followed my instincts and said no right from the beginning. Why didn't Jackie and Blake consult us and see how we felt about it before they named us in their Wills?"

That was only the opening two paragraphs of the rant. Finally, only when Jake stopped to take a breath, did Tyler respond. "I'm laughing, you moron, because this is the oldest trick in the book. Megan put us on defense, but she's goddamn smart, especially for a kid her age. Now she thinks that we'll have to tiptoe around her, and she'll get to do what she wants, or we'll be in trouble with the Judge. She thinks we can never tell her to do anything for fear that we'll be seen as 'being mean to her.'

"She just turned the tables on us, and she did it in such a clever way. She actually understood how much power the Judge has, and she's cleverly made the Judge an inadvertent ally. She somehow innately understood that the Judge is the most powerful adult in her life, and she maneuvered the Judge and maybe without realizing it, the whole legal system onto her side. Advantage Megan."

Harris sat back into his desk chair and let out a deep breath. He had always thought that Tyler was a bit of an idiot and a flake, but maybe he had misjudged Tyler based on his perpetually rumpled clothes and disheveled hair. Harris was the first to respond.

"Ya know, Tyler, you might be right. Megan might not be able to verbalize what she did and the effect of setting the ball in motion, but she somehow discerned it. I told her myself several times how important the Judge was and that the Judge was going to hear the story and decide about the case. Megan seems to have gotten that message loud and clear. I wish my own kids would take to heart the things I tell them the way Megan did about the Judge."

Now Jake interjected again. "Oh, for the love of God! Do you really think a nine-year-old can manipulate the legal system to help herself?"

Before Jake could say another word, both Harris and Tyler answered with a resounding "Yes."

Tyler said, "Jake, if for once you would see that everything in the world is not about you. Everything you said earlier is all about you. How this could affect your life. How charges could be brought against you. How your life was upended by having to become the Guardian. Blah, blah, blah. That's the problem right there. It's only about you and your viewpoint of the world. Not Megan's viewpoint or Megan's world."

Harris was extremely glad that Tyler had run point on this, because he said out loud what Harris was thinking. Harris would have had to be more diplomatic in how he would phrase it to Jake, but Jake's earlier rant only seemed to be about him and the effects on his life. Harris was waiting for another rant from Jake, but for the moment there was none.

Harris then explained that he would hear from the lawyer appointed as the Court Evaluator for Megan. Harris explained that the Court Evaluator is an independent attorney appointed by the Court to represent Megan's interests in this case, since presumably Megan's interests and Jake's and Tyler's interests might very well be different. The Court Evaluator would then submit a report to the Court. Based on the Judge's comments and her use of the pronoun "she" when referring to the Court Evaluator, Harris knew it was going to be a woman. Harris explained about the people the Court Evaluator would most probably want to interview. He also suggested that they get in touch with Dr. Moran, Megan's psychiatrist, and give her a heads up about what was going on, so she could handle the matter from her end. The Court Evaluator would undoubtedly want to speak to the psychiatrist.

"One more thing I have to bring up with both of you. The Judge wanted it made known that you are to cooperate with the Court Evaluator and that Megan is not to be punished for writing the letter. She's going to tell the Court Evaluator that, and I was supposed to tell you."

Jake asked, "Are we supposed to tell Megan that we know she wrote this letter to the Judge? What about who this Court Evaluator is and why she wants to talk to Megan?"

Harris said, "My suggestion is that you talk to the psychiatrist and see how she thinks we should handle it. Maybe she will broach the subject first with Megan, and then all of you will discuss it together with the psychiatrist. Let me know what the psychiatrist says and tell her I am going to want to speak to her myself as well.

Chapter 51

After the girls went to bed, Tyler and Jake shut the door to the den and gave Sheryl a copy of Megan's letter and explained what Harris told them about the Court Evaluator. The letter equally surprised Sheryl. Jake asked Sheryl if she had any indication of Megan's unhappiness or why she would have written such a letter. Sheryl said she had seen some of Megan's stubbornness around doing homework or pitching in to help around the house, but nothing that would have signaled anything like this. Sheryl said she had made some progress about the state of "disaster" in Megan's room. The tone in the room was somber since none of the three of them saw this letter coming from Megan.

Sheryl asked, "Do you think Kristin feels the same way? I know she was worried about Megan going to jail for driving the car. When we came back from Court and had that discussion with her that jail wasn't in the cards for Megan and that it had gone pretty well in Court, Kristin seemed satisfied with that answer and calmed down.

"Do you have any indication that Kristin is also unhappy with the living arrangements? The other thing we should do is get with Dr. Moran and see what feedback she's been getting from both girls."

Both Jake and Tyler agreed about speaking to Dr. Moran.

"Maybe we have to think about other arrangements for the girls." That comment from Jake resounded in the room with a dull thud.

"Look, Jake, I think you're getting way ahead of yourself. We really don't know if this is a nine-year-old with typical complaints or if it is something more. I also think that Tyler is right that Megan may have latched onto something and realized that she could make an ally of the Judge. She's a pretty smart little kid."

Tyler said, "I have another idea. Maybe it would be good to get the kids out of the house for a few days. I was going to ask them if they wanted to go camping with me for a long weekend. I have all the camping gear, so it's just a matter of getting some food to take with us. Have the kids ever been camping?"

Both Jake and Sheryl shrugged their shoulders. Sheryl spoke up first. "You can ask them if they want to go, but Megan is not the least bit athletic, so I'm not sure I can visualize her hiking in the woods. I heard some stories with her trying to learn to play tennis and basketball and it was a disaster. Kristin might want to go, but what happens if she wants to go, and Megan doesn't. Isn't the whole point of this to get them both out of the house, but especially Megan?"

Tyler thought for a moment. "Well, I'll tell them it's a package deal. I take them both or we do it another time. I thought of the fact that Megan isn't athletic, but I was thinking of going to a spot overlooking some terrific scenery and maybe Megan could bring her charcoals or pencils and do some sketching."

Jake said, "It might work."

"What about school? When can we go that doesn't interfere with school? Oh, and Kristin's practices and tennis matches?"

"We'll have to look at the school calendar. We'll have to know where you're going."

"Jake, you are such an asshole. You want to control everyone and everything, even if you're not involved. Maybe that's what Megan was referring to about being mean."

Jake flushed and spat out the words. "Someone has to be the adult around here, because it certainly isn't you. Everything you do is half- assed. Let me also remind you that Megan did not say I was the only one who was mean to her. She said it was her Uncles. Plural."

Sheryl stepped in. "Okay, okay, you two. This isn't getting us anywhere. If you both feel this way, then I suggest you slug this out with Dr. Moran. Clearly, you both have very strong feelings about this, and you better work it out.

"Don't think for a minute that the girls don't hear these comments and pick up on your feelings since they are barely below the surface. I'm serious. You two better get with Dr. Moran before this Court Evaluator wants to interview everyone. The Court Evaluator will pick up on this animosity and that won't be good. Let's call it quits tonight and you go to neutral corners.

"We've agreed that Tyler is going to ask the girls if they want to go camping, and tomorrow we can look at dates on the school calendar."

Chapter 52

There was an in-service day coming up for the teachers in about two weeks and the girls would have a Friday off, so that was the weekend they decided on for camping. Tyler broached the subject with the girls at breakfast after Jake left early for work. Sheryl watched the expressions on the girls' faces as Tyler laid out his plans for the camping trip.

Kristin spoke first. "Can we go swimming in the lake?"

"It will be cold in the mountains, but maybe I can borrow a boat and we can go out on the lake. If I can do that, I have some fishing poles."

"What do you think, Megan? You can bring your charcoals or your pencils and do some drawing. The sights are breathtaking. You could do some really great drawings."

"Would we have to hike really far? I don't want to do that or carry heavy stuff." Tyler glanced at Sheryl who was leaning against the counter drinking her coffee.

Tyler laughed. "I think we can work that out. You are going to be amazed by the scenery and it will be a great opportunity for you to draw."

"Can Aunt Sheryl come with us?" Sheryl had noticed that Megan was getting a little clingy with her. It was understandable considering the circumstances with the Court, and especially because of her mother's death. Megan turned expectantly toward Sheryl.

"How about you three go now and I'll come the next time?"

Megan's face fell. "No, I want you to come with us now."

Sheryl thought this was a bad idea. The trip was Tyler's idea and Tyler's time with the girls. She didn't want Tyler to think that she thought she should come to supervise him. The other nagging thought in her head was that at some point she was going to have to go home. She had already stayed longer now than she had planned. However, now with this new case hanging over everyone's head, Sheryl felt she should stay and provide some more stability in an otherwise turbulent house. If last night's skirmish between Tyler and Jake indicated the temperature in the house, then she felt she should stay and try to lower the temperature. Sheryl felt no animosity from Tyler toward her even though she and Jake were siblings, or after the guardianship contest.

"Look, you guys be the scouts. When you find the perfect place for camp, then I'll come next time. Besides, someone has to stay here and keep Uncle Jake company."

It did not persuade Megan. "Uncle Jake will probably like being here by himself. He'll like it that it's quiet and that nothing will get messed up. You'll have more fun with us."

Sheryl's first thought was "Out of the mouth of babes." Jake probably would like the peace and quiet. And more than that, he would like everything perfectly neat. And yes, she probably would have a better time with Tyler and the girls.

Maybe it was the only chance Sheryl would have to be with Jake alone and see if she could figure out what was going on in the house which prompted Megan to write the letter to the Judge. For all his laissez-faire attitude, Tyler seemed to be the one who intervened to tone down Jake's domineering and sometimes intractable stance. Maybe Tyler's lack of responsibility caused Jake to move in the other direction as a counterbalance.

Sheryl caught Tyler's eye from across the room. She ever so slightly shook her head no and Tyler saw it and nodded back to her. A smile crossed his face.

Then Tyler spoke up. "Megan, Aunt Sheryl is right. Let us find the perfect place for camping and then she can come with us next time. You and Kristin have to decide on the perfect spot before we take Aunt Sheryl."

Kristin, who had been surprisingly quiet during this whole back and forth, finally spoke up. "Okay, Aunt Sheryl, if you don't want to come this time, can I bring my friend Shelby?"

"Oh God," thought Sheryl. Tyler could probably handle the two of them quite well but introduce someone's friend and the whole mix could change. The two older girls could decide to do something together and exclude Megan and it could be a recipe for disaster.

Plus, Shelby's mother, Beverly, had been the one Kristin had called when Jake had the accident and went to the hospital. Beverly had cleaned up the blood, and she had taken the girls to her house for the night after Jake and Tyler returned from hospital. She had picked up on the tension in the house. She had broached the subject twice with Sheryl when they were watching the girls play in the tennis matches. Sheryl had been non-committal with her, but now Sheryl thought maybe she should rethink this. Sheryl wasn't even sure that Beverly would allow Tyler to take the three girls alone without another adult along. If Beverly said no, then this would open another can of worms.

Fortunately, Tyler spoke up again. "This is supposed to be a family trip. Our family. We can bring friends along another time. Maybe next time Shelby's parents would want to come with her for her family, and our family would include Aunt Sheryl. But that's a trip for another time. Okay?"

Sheryl nodded at Tyler and gave him a thumbs up. She couldn't have said anything out loud, because the lump in her throat was too big.

Chapter 53

Dr. Moran looked at her appointment schedule on her Ipad. She was normally busy, but it seemed the situation with Megan had exploded and everyone wanted to see her. Jake, Tyler, and now Aunt Sheryl. The attorney, Harris Mayfield, wanted to see her, and he told her he would soon get a call from the Court Evaluator who would also want to see her.

Dr. Moran decided that she wanted to hear from the two girls first and not have her opinion influenced by the adults. She decided to see Megan first, who was the epicenter.

Megan arrived with backpack in hand, which was usually a good sign. It meant that Megan had a new drawing for Dr. Moran to see. Sometimes the drawing provided a great jumping off point for their discussions and sometimes they were just good drawings. It was obvious that Megan hadn't fully dealt with or processed her parents' sudden death, but Dr. Moran wasn't sure it was correct to attribute every action of Megan to that and not just to the actions of an inquisitive and often stubborn kid.

"Hi, Megan, I see you have your backpack with you today. Does that mean that you have a new picture for me to see?"

Megan beamed. "Yeah, wait 'til you see it. It's a really good one."

As Dr. Moran came around her desk to sit at the smaller table and chairs she used with kids, she said, "Okay, I can't wait to see it, especially if you think it's really good."

Megan proudly pulled a drawing of a mountainous scene overlooking a fast-moving river.

"This is beautiful. Where is it?"

"I dunno. Kristin and I are going camping with Uncle Tyler and he says it's a really beautiful place so I can draw it. This is just what I think it will look like."

"That's great. When are you going camping with Uncle Tyler?"

"In a couple of weeks. I wanted Aunt Sheryl to come, but she said she'd come next time." The disappointment was evident in Megan's voice.

"What about Uncle Jake? Is he going too?"

"Nope, but I still want to see if I can get Aunt Sheryl to come."

"Are you happy about just the three of you going?"

"Yeah, Uncle Tyler said I don't have to hike really far or carry some heavy stuff. He says maybe he can borrow a boat and we can go out on the lake."

"So do you like Uncle Tyler?"

"Yeah."

"Why?"

Megan had been fiddling with a piece of a jigsaw puzzle on the table and she stopped and looked up. "I just do."

"That's not a real answer, Megan. If someone said you could have up to four ice cream cones, one for each reason you gave, which was true, about why you like Uncle Tyler, what would they be?"

"What flavors?" Megan was smart enough to know that she was being a wise guy and when she saw the serious expression on Dr. Moran's face, she folded her arms across her chest and stared out the window. Dr. Moran let the silence settle and waited.

"He's nice. He doesn't get mad over stupid things. He doesn't really care if I do all my homework or clean my room. Sometimes when Uncle Jake is mad, he tells him to calm down. When I was in the ambulance, he came in and hugged me. He looks like my Daddy. But he smokes and I don't like that."

"I know you were in the ambulance after you drove the car, but I didn't think you were hurt."

"No, the ambulance driver helped me get out of the car and he wanted to check me out in the ambulance to see if I was hurt. I banged my head, but mostly I was scared because the car got stuck on the lawn and I couldn't get it to move. When the ambulance and the police came, I knew I was in big trouble."

"Did you know why it was wrong to drive the car?"

"It's some stupid rule that you have to be sixteen to drive a car. I've seen everyone do it and it's not that hard."

"Megan, just like you have rules in school, there are laws we have to follow in society, even if we don't like them. The laws are in place for a reason. What would happen if every kid your age decided they were going to drive?

"Suppose you drove and had an accident and hit someone and they got hurt? You were lucky you didn't hurt yourself or someone else because you really didn't know all the things about driving a car. Adults take a road test to see if they are good enough to get a license."

Megan looked pensive, but she countered. "My Dad had a license and look what happened. He was driving, and the car went over the cliff." The tears welled up in her eyes and some tears rolled down her cheeks.

"You know that it wasn't anything your Dad did. The truck driver lost control and hit your parents' car. It was a tragic accident, but at least with adults, they have a lot more practice driving cars and trucks and probably have avoided lots of other accidents. Does that make sense?"

"It's not fair and I miss them a lot."

"I know you do, and it's okay to say that. We've talked about that it's okay to miss them and cry when you feel sad. Should we take a break for a minute and get some water? Then I'd like to take a few minutes and talk about Uncle Jake."

Dr. Moran and Megan each came back to the table with a bottle of water and Megan had two peppermint hard candies. These little pieces of hard candy worked as great little treats and incentives without hyping up kids on sugar, and without making a mess or leaving crumbs everywhere.

"Okay, so let's talk about Uncle Jake. You want Aunt Sheryl to go camping, yet Uncle Jake is not going camping with you, and you seem to be okay with that. How come?"

Megan busied herself with unwrapping the peppermint. Dr. Moran let the question hang in the air.

Finally, Megan looked up and answered. "He's always telling us about the rules and all the stuff we have to do. I think he's mad at us all the time. I don't care if the house is that neat, but he cares."

"Anything else?"

"Our house isn't the same as when my Mom and Dad were alive. I don't like living in the house now."

"Megan, you know that things are going to be different in your house and in your life because your parents aren't here. It's got to be different because of that huge change alone. But you also have to understand that people do things differently. It's a big adjustment for everybody. Do you understand that?"

"Yeah, but I don't want to live in the house anymore."

"Why do you say that?"

"I don't want to live with Uncle Tyler and Uncle Jake. They fight with each other, and it makes me scared. I don't think that they can agree on anything. It's better now that Aunt Sheryl is staying with us. I want to live with her. That's what I told the Judge."

"How did you know to write to the Judge about this?"

"Mr. Mayfield kept telling me over and over that it was very important to tell the Judge my side of the story, since she made all the decisions about whether I was in trouble. He said everybody had to listen to her. We learned how to write letters in school, so I wrote the Judge a letter. If she decided that I could live with Aunt Sheryl, then everybody has to listen to her. I want to live with Aunt Sheryl."

There was a finality in Megan's words and in Megan's tone of voice.

Chapter 54

Jody Gibson was the attorney assigned by the Court to interview the parties involved, including Kristin and Megan, based on Megan's letter to the Judge.

Jody was a woman who had been practicing law for almost eighteen years, and she devoted a significant percentage of her practiced to matrimonial and family law. Sometimes she surprised herself, because she had started her career as a young associate working in a law firm in New York City that did primarily bankruptcy work. After a year of that work, Jody was definitely convinced that bankruptcy work was not for her. In fact, she downright hated it. When she saw an ad for a firm in White Plains looking for an associate to work on matrimonial cases, Jody eagerly answered the ad. She wanted to work with people and help them with problems. She wanted to be in Court, not just crunch numbers on bankruptcy issues and work on motions on esoteric points in the Bankruptcy Code.

The interview went well because Jody's enthusiasm came through and she got the job. She had told herself that if she didn't like that firm, she could make another change because there were other areas of practice which interested her. However, she stayed at that firm and ultimately became a partner. She also stayed working at matrimonial and family law cases.

There were days when she went home exhausted mentally, emotionally and physically. The divorce cases were mostly acrimonious as the parties battled over custody and visitation of the kids, but also over money. Lots and lots of battles over money. Sometimes battles over things that seemed crazy like vases and sets of dishes. Sometimes battles over the dogs or cats. But at the end of the day, Jody liked what she did, and that she felt she truly made a difference in people's lives.

When Jody got the information from the Court, the facts surprised her. She thought that she had seen every situation, but this case presented with a new twist with the two uncles having been appointed by the Surrogate's Court as the Co-Guardians for the two minor children whose parents were recently deceased. Jody could read the Surrogate's Court file on the NYS e-filing system. She looked at the Death Certificates for the parents who died together in a car crash. Then she read the two Wills and saw the naming of the two uncles as the Co-Guardians. One uncle from each side of the family. Very unusual, Jody noted. At first, Jody couldn't tell from the Surrogate's Court files if the deceased parents had any other siblings.

She then read the subsequent Petition from the Aunt who wanted to become the Guardian in place of her brother or become the sole Guardian. She read the opposition papers from the husband's brother as a Co-Guardian, and she read the Court's decision keeping the named Co-Guardians in place.

Then she read the Family Court file about one of the girls driving a car at age nine. This little girl wrote the letter to the Court saying her uncles were mean to her, and she wanted to live with her Aunt. The same Aunt who petitioned to become the Guardian. And with that letter to the Court, they were off to the races.

Jody calculated that she had to interview both girls, both Co-Guardians, the Aunt now helping in the house, and the psychiatrist treating the two girls. The question was where to start and who to interview first. She thought about it for a day and then decided.

She decided to interview Megan first and then Kristin. She wanted to hear from the little kid who drove a car and then wrote a letter directly to the Judge. Jody thought it was pretty gutsy stuff for a little girl, and quite smart to understand that writing to the Judge would create waves. She may not have understood that she would cause a tsunami.

Jody had yet to decide if she was going to interview the Uncles or the psychiatrist next. She might get some valuable insights from Dr. Moran since she had been seeing the girls, yet she didn't want her own conclusions to be based solely on the psychiatrist's views.

Chapter 55

Jody called the office phone number provided to her and Jake answered the phone. She had already spoken to Jake's and Tyler's attorney and asked him to give them a heads up who she was and that she wanted to interview the family. Jody exchanged pleasantries with Jake and then said she would like to set up a schedule for the interviews. She asked to interview Megan first toward the end of the week since she seemed to be in the center of the maelstrom. Jake explained with some aggravation in his voice that Megan and Tyler were going on a camping trip over the long weekend.

Jody picked up on the aggravation in his voice and asked him if he was upset about the camping trip and why. With that, Jake went on a tirade about Tyler, his irresponsibility, his bad attitude etc. Jody was a little surprised that Jake let loose on the phone in their first phone conversation which she expected to be perfunctory about setting up interviews. Jake volunteered to be interviewed first since Tyler and Megan were going to be away. He was so adamant about it that Jody agreed to interview him first. He said he could provide context. Maybe this interview would highlight the major issues existing in the household. She would see if Jake's opinions of what was going on in the house were similar or in direct opposition to what the others had to say.

When Jake arrived in Jody's office, her first impression of him was that he was a well-dressed, well-spoken man. Jody asked him about his job and his hobbies to get some idea of what he was like. He answered her questions politely, but then rapidly wanted to move the conversation to discuss the girls.

"Look, Ms. Gibson, I'm going to be very frank with you. My sister- and brother-in-law's deaths were tragic, and I don't think any of us is over grieving for them. But the tragedy continues every day in other ways. They never spoke to Tyler or me about their plan to name us as the Co-Guardians. And they certainly should have spoken to us about it when they were doing their Wills. It's a lousy arrangement."

"How so?"

"It's just a stupid idea not to have consulted us beforehand and heard what our concerns were in advance. But it was an even stupider idea to name two Co-Guardians who weren't a married couple, who would have at least had the same philosophy on raising kids. I barely knew Tyler before their deaths. Neither of us is married and neither of us have kids. Suddenly, we're thrown into a situation with a nine-year-old and a twelve-year-old who are completely traumatized by the death of their parents. To make matters worse, I'm stuck with this idiot as a Co-Guardian who often acts like a bad adolescent himself."

"I'd like to hear some examples of what you mean."

"Tyler doesn't know how to raise kids. He takes the path of least resistance on everything involving the girls. He will let them do anything if that takes the least effort. What kids want to do their homework or clean up their rooms? Tyler doesn't care if they don't do their homework or if every piece of clothing they own could stay filthy lying on their bedroom floors. So that makes me the bad guy when I try to make some rules or try to enforce them. He's the great uncle who lets them do whatever they want, so of course they like him better. He won't back me up on any rules, so once again, he's the good guy and I'm the bad guy.

"My sister, Sheryl, and I tried to become the Guardians and Tyler could have resigned. He wouldn't agree to that and told me I could resign, and he would stay on alone. That would have been a total disaster for the kids."

"I read the Court's decision to keep in place your sister- and brother-in-law's decision in their Wills. Why do you think they named you two when you are not related to each other? You just said that you barely knew Tyler."

"I'm not really sure except to say that maybe they wanted one person from each side of the family."

"What about your sister Sheryl? Why don't you think they named her? The Court pointed out in its decision that although she petitioned to become the Co-Guardian with you, your sister- and brother- in-law never named her in any capacity in the Wills."

"I'm not really sure, except that she lives in Florida, and they didn't want the kids to be uprooted. She has been staying with us now and it's been a big help. She's won't stay forever. She's lived in Florida for a long time and her husband is in Florida. Sheryl has said that she sometimes feels like she's the referee in the house. That's not good. Yet I will not give up on what I think is best for the girls just because Tyler wants to take the easy way out."

"Why do you think Megan told the Court that her uncles were mean to her? She said, 'Uncles,' so that means both Uncles."

"I'm actually surprised that Megan didn't say that I was the one who was mean to her. I think she sees me as the enforcer. She picks up on the tension between Tyler and me. She's taken her parents' deaths much worse than Kristin. Maybe because she's younger. She seems to have latched on to Sheryl. Sheryl and Jackie look alike, and they have the same build. Right now, Sheryl is sort of stepping into the void Jackie left. She's acting as the Surrogate mother. As I said, this could create more problems when Sheryl goes home.

"Megan acts out. She can be stubborn, and she is manipulative. She knows that people feel sorry for her because her parents died and so she uses that."

The interview continued, and Jody understood many of the points Jake was making. Many of them seemed valid, yet something was clearly wrong in this household.

After Jake left, Jody added a few more thoughts to her notes. This situation was going to be even more complicated than she first thought.

Chapter 56

They decided upon the date for the camping trip. Friday was an in-service day for the teachers, so the girls had off from school and they could spend three days camping. Tyler had a lot of camping gear stored at a friend's house which he now moved in front of the garage doors much to the irritation of Jake. Once again, Sheryl felt like the referee between Jake and Tyler. Tyler wanted to leave the gear in the driveway, so he could check it and then move it onto the flatbed of his truck. Since there was so much equipment which had been sitting around for a long time, it looked like so much junk, and it of course, blocked Jake's access to the garage.

Sheryl brokered a deal that Tyler would move the equipment into his side of the garage, put what he wanted into his truck and then move the rest of the equipment back to his friend's garage or throw out what was old or broken. It was a deal that seemed better in the abstract than in reality. Tyler moved the stuff into the garage, but it seemed to ooze onto Jake's side of the garage, so he still couldn't park his car in the garage. This situation was emblematic of the many other issues which erupted in the house over large and small matters.

One night when the girls went to bed, Sheryl cornered Jake and Tyler in the kitchen.

"I need to speak to both of you. You're both intelligent people, yet I feel that I need to wear a referee's shirt and whistle in this house. The camping gear is the latest saga. Tyler, I know you need to sort through the gear, but you should have realized that it shouldn't have blocked Jake's ability to get his car in and out of the garage.

"Jake, you could have had a little patience with this process, since it won't last forever. It also isn't a tragedy if you have to park the car in the driveway. Now you both have agreed that Tyler would move the gear into the garage so he can sort through it.

"Tyler, somehow the gear has now taken over much more than your side of the garage, which infuriates Jake because you just moved the problem inside. Jake, you could have moved the stuff which prevented you from parking in the garage back to Jake's side of the garage. But both of you are so stubborn that you just stew about it and then explode.

"This is precisely what Dr. Moran is saying that upsets Megan. I really can't understand why you two can't see this and act like adults. Both of you need to grow up and stop getting stuck on petty differences and petty issues. Maybe you should discuss this with Dr. Moran."

Sheryl spoke with her husband Mike on the phone at least once a day. After her conversation with Jake and Tyler, Sheryl felt she needed someone to support her. For the first time in a long time, Sheryl felt emotionally spent and almost hopeless.

"Hi, honey, how did it go today?"

"Honestly, Mike, today I feel very down and frustrated. Jake and Tyler have completely different world views on just about everything. I can't tell if they do it purposely or if they just can't see what the other one sees. Kristin and Megan are caught in the middle of this drama. Kristin seems to handle this better than Megan, at least on the face of things. She's more involved in school and tennis. Megan has obviously internalized this and now it's erupted."

"No matter what you say, they don't seem to get it. It's not that they are stupid, so what's the deal?"

"I think it's that they never had to negotiate with someone in a situation even remotely like this and they don't seem to get it that their actions directly impact what is happening with Megan and Kristin. Neither of them is in a relationship at the present time, but they each have been in serious relationships before. And God help us, both are stubborn in their own ways. They should see that what each of them does irritates the other. I don't know if they don't see it or that or they simply don't care."

"Is there any chance that you can come home for a while? I miss you. How about coming home for a week, so we can be together, and you can get a break from the cauldron of emotions boiling there?"

"I don't think so, especially since we're waiting to hear about when the Court Evaluator is supposed to interview all of us. Since I'm now in the mix, I have to be interviewed as well. I just don't think I can leave now. There's also a certain amount of added tension in the house now that Megan sent the letter to the Judge. The tension is simmering just below the surface. I think I help keep the tension level down a bit. Why don't you come up here for a week?"

"I don't think you need to add another person into the 'cauldron."

"Maybe it would be a good thing if you came. You'd be a fresh face, a fresh voice. I'm sure the girls would love to see you. And most of all you are not a partisan. Maybe you could be a good influence on the two guys, since you're a guy.

"I'd really like it if you came up. Mike, it would help me too. Think about it."

Chapter 57

Two days before the camping trip, Jake got a call from Mr. Reece, the tennis coach, saying that Kristin had sprained her ankle in practice and that he should come pick her up. Jake called Sheryl who said she would go pick up Kristin. She arrived at the school to find Kristin with her leg elevated and an ice pack on her ankle. The school had crutches for just such an occasion and the nurse helped Kristin out to the car as Sheryl pulled the car right up to the front door.

"I don't think anything's broken, but I think you should take her to urgent care and have the ankle looked at to be sure," came the advice from the school nurse.

Sheryl asked Kristin how she hurt herself. "I tried to stop short to hit a ball and my ankle twisted."

"Is it very painful?"

"It hurts, but it isn't too bad if I don't stand on it. As soon as I do that, it really hurts."

The doctor in urgent care took an x-ray and concurred that nothing was broken, but it was a bad sprain. "Follow the standard protocol called RICE, which means, rest, ice, compression and elevation. I think you will be okay with some Aleve for the pain. But the most important things are to stay off it and keep it elevated. Ice on and off for twenty minutes at a time. Use the crutches and don't put weight on the ankle. If it's more swollen by morning or if it hurts a lot more, then you need to go see your orthopedist tomorrow."

"What about my tennis matches?"

"What about them? You certainly cannot be running around on this ankle. You couldn't run on this ankle even if you wanted to. When are these matches?"

"Next week."

"Well, next week is a long way off with a sprain. If you do what I just said with 'RICE' and the ankle isn't swollen and doesn't hurt next week, you can see if you can run. It all depends on how much you stay off it and how it feels next week. It's just too early to tell."

On the way home in the car, Kristin was dejected. Sheryl repeated, "The doctor is right. Next week is a long way off. If you are careful and follow everything he said, you may be able to play. A lot is up to you. If we think it's getting worse, then we go to the orthopedist."

"What about the camping trip?"

"Kristin, I think the camping trip is out of the question. I doubt you are going to be able to walk on the ankle day after tomorrow, no less go hiking on it. If you want to play in the matches next week, you are going to have to be very careful and very strict about what you do this week. Look at the bigger picture. I'm sure there will be other camping trips, but this one is too soon."

As they drove home in silence the rest of the way, Kristin mused about her chances of playing her matches, but Sheryl was musing about something completely different. She wasn't sure how Megan was going to react about going camping without Kristin and alone with Tyler. Megan might go, but Sheryl wasn't at all sure. If Megan refused to go, was this going to set off another round of problems? Tyler was looking forward to the trip and doing some activity that he truly liked with the girls. Was he going to feel bad if Megan now backed out? Did this have something to do with Megan not liking her Uncles? Was Jake going to throw up roadblocks to Tyler taking Megan alone?

Sheryl started feeling a tension headache coming on. She said to herself, "Why does everything have to be difficult?"

Chapter 58

Kristin had her leg elevated on a kitchen chair with an ice pack on the ankle when Tyler walked in. "Wow, what happened here?"

Sheryl realized that she should have called Tyler to tell him what happened when they were on the way to the urgent care facility. Sheryl told him what happened and then apologized, but Tyler brushed it off.

"It's not broken, and a sprain is not that serious, so it's okay. I'm sure you had your hands full. I went to the gym and my phone was in my truck because they have stolen things from the lockers. No big deal."

Kristin looked morose and then when Sheryl reiterated Kristin had to be off her foot for several days, it dawned on Tyler that she could not go camping.

"Yeah, that's some bad luck. We told Megan that we'd go camping again and take Aunt Sheryl, so now we definitely have to go again so you can come too. There isn't much choice here. You can't walk, so you can't hike." Tyler was not one to dwell over split milk.

Sheryl didn't know if she should broach the subject with Tyler that maybe Megan might not want to go without Kristin. Before she said anything, the kitchen door opened again and in walked Megan. They explained about Kristin's injury, as Megan busied herself with getting a snack out of the refrigerator. Tyler noted with some irony, that Megan retrieved a container of yogurt and didn't make a beeline for the cookies. Had they worn her down, or had Sheryl changed the culture?

Tyler said to Sheryl, "I guess you have been able to change the 'culture' here," referring to the fact that Megan was getting herself a yogurt. It only took Sheryl a moment to groan at the pun. Megan looked from Sheryl to Tyler, but the pun went over her head entirely.

Tyler said he had some calls to make and disappeared. It didn't even occur to Tyler that Megan might not want to go camping.

Kristin was going on about her tennis matches, which took the spotlight off the camping trip, at least for now. Kristin was going to stay in the kitchen to do her homework, so Sheryl got Megan settled at the dining room table for now to do her homework. This way she could keep an eye on both girls and start dinner. It also occurred to Sheryl with some annoyance that Jake had never called her to see how they did at Urgent Care.

At least for now, all was quiet on the western front. About twenty minutes later, Megan appeared in the kitchen with pencil in hand and blurted out, "What about the bears?"

"The what?" came the response.

"The bears."

"What bears are you talking about?"

"Suppose the bears come after us while we're sleeping?"

And we're off to the races, thought Sheryl. "Megan, I know Uncle Tyler will not take you camping to any place that has bears. He's been to this place before. Why don't we ask him to come downstairs and you can ask him your questions?"

A few minutes later Tyler came back to the kitchen with Megan in tow. "I told her there are no bears. This is crazy. We put all the food away properly so no animals get to it."

Megan's eyes opened wider with that statement. "What other animals? Like lions or alligators?"

Tyler looked at Megan for a moment to be sure she wasn't pulling his leg, but then he saw she was serious. "Megan, you need to learn a little geography. There are no lions. They are in Africa. You know, like people go to Africa to go on safari to see lions. Alligators stay in the south in the swamps. They are cold blooded. They wouldn't last in the winters up here. Geez, don't you learn anything about animals and their habitats in school?"

"So what animals?"

"Like raccoons or foxes."

Sheryl now figured it was time to intervene before Tyler mentioned bobcats, wolves or coyote. "Tyler, I think Megan is a little fearful of what animals there might be, but you are there to protect her."

"I've been to this place before and there is nothing to be afraid of. These animals keep their distance from us. There's nothing to worry about."

Now Kristin who had been quiet, piped up. "That's not true. I saw on TV that people in northern Jersey and northern Westchester have seen bears in their yards."

Tyler now shot Sheryl a worried glance. He was taking fire from both sides. "That's only in the early spring when they come out of hibernation and are really hungry looking for food. I'm telling you I've been to this camp before and there are NO bears."

Sheryl shrugged and looked at Tyler and said, "Megan, is there something else you're worried about? This is the first time you've mentioned being worried about bears. Is there anything else?"

"I want Kristin to come too."

"Well, you know Kristin can't come because of her ankle. Is that why you're scared?"

Tyler looked surprised by the turn of this conversation. Apparently, it had not crossed his mind that Megan wouldn't want to go without Kristin.

"We'll have a great time. You'll love it and the weather is supposed to be sunny all weekend. Remember that you wanted to take your stuff and draw all the beautiful things we're going to see."

Megan looked like she was going to cry. Tyler picked up on that. "Look, if you don't want to go, nobody's going to make you go, but you're going to be missing out on a lot of fun. Including s'mores over the campfire."

Sheryl was hoping for the middle ground. "Suppose you think about it. Uncle Tyler is right. No one is forcing you to go. You can decide to go and if you don't like it, you can come home. How about that?"

Now Sheryl looked at both Tyler and Megan for some sense of whether she struck the right balance.

Chapter 59

Over the next twenty- four hours, Sheryl thought she was going to get whiplash. Megan vacillated between wanting to go camping and not wanting to go.

"Look, Megan, if you don't want to go, it's okay. Uncle Tyler said no one is going to force you to go. But you have to talk to him and not just tell me. What makes you not want to go?"

Several of these conversations ended with Megan shrugging her shoulders or not giving an answer at all.

"I dunno, I just don't think I want to go."

"Is it because Kristin can't go?"

Jake came in and heard the tail end of this conversation. "I don't think you should go, Megan. Why don't you wait until another time when Kristin can go with you?"

"Jake, this is really Megan's decision if she wants to go."

"Like hell it is. I'm her Co-Guardian and I certainly have a say in this."

Sheryl gave Jake an "I'll turn you to stone look," but said in a calm voice, "Let me talk to you for a minute."

Sheryl and Jake walked into the family room which was two rooms away. "What the hell is the matter with you? It would be great for Megan to go camping and get to do some artwork, but she has to decide that for herself."

"Bullshit. I wasn't crazy about this whole camping thing from the beginning, but now I don't like the idea of Tyler taking Megan alone. He'll probably forget she's with him and leave her alone, or make her do something she hates, because he wants to do it. Megan is the least athletic kid I ever met. I can't see her hiking in the heat or sleeping outside in a tent or using some gross bathroom. Tyler won't even notice that she's unhappy. He's oblivious to everything."

"So you're saying that Kristin was going to be the police force for this trip? That's quite a responsibility for a twelve-year-old. If you think they need a chaperone, then you should go, since you're so hung up on being the Co-Guardian." The last sentence was dripping with sarcasm.

"I didn't ask for this job, but since I have it, I'm going to do it the right way."

"That's the problem, Jake. You think the right way is always your way."

"Okay, then you go with them. There needs to be an adult, and you should be it because Tyler is not the adult, especially since they are going to be in the wilderness."

"I am not going camping. I never said I wanted to go, and it would have been good for the kids to learn something new and spend some time with Tyler doing something he likes and is good at.

"Whether or not you recognize it, there is tremendous tension in this house that is simmering just below the surface. I can feel it and I try to diffuse it where I can. I think the kids can feel it and that's why I think Megan wrote the letter to the Judge. If you block this camping trip merely because you can, you're going to turn up the heat and the tension some more. Think about it before you pontificate."

With that, Sheryl turned and walked out of the room.

Chapter 60

After much hemming and hawing, Megan decided she wanted to go camping. Sheryl got Tyler alone and said, "Tyler, are you okay if Megan gets there and decides she wants to come home? Because she may do that, especially without Kristin there."

Tyler frowned and thought about it for a minute. "Look, it's about a three-hour drive and then there's the time to set up the camp. I'd be okay if she would at least agree to stay one night, so I don't have to do another three-hour drive back. I won't be happy, but I would come back the next day."

"Do you think we should discuss this with her now before you go?"

"I really don't want to put that idea into her head, but if she wants to come home, I'd come back early on Saturday. I'm kinda hoping that when she gets there and sees how beautiful this place is, that she'll want to stay and do some of her drawings."

"Just one more thing. If you go for a long hike or she has to carry a heavy backpack, I think she'll be done for and then she'll want to come home."

"Yeah, I thought about that. I'm going to tell her to put her drawing stuff in one small backpack, so it won't be heavy, and I'll carry the rest of the gear to the place where we'll have the best view for her to draw. I'll carry what we'll need for lunch and plenty of drinks. I've learned the hard way when Megan gets stubborn and digs in her heels, that nothing can budge her. Believe it or not, I think she might actually like this. Wouldn't that be a kick in the head!"

"This is going to be a whole new experience for her. She's never been camping before. She's never been away from home without Kristin, and she's never been alone with you for three days. That's a lot for a little girl. None of us should forget that the greatest change of all is the loss of her parents. Her whole life has turned upside down and we're all trying to pick up the pieces. For a little girl, and that's what she is, a little girl, to lose her parents so violently and so suddenly, has to be terrifying. Nothing is ever going to be the same. Sometimes when she gets exasperating, I take a deep breath and remind myself of that horrible fact."

Tyler stood there for a moment staring at Sheryl. There wasn't any expression on his face. Sheryl wasn't sure if she had overstepped some boundary and if or how Tyler was going to react. It was a long few seconds of silence.

Finally, Tyler said, "Yeah, I hadn't thought about all of it that way. Okay."

With that, Tyler shook his head yes, picked up his can of soda and walked out of the room.

Sheryl stood there for a moment, not knowing exactly what to make of the conversation. As she replayed it in her head, she thought Tyler had heard her. She just hoped that the message had sunk in and that he would retain its meaning throughout the camping trip.

The sound of crutches on the floor disturbed her thoughts as Kristin navigated through the doorway. Kristin had been morose since the ankle sprain. Sheryl was not sure whether the bad mood was her not being able to go on the camping trip or the uncertainty about being able to play in her tennis matches. Maybe both.

"Hey, how does the ankle feel? Does it still hurt?"

"It's still throbbing."

"Well, I think there's been enough time so you could probably take another Aleve. You should probably ice it again. Let me go get the ice pack and some Aleve."

Kristin sighed. "And I'm bored. There's nothing to do."

The thought that went through Sheryl's mind was "this place is a shit show."

As she went to get the ice pack, her cell phone rang, and it was Mike.

"Hey, how's it going with the patient?"

"Which one?"

"What do you mean, which one?"

Sheryl walked into the family room away from where Kristin had parked herself and her crutches in the kitchen, so that Kristin couldn't hear. Sheryl described the back and forth with Megan about wanting and not wanting to go on the camping trip, Jake's opposition, Tyler's good intentions, but somewhat clueless understanding of the situation and Kristin's feeling sorry for herself about her ankle.

"I feel like I'm the patient too, since I'm being battered on all sides."

"Jeez, this really sounds awful. I hoped that my news would make you feel better and less like a patient yourself. I thought I'd come up on Monday and stay for the week. If Kristin feels better, maybe you and I will go stay in a hotel for a few days and do some things you want to do."

"Mike, that's great. I doubt we will be able to go to a hotel, but it would be so great to have you here with me. I have most of the day free while the girls are in school, and the 'bigger boys' are at work. I'm going to be so glad to see you. I need reinforcements. The girls are going to be glad to see you too. They have been asking why you haven't come up."

Chapter 61

On Friday morning the sky was blue with high clouds. The temperature was in the high fifties and promised to warm up to the low sixties. Sheryl had checked and double-checked Megan's clothes. She wanted to make sure that Megan had layers of clothes she could put on or take off if the weather warmed up or cooled off. She also made sure that Tyler knew what she had packed for Megan.

Jake made what appeared to be an excuse and said he had an early morning meeting at the office. Sheryl wasn't sure if he was avoiding another fight or if he didn't want to be bothered with all the commotion getting Tyler and Megan off on their trip. Sheryl thought Jake had been somewhat cool after their conversation about the camping trip where she came down on the side of letting Tyler take Megan alone. It was hard to tell with Jake how much of a conversation sank in. Sometimes he just wouldn't budge from his position. Sometimes Sheryl thought it was that Jake wanted to save face.

"Jeez, how much did you pack for her? It's Friday morning and we'll be back Sunday afternoon. How much do you think she can wear?" Tyler asked.

"Nothing is going to make Megan crankier than if she's hot and gets overheated. You're going to have her all to yourself, but that also means that you have to deal with the whining and the stubbornness all by yourself as well. I'm just trying to save you."

Tyler rolled his eyes, but said, "Thanks, you're right."

Shortly thereafter Megan came into the kitchen, and she looked happy. Tyler said, "Megan, let's eat breakfast here before we go, so we don't have to waste time looking for a place to eat. I already have some snacks in the truck so we have something to munch on. It's going to take some time to set up our camp when we get there, so I don't want to waste time now."

After a quick breakfast, they were almost on the way out the door when Megan bolted out of the kitchen saying she had forgotten something. Tyler looked at Sheryl with a questioning look. Sheryl shrugged an "I don't know" look in response. Shortly thereafter, Megan returned to the kitchen with a small stuffed animal dog with floppy ears. "Lulu wants to come too. She sleeps with me at night or she gets lonely. She doesn't want to miss the camping trip."

"Okay, but you have to be careful not to lose her on the trip." Sheryl had visions of Lulu being dropped off a cliff by mistake and Megan refusing to come home without her. It was a Megan scenario that seemed very plausible.

"Wait, one more thing." Megan again bolted out of the kitchen before anyone could say anything else.

"What now? We need to get this show on the road." Tyler plopped himself down into a kitchen chair. "Jeez, Louise, we're going for two and a half days, not an artic expedition."

"In case you haven't figured this out, Megan has a lot of ambivalence about going. If you don't let this play out, she's going to be crying and she won't go."

"Crying about what? It's two and a half days and if we don't get going soon, it's going to be one day!" Tyler was clearly getting exasperated.

"Tyler, don't forget she's a little girl. I know I've said this, but I think it bears repeating. This will be the first time she'll be away from home since her parents died, and she's going with you alone and she's never been camping before. She does everything with Kristin and Kristin is not going either. She's apprehensive about everything, but she doesn't know how to express it."

Megan reappeared shortly thereafter, but her eyes were glistening. "I wanted Kristin to come downstairs to say goodbye, but she doesn't want to. She said she wants to go back to sleep."

Now Megan's lower lip was quivering, and it was only the proverbial hop, skip and a jump before the tears started flowing.

Tyler hit himself in the head with his hand, but his recovery was quick. "Kristin feels bad that her ankle hurts and she can't come camping. She's also worried that her ankle won't be better for her tennis matches next week. We gotta cut her some slack because she feels bad about everything. She's unhappy that she is going to miss out on all the fun."

Something Tyler said struck a chord. In Megan's mind, maybe she was going to get to do something new and exciting and Kristin was going to miss out. A way to lord it over her sibling. The waterworks ended.

Sheryl nodded and winked at Tyler.

"I'll be right back."

Both Sheryl and Tyler said in unison, "What now?"

Megan looked at them as if they were both the village idiots. "I have to go to the bathroom. You're always telling me to go to the bathroom before we leave the house."

The bathroom trip completed and then they were in the truck and on their way.

Sheryl also had mixed feelings about the camping trip. She thought it would be good for Megan and Tyler to do something alone together. She also knew that Megan could be stubborn and difficult, and sometimes it took more than one adult to deal with her to resolve the issue. Sheryl gave Tyler points for being brave and trying. She also thought that it was important for Tyler to assert himself with Jake and not buckle under to Jake's objections to the trip. She had, however, clearly come down on Tyler's side on taking the trip. Sheryl had also noticed that Tyler often just ignored Jake and did what he wanted. The problem with that behavior was that no one dealt with the problem, and so reared its ugly head at another time.

As she walked through the dining room, she also found a sheet of paper on the dining room table with Tyler's cell phone, the name of the campground, the address and front office phone number. She and Tyler had discussed that he would leave the info with her, but with the commotion of getting them out of the house, she forgot to ask about it. "Good going, Tyler. You can be a flake, but this time you are acting like an adult."

Chapter 62

A little after one pm, Sheryl's cell phone rang, and it was Mike. "Hey, it's me. Do you want to have lunch?"

"What do you mean, lunch?"

"I wanted to surprise you and come up a few days earlier. The plane just landed and we're taxiing to the terminal. Should I take a cab to the house or check in to a hotel?"

"Are you serious? Which airport?"

"Westchester. It's not that far from the house, right? But I didn't want to show up at the house in case you're not there and I'd be sitting out in the cold."

"I can throw a coat on and be there in fifteen minutes. And no, you don't need to check into a hotel."

"And does your room have a bed big enough for two? I'd like to see what my wife looks like in bed."

"Nice try, slugger, but I'm not alone in the house. Megan went on the camping trip this morning with Tyler, but Kristin is here nursing her ankle. They had a day off from school for the teachers' in-service day. Tell me which terminal and I'll pick you up."

About an hour later, Sheryl, Mike and Kristin were sitting around the kitchen table as Mike ate lunch. All three of them seemed to be in better spirits. Sheryl had never been so glad to see Mike. Mike was upbeat, and she needed that breath of fresh air.

They had never been separated this long during their marriage except for the time Sheryl had now spent in New York. They each missed each other, and Sheryl felt she was getting reinforcements. Maybe Mike would be a calming influence on the tension in the house. Kristin was still upset about missing the camping trip, but most of all about the possibility that she was going to miss the tennis matches. Now she was telling Uncle Mike about the previous season in tennis and her mood was much better. Maybe her ankle would be good enough for her to play, and Uncle Mike could see her play in the match.

"Do you think your ankle would be okay to go out for dinner and the movies tonight?" Mike was a terrific organizer, and he didn't like to sit around. He made something as mundane as a movie and dinner seem exciting. "Can we go to the movie where you reserve your seat in advance? If so, we'll reserve a seat in the row ahead of us so you can keep your foot elevated. Megan and Tyler will freeze their asses off in the cold tonight and we'll be having a great dinner and watching an exciting movie."

As Mike was finishing lunch, Kristin's cell phone rang, and she stuffed the cell phone in her pocket and hobbled on the crutches into the next room to talk to her friend. Mike took Sheryl's hand in his and said, "So tell me what's going on here. It always sounds tense every time I talk to you."

"It is. Tyler and Jake can't agree on what day of the week it is. There's a tug of war between the two of them about virtually everything. Even small stupid things. And the girls are the ones in the middle of the tug of war. Kristin seems to do better than Megan. They both are so young to have lost their parents, but I think Megan has taken it far worse.

"Even with seeing the psychiatrist, I think Megan has a lot of trouble expressing her grief and it comes out as defiance and stubbornness. None of us know what thing is going to be the battleground on any day. So you have that added to the fact that Jake and Tyler can't agree on how anything should be resolved.

Jake is so anal about everything, and Tyler couldn't care less about anything. Jake was trying to throw his weight around as the Guardian about not letting Tyler take Megan on the camping trip. I spend my time trying to get both to be reasonable. I'm exhausted from the stress of it all."

"Maybe it's time for you to step back. They didn't name you as the Guardian or Co-Guardian, so maybe this is not your job or your responsibility. This is Tyler and Jake's job and they have to figure it out."

"That's easier said than done. And the losers are going to be Kristin and Megan."

"Yeah, but maybe they won't be able to figure this out if you are here always picking up the pieces."

"While things aren't smooth sailing, they are certainly better now that I'm here. And we cannot forget that the Court ordered an investigation based on the letter that Megan wrote to the Judge that her uncles are mean to her. From what the lawyer tells us, the Court takes these statements very seriously. The Court is charged with what doing what is in the best interest of the child. This whole can of worms started with Megan driving Jake's car."

Mike grinned. "It was a kid's prank. Every kid does something stupid growing up."

"Don't laugh at this, Mike. It involved a minor driving a motor vehicle, and the Court didn't think it was funny. Megan was just lucky that no other car was involved, and no one got hurt.

"Megan understood the Judge had all this power because we told her that multiple times. We told her she had to listen to everything the Judge said. We told her the Judge might want to talk to her, so this was important that she understand what was going on and that she shows the Judge she was sorry. She somehow was smart enough to turn the tables and manipulate the situation to her advantage by writing a letter to the Judge. The Court appointed a Court Evaluator who is going to interview all of us. We all have to speak to Jake and Tyler's attorney and the psychiatrist before we meet with the Court Evaluator. I certainly can't leave now."

"I'm not sure I see why not. Your sister- and brother-in-law did not name you as the Guardian. They named these two clowns. It's their mess, not yours."

"Didn't you hear anything I just said about this situation?"

"I certainly did, but with the best of intentions, you have gotten yourself in the middle of a very screwed up situation, not of your own making. You keep ignoring the fact that your sister- and brother-in-law did not name you as the Guardian of the kids. You keep forgetting that. You didn't cause the problem, and it's not your problem, yet you have taken it upon yourself to fix it. No one asked you to fix it. You may not be able to fix it."

"I didn't cause the problem. The untimely death of Jackie and Blake did. I'm worried about Kristin and Megan."

Chapter 63

Tyler came out of the camp office and got back in the truck where Megan was waiting. "There's been a screw up and even though we had a reservation, they somehow gave away our campsite. Surprising that it's full this time of year, but the weather is still nice, so I guess people want to get in that last weekend or two before it gets cold. And of course, there's the leaves. People gotta see those leaves in the fall. But it's okay, I know some other places where we can go. Might even be better. Give me a minute to look. The other campsite near here is shitty, so I don't want to go there."

Tyler was now scrolling down on his phone as he spoke to Megan.

"Do we have to go home? I don't want to go home."

"Nope, we don't have to go home. I think I remember another place I went to with some friends a few years ago. Okay, I found it."

Tyler started the truck and pulled out of the parking lot. "So you drove Jake's car. How come you thought you could drive it?" Tyler looked at her and grinned.

Megan looked straight ahead and didn't answer for a few seconds. Tyler thought he'd try it, but maybe the moment had passed.

Finally, Megan turned toward Tyler and said, "I've seen everybody drive cars. I know what to do. It didn't seem that hard." She shrugged.

Now that Tyler had her talking, maybe he could get more out of her. "So do you think you could drive this truck?"

"No."

"No, why not?"

"I don't know how to drive a stick, but I've been watching you. So maybe by the time we get home, I'll know how. Uncle Jake's car is smaller. Sometimes I had trouble seeing over the dashboard, but I sat up really tall and I moved the seat way up."

"I'll tell you something cool about this truck. I like using the stick, but you can put it in sports mode where you don't have to drive it using the stick. It's kind of like automatic. See it's right here on the console between us." Tyler pointed to the spot between them.

"Then it would be easy to drive just like Uncle Jake's car. The person who thought that up was pretty smart."

Tyler had to suppress a laugh. "I think you're pretty smart. You know that?"

Now it was Megan's turn to grin. "Yeah, I am. The grownups don't think I know anything, but I know a lot."

Now Tyler felt they were in a chess match, and he was about to be checkmated. He took a few seconds to gather his thoughts, and he was aware of how his answer could be very important.

"Oh, the grownups think you're very smart. Maybe you're smarter than you're supposed to be at your age. What you need to remember is even though you're smart and you understand what's going on, there are some things that you can't do based on your age. Like driving a car or drinking."

Tyler was hoping they were on a roll, so he continued. "What else do you think you know the grownups don't realize?"

Megan shrugged her shoulders again.

"C'mon, what else?"

No answer. Maybe the moment had passed. If Megan didn't want to answer, nothing could drag it out of her. Perhaps he would broach the subject again on the way home if he talked to her about driving a stick and the clutch.

"I'm going to tell you something about your Dad and me when we were kids that no one else in the entire world knows. But it's got to be our secret."

Megan swiveled in the seat like her body was on a pivot. She was now facing him, and he clearly had her attention.

"Nobody talks about my Daddy anymore and I miss him." The tears welled up in her eyes and her voice quivered.

The thought flashed through Tyler's mind, "Oh, God, I'm going to make the kid cry and I'll ruin the whole trip. I don't want the kid bawling the rest of the way."

Tyler recovered fast enough to say, "It's kind of a funny story. We were about eight and ten years old and it was late in the afternoon on a Saturday in the summer. Our parents, your grandparents, were invited to a barbecue down the street from our house. We didn't want to go, so our parents said Blake and I could eat dinner at home and then our parents would go to the barbecue. We could stay home alone since they were only at a neighbors' house.

"It was still daylight when they left for the neighbors' house. We were playing basketball in the driveway when they left. When we finished playing, your Dad said he wanted Carvel. Our house wasn't all that far away from the Carvel, but not close enough to walk. I don't remember which of us first decided that we could drive there, but we both thought it was a good idea."

Megan was hanging on Tyler's every word.

"We knew we had plenty of time to drive to the Carvel, get the ice cream and be home before our parents got back. They would never know. I knew where Dad kept his car keys, so I went into the house to get them. Blake put himself in the driver's seat since he was older and taller. I came back with the keys, and we were both siting in the car about to turn it on when Dad came home. The neighbors ran out of something, and Dad came home to bring it back to their house. If Dad had come back two minutes later, we would have taken the car and been gone. And we would have been in big trouble.

"He wanted to know what we were doing in the car. Fortunately, Blake was quick and said we were pretending we were at the Indy 500. Dad looked at us like we were idiots and told us to get out of the car. Dad didn't notice that the keys were in the ignition. After he went back to the barbecue, I put the car keys back in their place in the house."

Megan looked at Tyler with an expression of disbelief on her face. "You and Daddy were going to take the car, even though you didn't have a license and were too young to drive?"

"Yup."

"My Daddy was going to drive the car?"

"Yup."

"Would you have gotten into trouble?"

"Big trouble! Look, Megan, I'm telling you this story not because it's okay to drive a car as a kid, but because kids often do stupid things. Your Dad and I were about to do a stupid thing and because our Dad came home when he wasn't supposed to, we got lucky. One of us could have gotten hurt or we could have hurt someone else. The point is you have to think about what you are going to do before you do something stupid or reckless. This is going to apply, not just now, but as you get to be a teenager too."

"Why didn't you tell me this story when I drove the car?"

"Because I didn't want you to think it was funny or that because we had tried to drive a car when we were kids, that it was okay.

You told me earlier that you're a smart kid. I think so too, and so I think you can get the more important meaning of the story."

As Tyler was concentrating on telling Megan the story, he wasn't paying full attention to the map on his phone. The service was spotty up here, and where they were, the GPS wasn't all that good. Tyler took the wrong turn to the right.

Chapter 64

"Where we're going isn't a typical campground like we were supposed to go. It's going to be a little more rustic, but since those idiots gave away our reservation, we're going to have to improvise. We either go here or we'll have to go home. If I remember correctly, the view is better, but we may have to hike a little way. You were looking for a spectacular view to do your drawing and this will be it."

They drove in silence for a while and then Tyler turned off the main road. The main road was a two-lane highway, and once they turned off, the road, such as it was, became very bumpy. Tyler backed up and turned around a few times as he tried to find the camp site he remembered.

Finally, they came to a point where the truck could go no farther. It wasn't what he remembered, but he said to himself that it had been a few years since he had last been there and that nature had a way of growing and changing, especially in an area that was wild and untamed to begin with.

Finally, Tyler stopped the truck and turned off the ignition. Megan turned to look at him and said, "Where are we?"

"We're here."

"Yeah, but where is 'here?' There's nothing here." Megan's tone of voice was a mixture of questioning and anxiety.

"I told you that this was off the beaten path. In the other campground, we were kind of close to each other. Here we've got the whole place to ourselves and it's really beautiful."

"I don't see anything here except weeds and overgrown trees."

"Just be a little patient and we're going to take a walk and find the exact place where we'll pitch the tent. You'll like it."

They walked for a few minutes and then saw a partial clearing in the undergrowth. "How about here? We're not that far from the truck so it won't take us long to bring the stuff here." Tyler realized that this was not the place he had been to before. He didn't know where they were or where this was relative to the campsite he had been to a few years before, but it looked like a good place.

They could see the mountains in the distance. Tyler said, "Listen, I hear running water, so there must be a stream or river nearby. We can go explore that. Aren't those mountains beautiful?"

Megan got caught up in the view and some of her anxiety lessened.

"You can draw those mountains. When we find the river or stream, that will be great to draw too. C'mon, let's go back to the truck and get the gear."

After the third trip back and forth to the truck, Megan sat down on one of the bags. "I'm too tired to make another trip back to the truck. And I'm thirsty."

Tyler was about to say something about needing help and a few more round trips when he caught himself. "Okay, stay here and I'll get the rest of the stuff."

"No, I'm afraid to stay here alone."

Sometimes with Megan, when she said things like this, he wasn't sure at first if she was pulling his leg. He also didn't have anyone here to help him deal with her. "Okay, you can decide what you want to do. If you're tired, you can stay here and rest, but I have to finish unloading the gear. If you're afraid to stay here alone, then you can come with me. You choose."

For as smart as Megan was, she didn't seem to get the irony of the situation. It was the proverbial "If I go, who stays and if I stay who goes?"

Tyler looked at Megan for a few more seconds and then turned around to head back to the truck without saying another word. Another second or two elapsed and then Megan yelled, "Wait, I'm coming with you," and bounded after him.

When they arrived back at the truck, Tyler opened one cooler and pulled out two bottles of water. He handed one to Megan who opened the bottle and gulped the water. Tyler took a long swig from his bottle. He handed Megan a backpack and grabbed some more gear from the back of the truck. Tyler didn't say anything to her, but just walked off toward the newly discovered campground. Megan tagged along behind him.

Tyler thought to himself that maybe he had found an important key in dealing with Megan. Don't argue with her, which only seemed to make her dig in her heels. Continue with the activity at hand and she could join in or not. Don't make a big deal about anything with her and give her a chance to act up.

After they reached the campground, Tyler put down the gear he was holding and headed back toward the truck. Megan followed again. By the end of the second-round trip after the water break, Megan slumped down and sat on the gear. Tyler turned around again to head back to the truck when Megan said, "I'm too tired to go back again."

"Okay," came the response.

"Are you going to leave me here alone?" This time the tone was whiny.

"You can come with me to the truck, or you can stay here, and I'll be right back."

"What about the bears?"

"I've told you there are no bears."

"You'll be sorry if the bears eat me."

"Yes, I will."

Tyler returned after a few minutes with the last of the items from the truck. Megan was still sitting where she was when Tyler left her. "Glad to see no bears came by." He said with a big grin on his face.

Chapter 65

Tyler set up the tent and put the air mattresses and sleeping bags in the tent. He cleared an area for the stove and was taking things out of duffel bags. Megan watched him but didn't offer to help. Tyler continued unpacking and setting up with Megan occasionally asking him what they used a piece of equipment for.

Tyler turned toward Megan and said, "How about we have some lunch?"

"I have to go to the bathroom before we eat lunch."

"Okay, so go. There's a roll of toilet paper right over there."

Megan looked at Tyler and then looked over to where Tyler was pointing. She then did a double-take back to look at Tyler.

"What do you mean, there's toilet paper over there?"

"Well, you're going to need some, aren't you?"

"Don't they have any in the Ladies room?"

Tyler could not suppress a laugh. "Megan, there is no Ladies room. We're in the middle of the woods. There are no buildings anywhere around here, so there are no Ladies rooms. Go behind a bush and take the toilet paper."

Megan looked horrified. She just stared at Tyler. "I can wait."

"Listen to me. Today is Friday. We're not going home until Sunday. You are going to have to go sometime before then. No one's around. Just go over in that direction. There's plenty of bushes. No one's around, so no one can see you."

"What about the bears?"

"Again with the bears? There are no bears. Besides bears don't care if you go to the bathroom in the woods."

Tyler was about to state the adage about a bear taking a shit in the wood but decided against it. He felt it would just open a new can of worms.

Tyler walked over to one cooler and started taking out some cold cuts and mustard and mayo. From another bag, he took out jars of peanut butter and jelly.

"We have whole wheat bread and rye bread. What would you like to eat? You can have some turkey or roast beef for lunch, and I have chicken and hamburgers for dinner. Or you can have peanut butter and jelly. We can eat the perishable food first and tonight we'll do some cooking. I also brought marshmallows and Hershey Bars and we can make s'mores."

Megan just looked at Tyler but didn't say anything in response. "What do you want to eat?"

A tear rolled down Megan's cheek and her lip quivered. "I want to go home."

"Why? We haven't done any of the fun stuff yet. It took us time to get here and setting up camp isn't exactly fun. But now that we're set up, we can eat lunch and then go exploring."

"I want to go home."

"Why?"

"I'm not going to the bathroom in the woods."

"Oh, for God's sake, Megan, you just go and it's over. It's nothing to get upset about. No one can see you."

"No. I'm not doing it."

"Okay, but if you don't go, you're going to be very uncomfortable."

Megan wasn't budging, so Tyler didn't know quite what to do.

"Well, I'm hungry, so I'm going to eat lunch. You can do what you want. By the way, I also brought some fishing poles, so when we find that stream, we can go fishing."

Tyler started making himself a sandwich and then pulled a bottle of water out of the cooler. He sat down in one of the folding chairs and took a bite of the sandwich. He didn't know what to do. Should he just eat his sandwich in silence, or should he try to make conversation with Megan?

He was about halfway through his sandwich when Megan finally spoke. "You are so mean that you're going to make me go to the bathroom in the woods!" Megan emphasized the word "mean."

Tyler laughed and almost chocked on the food. "Look, I'm not MAKING you do anything. There is no real bathroom here and probably isn't one within miles. You don't have much of a choice. You either go in the woods or hold it. It's going to get pretty uncomfortable holding it."

They sat in silence for a few more minutes. Tyler finished his sandwich and started to put the food away. Megan finally said in a meek voice, "I'm hungry."

"Okay, what do you want to eat?"

"Peanut butter and jelly."

"The jars are right there and here's a knife. Make a sandwich."

"No, I want you to make it for me."

"C'mon, Megan, you can make a pb and j sandwich for yourself." More tears.

"Okay, okay, a pb and j sandwich is not something to cry over. I'll make the sandwich."

As Tyler was making the sandwich, he was worried how the next two and a half days were going to go. Maybe Sheryl did a lot more for Megan than he realized.

Megan ate the sandwich in silence. Tyler was considering his next move. No question Megan could be stubborn. But was she always this needy?

When she finished with the sandwich, Megan said almost in a whisper, "I still have to go to the bathroom. I want you to come with me."

"Really, you can just go over into the bushes and I'll be right here. You don't need me."

More tears and now Megan had slumped back down onto the folding chair. Tyler didn't know what to do. Now he really wished either Kristin or Sheryl were here to help. In fact, he wished both of them were here. He didn't want Megan crying the entire weekend, but he didn't want to give in to her every time she started crying.

"Here's the deal. I will come with you this one time, so you get the hang of it, but I'm not coming with you every time you have to go. And if you keep crying over every little thing, then I'm not taking you when I go exploring or fishing or to the beautiful places that would be great for drawing. Is that a deal?"

Megan nodded slightly. They took the roll of toilet paper with them and headed off into the woods. When they found a suitable spot, Tyler said. "I'll look the other way and you go over to that spot."

A few minutes elapsed and Megan came back crying. "Now what?"

"You didn't tell me I had to move my underwear and jeans, so now they're all wet!" Next came the wailing.

"Jesus, Megan, you know how a girl's plumbing works and it's different from a boy's. I shouldn't have to tell you things like that."

More wailing. "Okay, okay, stop crying. We can't have the waterworks every five seconds. I know Sheryl packed clean underwear and pants for you, so you can change."

Chapter 66

Sheryl, Mike and Jake sat in the family room. Mike poured each of them a glass of cabernet. They had dropped off Kristin, who now was spending a few hours at her friend Shelby's house. Her mother, Beverly, had promised to drive Kristin home by 11 pm on this Friday night.

Mike asked, "Jake, how's work going?"

"Pretty well. I've been working on some big accounts and the clients like me, so that certainly will be a boost when I come up for partner. Thanks to Sheryl, I have been able to put in the hours I need. I'm not sure what I would do if I had to leave the office early on a regular basis. Sheryl has been a godsend with all her help. The girls really love her."

"Well, I suppose you'll hire a housekeeper when Sheryl comes home, which I hope will be soon." Mike made that comment purposely both for Jake and Sheryl's benefit. Sheryl pretended she didn't hear the comment.

"Between you and Tyler sharing the responsibilities, that should give you enough coverage with a housekeeper."

Jake rolled his eyes. "Only Sheryl and I are the adults here. Tyler is like an adolescent. He does what he wants when he wants. He doesn't help us, and he blatantly disregards any rules we have in place, so it makes it very difficult for us to enforce the rules with the girls."

After Jake finished, the silence hung in the air for a time. Sheryl thought about picking up the proverbial ball and running with it because she had made it known to Jake that she thought some of his views about the house and girls were too extreme. She didn't think prolonging this conversation was going to accomplish anything. She could voice her views to Mike later when they were alone.

Sheryl wanted to change the conversation to another subject because this was rehashing views which they had been over countless times. She changed the subject to the camping trip.

"I wonder how the camping trip is going. We haven't heard anything from them today, so I think that's a good sign. And they haven't come home, which is another good sign."

Mike asked, "Has Megan ever been camping before?"

"No, that's why I thought it was a good idea for her to experience something new. Megan is not athletic, and her hand eye coordination is pretty terrible. This is a chance for her to be outside in the fresh air without having to be playing a sport."

Mike nodded and said, "Sounds like it will be a good thing for her."

"It's also good that she does something without Kristin. There's always a certain amount of competition between siblings and for anything athletic, Kristin wins. It's good for Megan that there isn't competition. Tyler told me he brought fishing rods, and he was going to take her fishing. If both kids were there, it would turn into a competition about who caught the most fish. I just want Megan to enjoy something for itself without having to compete."

"I can understand that. Brian didn't have siblings, so he was always competing with me when he was a kid. The father/son rivalry. Who hit the most shots in the backyard playing basketball, who got the most hits in the batting cage, who won the tennis match and who had the better golf score."

Sheryl laughed. "You think the competition is over? It still goes on even now. It's just that Brian lives in a different city, so the competition is not daily. It's very much alive and well when he comes home, and you guys go to play tennis or golf.

"I can remember the first time he beat you in tennis. You would have thought that he won Wimbledon or the U.S. Open."

"Yeah, I remember that. He was getting bigger and stronger. His serves were tremendous, and I couldn't return them. But he has yet to beat me at golf. He still thinks that he has to hit every shot at a hundred miles an hour, and because of that his ball often ends up in the woods or out of bounds. That is still my secret weapon.

"I'm going to head upstairs. Even though it was a short flight, flying always exhausts me. All that great recycled air. C'mon, sweetheart, let's go."

Sheryl looked at Jake. "Kristin should be home in about a half hour. Are you okay to wait up?"

"Yeah, sure. See you guys in the morning."

"She's probably going to need help with the crutches going up the stairs."

"Yeah, no problem."

Chapter 67

Saturday morning was another sunny and bright morning. Tyler started making bacon and egg sandwiches and the smell of the bacon awakened Megan.

Megan poked her head out of the tent and got a better whiff of the food cooking. As she emerged from the tent, she said to Tyler, "I didn't know you could cook."

"I barely can. It's a good thing that we're only going to be here for two more days. In that short time, you will see the full extent of what I can cook. It's pretty basic stuff."

"What are we going to do today?"

"I was thinking of a few things. How about after we eat, we take a walk, and you bring your pen and paper so you can do some drawing? The mountains are over there in the distance, but I think we can get you a better view of them if we walk that way." Tyler was pointing to his left.

"Then we can come back here and eat lunch. I have an idea where there's a stream and it should also be pretty there too. You can draw, but we can also do some fishing. Have you ever been fishing?"

"No, but I don't want to bait the hook with worms. That's disgusting."

"Go get the orange juice for yourself. Your sandwich is almost ready.

"You don't have to bait the hook with worms. We're doing fly-fishing, which means you don't use worms. It's really fun."

Tyler thought he was making some progress since not everything with Megan was a battle, nor was she crying over everything. The bathroom situation was still an issue, but Tyler hoped that Megan would like the activities they were doing and hopefully that would overshadow having to go to the "bathroom" in the woods.

"Okay, I'm finished eating, so let's go."

"Hold on, kid, we still have to clean up. We can't leave food hanging around which might attract animals."

Megan's eyes got wide at the mention of the word "animals." "You said there were no bears."

"I said about a million times that there are no bears, but there could be other animals."

"Like what, something that could eat us?"

"Nothing that will eat us."

"Then what?"

"Geez, Megan, you're like a dog with a bone. There could be coyote or foxes, but it's unlikely that they'll come near us if they don't smell food."

"I'm scared of them. We should go home."

"There's nothing to be scared of. If we put the food away, no animals are going to come. I want to take you fishing. I think you'll like it. It will be fun for you to try something new.

"I want to tell you a story. Once when I was ten, I got hit by a ball in Little League. The pitcher didn't do it purposely; he was wild. I got hit on the arm. I had this enormous bruise, and it was all black and blue. I didn't want to go to the next game for fear I'd get hit again. My Dad tried to convince me it was okay to play in the next game and that I wasn't going to get hit again. I was still really scared, and I wasn't going to go. But it was YOUR Dad who said to me that just because something is hard or even scary, that you can't just bolt and run away. He said if we face what's scary, then suddenly it isn't scary anymore."

"So did you go to the game?"

"Yup. And this was a different team and a different pitcher. I almost got hit again. And you know what happened? Because I faced what was scary, and I stood in that batter's box for the next pitch after that, I hit a double and drove in two runs."

"My Daddy taught you that?"

"Yes, and he was the one who was cheering the loudest for me as I was running to second. I could hear him over all the other kids' voices. So maybe when you're scared, think of your Dad and know that he's cheering for you, so you shouldn't bolt and run."

Tyler could see he struck a chord, because the tears starting streaming down Megan's cheeks. Every time Megan started to cry, Tyler got very nervous because he didn't know what he should be doing.

"I think your Dad helped me to remember that story now because it's important for you. I hadn't thought about it in years. I bet he's with us right now. Your Dad loved to go on adventures too, so that's what we should do now in his honor. Grab your art supplies, and I'll get the backpack with some water and snacks, and we'll find a place you like, and you can draw a picture your father would like."

Chapter 68

Tyler wasn't totally sure where they were going. He was walking in the general direction of the mountains hoping for a place where they would get an unobstructed view. After about a half hour of walking, Megan announced she was tired and wanted to stop walking.

"Okay, take a drink of water and we'll stop for a while."

"No, I want to go back; this is too far."

"Hey, what did I tell you about your Dad and not bolting and running. I think we're getting close to a great spot for you to draw."

"You said I shouldn't bolt and run if I'm scared. I'm not scared. I'm tired and hot and I don't want to walk anymore."

Tyler could feel his own aggravation boiling up within him. "The story wasn't just about being scared. It's about not giving up when things are scary or hard. Sometimes you have to push yourself."

Megan made a face. Tyler had seen that face many times before. It was a precursor to her digging in her heels and refusing to do something. Once that happened, then no amount of pleading or reasoning with her did much good.

"How about we make a deal? We walk for another fifteen minutes and if by then we don't find a good place, then we can go back. We could find a great place in the next three minutes and it would be a shame to miss it."

Megan eyed him warily. "You're just trying to make me do something."

Tyler could feel his aggravation turning to anger. Megan might very well miss out on something great because she didn't want to, and couldn't be convinced to, take another step. She was stubborn, and that was going to be her downfall in a lot of things in her life.

"Ten minutes."

"What?"

"I'll walk for ten more minutes and if we haven't found a place, then I want to go back."

"Okay, ten minutes it is."

"And don't try to trick me. I know what ten minutes is."

Tyler wasn't sure how she would know when ten minutes was up because she was not wearing a watch, but at least the negotiations yielded something fruitful.

Tyler wasn't one for praying, but as they walked, Tyler implored the universe and his dead brother to help them find a spot and find it quickly.

About four more minutes into the walk, they came upon a clearing with what was a panoramic view of the mountains against a backdrop of beautiful trees.

"Wow, look at this, Megan. It's gorgeous. This was worth walking for a few more minutes. You have something great to draw here."

Megan was already pulling her pad and pencils out of her backpack.

Tyler was silently thanking the universe and his brother and whoever else came to his aid.

Chapter 69

After Megan worked on her sketches, they headed back to their camp. Megan told Tyler that she did a number of what she called "early sketches" and then she would work on them later, some in color and some in black and white. As Tyler looked at them, he realized they were good, especially for a little girl. She had talent, and he believed her work would only get better as she got older. Tyler saw that when she was working on sketches or other drawings, she was a different kid. She was much easier to deal with. He said to himself that when they got back, he should talk to Jake and Sheryl about getting her art lessons on a regular basis.

Lunch was uneventful since Megan was in a very good mood about her drawings. When they finished eating lunch, Tyler asked her if she wanted to go fishing. Megan made a face.

"Here's the deal. You can try fishing and if you like it, great. If not, you can do some sketching by this stream. It will look totally different from the view of the mountains and will give you something new to draw. You didn't want to go to the clearing this morning because it was too far, yet when we got there, you loved the view of the mountains and it was worth the walk."

Tyler was careful to us the word "walk" instead of "hike." For some reason, the word hike had a bad connotation with Megan. Maybe she had been forced to go on a hike with the Brownies or some other group, and apparently it was anything but a hit with Megan. Even though Megan could be cute, and she was definitely smart, Tyler was finding it exhausting trying to navigate the minefield that was Megan. He was glad that they were more than half-way through the camping trip. Tyler now realized that Sheryl had subtly warned him that dealing with Megan all by himself for three days, might prove to be a handful. Now he realized it was a very big handful.

Tyler was also wondering if Megan had been this difficult before Blake and Jackie's deaths. He knew that there had been some sports disasters with tennis and basketball, and there may have been a few others. Tyler also knew that Jackie inadvertently had gotten Megan into art as a diversion from the sports disasters and it had been a success. Tyler realized that he didn't know much about the kids before the deaths, because he hadn't been around them all that much.

It made it even more curious that Blake and Jackie had named him and Jake as the Co-Guardians and that they had never spoken to either of them about it when they were preparing their Wills. He thought Sheryl would have been the more logical and better choice as the Guardian. Another curious thing in Tyler's mind.

Tyler wasn't even sure he wanted to do this parenting thing long term. He might want to move to Florida or California, where the weather was better all year round. He could do his carpentry work anywhere. A good carpenter was always in demand. Tyler liked it that he could work when he wanted and where he wanted. He had a few contractors who called him, and that was fine.

It would also be a pleasure to get away from Jake, who was a royal pain. Tyler felt he had never met a person more concerned with cleanliness and rules than Jake. No wonder that Jake hadn't been in a serious relationship long term in a while. He would probably drive the other person crazy.

Tyler knew that he himself was a slob and frankly, he didn't care. Sometimes he just threw things around or left a mess precisely because he knew it would irritate Jake. Hard to believe anyone could be that obsessive compulsive. When Jackie was alive, the house was always clean, but Tyler didn't remember her going crazy over every spill or mess. Sheryl had been staying with them for a while now, and Tyler didn't see her getting nuts over everything in the house. Jackie and Sheryl were Jake's siblings, so they grew up in the same house with the same parents and the same set of rules. What had happened with Jake to make him such a clean freak and so obsessive about every detail?

Chapter 70

"You ready to go?" Megan's question tore Tyler out of his musings about his life and the people who were suddenly such a big part of it. Apparently, they would not have a tug of war about going fishing.

"Yeah, let me get the fishing gear and something for us to drink."

This time they went off in a different direction from the "hike" to the mountains. Tyler was again careful just to call it a walk. Tyler had a pretty good sense of direction, and he could see that as they were walking, they were going to a lower elevation, where he thought the stream was located.

This walk to the stream wasn't as far as the mountain walk from this morning. Tyler stopped walking and said to Megan, "Listen."

Megan stopped and looked at Tyler. "What? Do you hear bears?"

"God, no bears. Shhh. If you're quiet, you can hear the stream. We're getting close."

In a few more minutes, the sound of the stream rushing was apparent, and then they saw it. Another unspoiled sight in nature.

Tyler unpacked the fishing rods and the lures. That there were no live worms was going to be a plus to get Megan to try fishing. Tyler saw that if they stayed on the bank, the water was too shallow and rocky for them to catch anything. They didn't have waders, so they were going to have to venture out on the rocks in the stream. Before they left the bank, Tyler showed Megan how to cast the rod into the water. Tyler thought there was nothing Megan could do wrong in casting. It might not be perfect, and it might not even be that good, but gravity and the weight of the lure would make the line hit the water. It might even be a positive experience for Megan to do something somewhat athletic and succeed at it.

Megan watched Tyler do it a few times and then he put his hand over hers on the rod to get her to feel what it was like as he cast. Megan then tried it a few times herself with mixed success. The first few times she didn't cast it hard enough, and the lure bounced off the exposed rocks. After a few more tries, she was getting better.

"Okay, so you see that we're too close to the bank and the water is too shallow here for the fish to come in. All we have to do is take a few steps out onto the rocks and then when you cast, the line will be in the deeper water."

Megan eyed him suspiciously. "You want me to go out there in the water?"

"Not in the water. On top of those rocks right there so you can get your line into the deeper water. It's only a couple of feet deep there. How about I hold on to you and help you get to the rocks so you don't fall?"

Megan hesitated again. Tyler was afraid he was going to lose the momentum he had built up with her. Megan had seen that it wasn't that difficult to cast the line, and it didn't have to be perfect.

"Megan, think of your Dad and what he said. You've got to stand in there and not bolt and run. It's just like I did in the batter's box. C'mon, I'll help you. You can do this."

Tyler reached out his hand and Megan took it. "Look where you're stepping. We're going to step rock to rock."

Miraculously, Megan made it rock to rock and ended up on the rock Tyler wanted her to be on. "Just stay here for a minute and I'll get the rods."

Tyler went back to the bank, grabbed the two fishing rods and then made his way back to a rock near where Megan was perched. He handed Megan a rod and said, "Okay, now cast as we practiced. If you don't get it the way you want, you do it again. No big deal."

Megan tried it a few times and her casting wasn't bad. Tyler felt a tug on his line and tried to reel it in, but the fish got away. Megan watched Tyler try to reel the fish in.

"What happens if I get a fish on the line?"

"We'll try to reel him in. You saw I got a bite, but he got away. It happens sometimes. That's the fun of it. Sometimes you win and sometimes the fish wins. You never know."

They both cast their lines and suddenly, Megan screeched, "I have something on the line!"

"Start to reel it in."

Megan got too excited and jerked the line. As she did so, she lost her balance. She fell off the rock and landed with a huge splash into the water. Fortunately, the water was probably about four feet deep, so she would not drown, but Megan was startled by her fall, and the water was extremely cold.

She started screaming as she fell. Tyler saw Megan fall, but he was powerless to do anything about it. He was too far away to grab her. He jumped into the water but had to wade his way to her and the water was providing considerable resistance. As he hit the water, the cold water shocked him. It took his breath away, but he kept moving as fast as he could. He was pretty sure she would not drown, but he thought that Megan may not have been athletic enough to grab onto something and stand up, especially in wet heavy clothes.

As Tyler reached Megan, he grabbed her by the sweatshirt and yanked her up toward him as hard as he could. She got a mouthful of water on her way down, so now as Tyler pulled her up, she was coughing and crying at the same time.

"Stand up, Megan, the water isn't that deep! Get your feet under you!"

Finally, with Tyler pulling her up, Megan got her feet down on the stream bed. Tyler also saw that her forehead was bleeding and so he half dragged half pulled her toward the bank. As they reached the bank, Tyler climbed up and then pulled her out of the water toward him. Megan was now wailing uncontrollably.

"Let me look at you. Are you hurt?"

The gash on her forehead didn't look that deep, and she had skinned both palms trying to grab the rocks as she fell.

"Megan, you're okay. You've got some scrapes on your forehead and your hands, but that's about it. You're scared and shaken up, but you're okay. We're both cold and wet, but that's it."

Megan was still crying, but she was slowly stopping. Tyler had his arms around her. Megan finally stopped burying her face in his jacket.

"C'mon, we have to get both of us out of these wet clothes. Let me go get the two rods out of the water."

Tyler really didn't want to go back into the cold water, but he didn't want to lose the rods either. He could pick up one rod while standing on the rocks, but he had to go into the water to get the other. He felt as if someone was stabbing his legs as he got back in the cold water.

They trudged back to the camp in stony silence. Tyler didn't know if he should say something and try to lighten the mood or stay silent. He was shivering, so he picked up the pace a little.

The first time Megan said anything was as the camp came into view. "I guess the fish won today like you said, but do you think my Daddy would be proud that I learned how to fish and even went out on the rocks?"

"He would be so proud."

Chapter 71

Tyler woke up Sunday morning and his first thought was he was glad it was Sunday. This felt like a much longer weekend than he had expected. Megan required a lot of hand holding. She was needy and often difficult. Tyler tried to remember what it was like being a nine-year-old. His memories were mostly about playing organized sports and playing with Blake and the neighborhood kids in the back yard. Maybe he was oblivious because he was a boy or maybe it was just a different time.

Kristin didn't seem to need as much attention or hand holding. Tyler didn't know if Megan had been like this before Jackie and Blake's deaths. He had talked about Blake more this weekend than at any other time and while it felt good to remember things, he also realized that he had never truly mourned for his older brother. He just kept pushing it to the back of his mind. Now some of the sadness crept in and he didn't push it away.

"Hope you liked this weekend, Blake," he said half under his breath. "Hope I helped this little kid. I didn't realize, but I did it for you."

Tyler thought he would let Megan decide what she wanted to do. If she wanted to take one more walk, and God forbid he say the word hike, they could find another place and she could do some drawing. If not, then they would pack up and head home a little earlier. Even if they found another place for her to sketch, it would take some time to pack, but they would still leave in the afternoon.

Megan had said very little when they returned to camp after her fall in the water and she had been quiet while they were eating dinner. Maybe she wasn't as traumatized about the entire afternoon as he thought. There was no more crying or wailing and they had quickly changed into warm dry clothes. Megan had gone through almost all her clothes, so that was another reason to go home, what with the first bathroom situation and now the fall into the stream. Tyler thought she would be more animated over the s'mores, but she ate them and didn't say much. They both were tired and although he didn't like to admit it, he was emotionally spent from the episode at the stream. It could have turned out much worse and the cut on her forehead stopped bleeding even before they got back to camp. She fought him a little when he cleaned off the cut with antiseptic.

Tyler got up to make some much needed coffee and breakfast. After a while, Megan came out of the tent. Her forehead looked raw near the gash, but Tyler didn't want to make too much of it in front of Megan and start a drama. He had cleaned off the wound, so he didn't think it would become infected, but they could take her to urgent care, if necessary, when they got home.

"What do you want to do this morning? Do you want to go find a place for you to do some sketching and then we'll pack up and go home, or do you just want to get ready to go home?"

"I'd like to do some more drawing, but I don't want to walk for miles and miles."

"I don't think we've ever walked for miles and miles as you called it, but we can find a place that's not too far. Let's eat and we can get ready to take off."

Tyler finished eating first and then started bringing things to put away in the truck. He noticed that suddenly, Megan disappeared. Tyler realized that Megan had gone into the woods. Tyler thought to himself that they had made some progress with the "bathroom situation." She had complained for most of the two days they were here at the camp, but there was really nothing else they could do.

Megan reappeared and said, "This is so gross. Next time we go camping, I want to go somewhere that has a real bathroom and a shower. I know I got a bath yesterday, but that isn't what I wanted."

"Well, I'm glad to hear you want to go camping again."

Chapter 72

For their third and final walk, they set off in a third direction. This was unfamiliar territory they had not been to before. Tyler wasn't sure exactly where they were heading, but they had managed quite well on their two previous walks. He had a pretty good sense of direction.

It was cooler this morning and maybe that was good, because Tyler was sure they had walked farther than either of the two previous walks, and Megan wasn't complaining yet that she was too hot or too tired. Tyler knew he was on borrowed time, and it was only going to be a matter of minutes before Megan started complaining. He was hoping to find a spot with a good view and then she could start drawing and all would be well. But they had to find the spot relatively soon.

After a few more minutes, the inevitable happened. "How much farther is this? We've been walking for miles and miles. It's too far."

"Almost there." Tyler didn't know where "there" was, but he was hoping "there" was close. He was hoping for a lucky break and that the lucky break would come soon.

After a few more minutes, Tyler found what he was looking for. The woods opened to a clearing on what looked like a promontory.

"Wow, look at this spectacular view of the mountains against that gorgeous sky."

Tyler stepped farther out onto the ledge and with that the ledge gave way and he fell. Tyler screamed and his fall was probably a good thirty plus feet. Megan saw him disappear from view and she heard his scream. His scream caused her to scream too.

Something in Megan was smart enough to realize that if the ledge had given way under Tyler, that it probably wasn't safe to go out on to the edge, but she was so terrified that she had to see what had happened. She started screaming "Uncle, Tyler, Uncle Tyler" at the top of her lungs. The terror in her voice was apparent. He wasn't answering her, which made her all the more hysterical and she tried to yell even louder.

There was some rational part of her brain which was working, but that part of her brain was fast losing ground to hysteria. She knew she didn't weigh as much as Uncle Tyler, and she had seen scenes of rescues on the ice on television. She had seen the rescuers lie down on the ice and inch forward on their stomachs toward the drowning person, so she got down on her stomach and inched her way toward the edge. She could see the jagged edge of earth and some tree roots where the ground had given way. She was getting close.

When she finally got to the edge, she mustered her courage and looked over. What she saw, made her gag. Tyler was lying on his back with his eyes closed, but the worst part was that there was a tree limb sticking out of his leg. Around where the tree limb was sticking out, she could see a widening circle of red.

For a few seconds, her fear paralyzed her. She tried to scream again, but nothing came out. Finally, she was able to scream, "Uncle Tyler, are you okay?" She screamed his name three times, when he half opened his eyes in response.

"Uncle Tyler, you fell. Can you move?"

Tyler opened his eyes full this time and tried to move, but the pain shooting from his leg almost made his pass out. He looked at his leg and knew the wound was terrible. The pain snapped him back to reality.

"Megan, I can't move, and I must have hit my head pretty bad too. My vision is blurry, and I have a pain in my head." As Tyler said that, he had his hand on his temple.

"Your leg is bleeding."

"Yeah, I know."

"What are we going to do?" Megan now sounded frantic.

"Megan, I think you have to go for help. I won't be able to free myself. Even if I could, I don't think I can walk on my leg."

"Where will I go? I can't leave you!"

"You're going to have to. There's a tree limb sticking out of my leg, and I'm bleeding. I'm stuck down here and you're up there. You're the only hope. You've got to go for help."

Now Megan started to cry. "I can't. I don't know where to go and I'm scared. I don't want to leave you."

Tyler was feeling nauseous from what was probably a concussion, but he knew that if she lost it, he was probably going to die there.

"Megan, listen to me. I know this is really scary and I'm scared too, but I'm also badly hurt, and you are the only one who can help me. If you stay here, you're not helping me. You've got to get back to the camp and call for help on my cell."

"How am I ever going to find the camp? I don't know where we are!" Now she started to wail.

"Megan, please, don't cry. You've got to think. If you keep crying, you can't think straight."

"I don't know which way to go!"

"Okay, okay, calm down." Tyler was trying to think about this himself and how to tell her where to go. His head was throbbing unmercifully which was making it that much more difficult for him to think.

"When we walked to this spot, the sun was hitting us in the back. Now when you walk back to the camp, you need to keep the sun in your face. If you see anybody, yell for help. If not, when you get back to the camp, my cell is in the green backpack rolled up in a gray sweatshirt. You may have to fish around in the bottom of the backpack, because the sweatshirt may have moved.

"It's possible that there may not be good cell service, so you may have to walk toward the main road to get service. The cell is charged. If you call 911, they should be able to find you based on the signal from the phone."

Megan nodded, but the tears were rolling down her cheeks, even though she was not openly sobbing.

"Do you have a belt on?"

"No."

"What do you have on underneath your jacket?"

"A sweatshirt and a long sleeve shirt."

"I need you to take off your shirt and throw it down to me. I'm going to have to try to make a tourniquet out of it to stop the bleeding. You should be warm enough with the two layers until you get back to camp and then you can grab something and put it on if you're cold."

Megan started stripping off her layers and peeled off the shirt. She could feel the cold air on her body as she took off each layer.

"Megan, listen, you can't just throw the shirt because I may not be able to reach it. Can you find a long stick or a limb and put the shirt on the end so when you drop it, it falls close to me?"

"I can't do this. I can't do this. It's too hard."

"You've got to try. If you don't, I may bleed to death. You can do this. C'mon, Megan, hold it together. Go find a stick."

Megan was even more horrified when she heard that he might bleed to death, but that spurred her to try. She found a broken limb which was fairly long, but not all that heavy, so she was able to maneuver it.

"Okay, I have it."

"Now put the shirt on the end of the stick. Come to the edge again so that you're in line with my head. Then you're going to shake the stick and the shirt will fall off close to me so I can grab it."

Tyler knew how unathletic Megan was and that her hand/eye coordination was poor. He knew they only had one chance. Megan lined herself up as Tyler said. As she shook the stick, the shirt fell. Miraculously, the wind blew the shirt toward Tyler. He was able to grab it.

"Great, Megan, you did it!"

"Yeah, I did it!"

"Now take some water bottles with you in the backpack. You can do this."

"I'm afraid. I don't know where to go. I'll get lost and I'll die."

"You can't just stay here or we'll both die."

Megan gasped when she heard that from Tyler.

"Remember what we talked about with your Dad. You have to stand your ground and stand in the batter's box. You can't bolt and run just because it's scary. Make your Dad proud of you."

A very meek response came from Megan. "Okay, I'll go."

Chapter 73

"Megan, you can do this. Remember to try to keep the sun directly into your eyes.

"Do one more thing before you go. Throw down a bottle or two of water. I know I had at least four bottles with us."

Megan edged her way again toward the edge of the shelf. She replicated what she had done with the shirt. She lined herself up with Tyler's head.

"Ready, I'm going to drop the bottle of water."

"Okay, fire away."

Megan dropped the water bottle and bounced off Tyler's head, but he was able to snag it. Getting hit directly in the head with a water bottle, didn't help the pounding in his head, but at least he would have some water.

"Sorry, did that hurt?"

"No, it's fine. Can you drop the second bottle?"

"Here it comes." Megan dropped it but this time the bottle bounced off his chest and rolled just out of reach.

Tyler knew he would have to decide how much pain he could endure to try to reach the second water bottle.

"Take the backpack. There are some snacks for you in there. You should really get going now."

Megan turned away from Tyler to start walking, but her eyes were blurry from the tears. Tyler wiped his eyes as well. In his mind he didn't know if Megan could find her way back to the camp or if she would get disoriented and be lost in the woods. He had tried to hold it together in front of Megan and appear calm, but he was anything but calm.

His head was still killing him, so he was pretty sure he had a concussion. He did his best to try to stop the bleeding with the shirt, but he had been impaled with the tree limb, so he could barely move the leg to get the shirt underneath to tie the knot. The pain was excruciating as he did it and he vomited off to his side from the pain. He hoped he wouldn't bleed to death before anyone found him.

Then another sickening thought crossed his mind. The information for the campsite he had given Sheryl was now totally wrong. They hadn't gone there since the campsite had screwed up their reservation. Sheryl and Jake would have no idea of where they were. It had crossed his mind a few times to call or text them, but he had forgotten to do it.

Tyler now realized that both of their lives were in the hands of a nine-year-old girl. And a nine-year-old who had never been camping before and did not know how to survive in the woods. Tyler was pretty sure that Megan wasn't paying any attention to where they were walking. She was merely following Tyler's lead. Tyler had always had a good sense of direction, and he mostly walked through the woods on feel. He couldn't expect the same from Megan.

Tyler believed that even if Megan couldn't find the camp, she would eventually stumble onto another hiker or maybe find her way to a road. At worst, when they didn't show up at home, Sheryl or Jake would call Tyler's cell and when it continued to go to voicemail, they would call the campsite. They would realize that something was wrong and call for help. The question was how long that would take and how long would it take to mobilize the authorities to look for them.

The only good thing that Tyler could think about was that he told Sheryl they would be home before dark, so when it got dark and they hadn't arrived home, maybe that would be another cue that something was wrong. Even though that thought had some comfort attached to it, he also realized that he probably would spend a night out in the woods with his leg impaled with a tree limb. Unless Megan got incredibly lucky and found her way and found it fast. In his heart of hearts, Tyler knew he could hope for that, but he could not rely on it.

Tyler felt that he was in this situation for a while. The more he lay there, the more the dire thoughts haunted him. He needed to stay still to keep the tourniquet in place and it seemed as if the red stain on his pants leg was not getting larger. He knew he was most probably going to endure a cold night exposed to the elements. He reached into his jacket pocket and to his great surprise and delight, he found two protein bars. So at least he had some food and water. He would have to ration what he had because there was no telling how long he would be there.

Then he started worrying about how much food Megan had in the backpack. If he had two protein bars in his jacket, did that mean that he hadn't put any in the backpack Megan had? He tried hard to remember, but his brain was still fuzzy. Had he put some protein bars in the backpack, and these were extras? The more he thought about it, the less certain he was and he was getting more upset.

As his mind wandered, he worried about animals. He had told Megan a bunch of times that there were no bears, but now his fears rose. Suppose there were bears? Even if there were no bears, there could be coyote or wolves and he was a sitting duck. He would be easy prey, especially if there were a pack of coyotes. Tyler felt his heartbeat speed up, and that was bad, especially since he was still bleeding.

Tyler thought he needed to get his mind off this track. There wasn't much he could do. Suddenly, he had a thought. "I'll sing," he said out loud. Tyler didn't know if he had a good voice, but right now he didn't care.

He tried to think of a song, but his mind went blank. He couldn't think of one song. Then without further thought he started singing the National Anthem. He couldn't reach the high notes, but he kept on singing. The next song was America the Beautiful. He couldn't think of the title of the next song, but he knew it started with the word, "Mine eyes have seen the glory of the coming of the Lord." He sang the whole song. He thought about the words and didn't know what the words, "the grapes of wrath are stored" meant. Finally, he remembered that the song's name was the Battle Hymn of the Republic.

These must have been songs he learned as a kid in grade school. He hadn't thought about them or sung them in years.

The next song he remembered was Bye, Bye, Miss American Pie. There were a lot of words to that song and a lot of verses. That kept him busy for a while trying to remember all the verses.

Next, he moved on to James Taylor songs. He knew there were a lot of them, and he was getting tired. By now his heart rate had come down and he wasn't as afraid. James Taylor could wait for now.

Chapter 74

Megan cried for the first ten minutes as she started walking. She was freaked out by seeing Uncle Tyler hurt with a tree limb sticking out of his leg. She was freaked out by walking in the woods alone. She was freaked out since she still expected to come face to face with a bear. She was freaked out because she had no idea of where to go to find the camp.

All Uncle Tyler had said was keep the sun on your face. That didn't give her a very good idea of where to go, so that freaked her out too. She could hear Uncle Tyler's voice in her head saying that he was going to die there if she didn't get help. That freaked her out the most since she had never been in the woods, no less in the woods alone. If he died, that would be her fault. Now she cried harder. Her Mom and Dad had died and left her and now Uncle Tyler might die and leave her too. She stopped walking and leaned against a tree with all these thoughts and emotions swirling inside her.

Now Megan was talking out loud. "Uncle Tyler, you can't die. Don't die. I miss my Mommy and Daddy so much and then I'd have to miss you too. Don't die.

"You said my Daddy said to not to bolt and run. I have to stand in the batter's box."

There was a long pause before she said out loud, "Okay, I'll try."

Megan decided to walk, and within about twenty-five yards thereafter, she kicked a branch with her foot. She looked down at it and thought it might help her push aside the dense underbrush, so she picked it up. She had seen pictures of people with hiking sticks, so maybe this would be good. As she stood back up with the branch in hand, she realized that the sun was not directly in her face. The sun was hitting her on the right side of her head. She would make the adjustment.

"This might be my lucky stick. Yeah, it just might be. Maybe it's a magic wand like in Harry Potter." Saying those words out loud made her feel better. She wiped her nose on her sleeve and kept walking.

She was trying to remember how long it had taken them to walk to the place where Uncle Tyler fell. She didn't think it had taken them an hour because she thought she would have been too tired by then. She remembered Uncle Tyler telling her they were almost there. Now she was trying to determine how long she had been walking now, but she was not sure.

The bushes and branches were making it difficult to walk and her progress was slow. She really didn't know how far she had walked and if she was walking in the right direction. That was the scariest part. She didn't know where she was going.

Now she was getting panicky. Was she walking in circles? Was she even walking in the camp's direction?

Megan continued walking and pushed a tree branch back with her new walking stick. Unfortunately, she didn't push it far enough, and it snapped back and hit her in the arm with a resounding thwack. "Ouch, that hurt."

As she looked down, she saw that the branch had skinned her hand. It was just on the verge of bleeding. "That was so mean," Megan blurted out to herself or to the universe.

She stopped for a minute and took off her backpack. She pulled a bottle of water out of the backpack and took a long drink. She put the bottle back in the backpack since she thought she needed to use both hands while walking.

Megan had no way of knowing if she was covering a lot of ground or not. To her it seemed as if she had been walking forever. She didn't have a watch, so she had no actual sense of time. It was getting warmer as the day approached noon time. Megan was aware of the temperature since she was starting to sweat. When they had left the camp this morning, she had on three layers. She had given Uncle Tyler her shirt to use as a tourniquet, so she was down to two layers, and now she unzipped her jacket, which was one of the two remaining layers. Normally, Megan hated being hot, and she got cranky in the heat. She wanted to complain that she was hot, but there was no one to complain to.

She remembered that when she pulled out the water bottle from her backpack that she had seen a baseball cap. Now she pulled the backpack off her shoulders again and took the baseball cap out and put it on. The logo on the cap was the interlocking NY which she knew meant the New York Yankees. She knew they were a baseball team, but not much else. If she knew more about baseball and the history of the Yankees and their many World Championships, that might have encouraged her that she could win against the woods around her and find the camp. But Megan didn't know any of that.

Megan didn't realize that she was subtly giving herself small pep talks.

"The Yankees play baseball, so they hit the ball. That means they stand in the batter's box, just like my Daddy said you do."

She continued trudging through the woods. Time passed by, but Megan didn't see anything familiar, nor did she see any other hikers. She kept walking, but she had paid no attention to where they were going when they left the camp, so even if she was on the route they had taken, Megan didn't know it.

Megan tripped on a tree root and went airborne. She landed on her stomach, even though her reflexes had her hands go forward which broke her fall a bit. The landing knocked the wind out of her and as she got up, she saw that she had skinned both of her palms. She sat there for a few minutes as she caught her breath, and then she started to cry.

"I want to go home. I hate this place. I hate camping. I want my Mommy." With that Megan started sobbing.

When she finally collected herself a bit, she realized she could cry, but that wasn't getting her any closer to the camp. She got up and walked even though she was crying and miserable.

Chapter 75

Sheryl realized that with all that had gone on with the weekend with Kristin still moping around on crutches and Mike being up from Florida, that she had not heard from Tyler and Megan. She didn't want to call them and make it seem as if she was checking up on them, but she had kind of hoped that one of them would call.

Megan didn't have a cell phone, but Tyler would certainly have let her call on his phone. When she broached the subject with Mike, his reaction had been, "Maybe it's a good thing that you haven't heard from them. Maybe they're having a good time and they don't need to call."

Sheryl thought about that statement. She didn't know if the campsite had a real bathroom and a shower. Somehow she couldn't imagine Megan going to the bathroom in the woods. They also hadn't mentioned the insects. Megan wasn't an outdoorsy kid. She got cranky easily if she got hot or tired. Mike's statement that maybe Megan was having a good time camping seemed implausible to Sheryl. Sheryl thought to herself, "And maybe pigs will fly."

Sheryl said to Mike, "I guess it's possible that Megan likes it, but I had more doubts than beliefs that this was going to work out well. Tyler was excited about taking her camping and he likes it. Once Kristin got hurt, I sort of doubted that Megan would go alone. She vacillated a lot, and I didn't think she would go. She surprised me that in the end she said yes that she'd go alone with Tyler without Kristin, who is often the buffer. I thought it was something he was good at and liked, so it was nice he could share that with her.

"But I tried to warn Tyler that he was going to have to handle her alone. He didn't seem to get that, or he didn't care. He shrugs off a lot of stuff and then it can come up and bite him in the butt."

"What do you mean 'handle her alone?' What's that about?"

"She is really, really stubborn and when she gets like that, it's better that there are two of us as the adults to handle it. My sister, Jackie, was like that. I can remember her ending up in pitched battles with my father especially, since both of them were stubborn. I guess this is a case of the apple not falling too far from the tree."

"So call them and see what time they plan to get back here. Let's take them out to dinner to someplace they like. That way you don't have to cook. I'm willing to bet that both of them will be happy for a hot, well-cooked meal. They probably have had their fill of hamburgers and hot dogs. This way we can make a reservation if we know what time they'll be back."

Sheryl called Tyler on his cell, and it went straight to voicemail. She left the message and asked Tyler to call back. About two hours later, she tried Tyler's cell again and again it went straight to voicemail.

"I wonder if they have good cell service up there. It may be spotty. At least I left messages on his cell so when they get to a place with better cell coverage, he can call me back."

"Do you have the number of the campsite? Call them and see if they checked out. That might help you figure out what time they could be back here."

"Good idea. I know Tyler left it for me. I'll call."

A few minutes later Sheryl came back to the family room where Mike was watching the game. "I called the campsite, and they said there was a problem with the reservation and they didn't check in. That's not good."

"Those snafus happen all the time. Sometimes the people taking the reservations are not all that swift or they double book and run out of space. They just went somewhere else."

"I dunno. This makes me worried."

"It's a little too soon to get worried. He'll get the message and call you back when he gets service."

"I hope that's true, but now I can't shake the feeling that something is wrong."

Another few hours passed, and Sheryl called twice more with no response.

"Tyler told me they would be home before dark. No sign of them and now I'm officially worried. Don't tell me not to be worried. It's getting late in the afternoon. By now they have to be in a place where he could call."

Mike didn't say anything because anything he said to try to placate her would ring hollow. He understood why Sheryl was worried.

Chapter 76

Megan was tired and sat down on a large rock. She pulled the backpack onto her lap and fished around inside. She came up with a protein bar, unwrapped it and took a bite. She was tired, hot and scared. She had no idea of how far she had walked or how long she had been walking. With every minute that elapsed, she was getting more frightened. She didn't know if she was close to the camp or if she truly was going in the right direction. The thought crossed her mind that she could be close to the camp and miss it because of the dense vegetation. Then she got even more afraid that she would be lost in the woods and no one would ever find her. What happened if she was lost in the woods and it got dark? The thought of spending a night alone in the woods made her shiver even though she was hot and sweating. So far Uncle Tyler had been right that they hadn't seen any bears, but it scared her that might change in the dark.

Right now she hated the woods, she hated camping, she hated being hot, and she hated being alone. She thought that if only Kristin had come on the trip, Kristin would know what to do. If Kristin were there, at least they would be together in the woods. Megan had been hoping that she would come upon some other hikers who could help her, but she hadn't seen a soul.

While she was inclined to stay put for a while, the thought of being alone in the dark tonight got her on her feet and walking again. Fear was a powerful motivator.

For Megan's sake, it was probably fortunate that she didn't have a good idea of how serious Tyler's injury was or how much blood he could lose. While fear was a powerful motivator, hysteria was the enemy of survival.

Megan kept trying to keep the sun in her eyes, but she didn't really know how to do it, since her experience in the woods was zero. In the same way that the universe had been very unkind to Tyler and Megan when the shelf he had been standing on gave way, now the universe seemed to want to even the score.

As Megan walked, a bush with some red flowers came into view. Megan was sure she had seen that bush when they left the camp that morning. Now she was encouraged because she had some sign that she was on the right path. Megan did not realize that she was close to the camp and had been close for some time. She had been walking in a wide circle around the camp, without realizing it. Suddenly, something caught her eye. She thought she saw something bright blue to her left. Everything around her had been green, and nothing had been bright blue.

Now Megan made a sharp left turn and scrambled toward the "bright blue." The "bright blue" was Tyler's truck. The truck was perhaps twenty-five yards or thirty yards from the camp itself. Megan scratched her arms on the brush as she pushed anything in her path aside to get to the "bright blue." Nothing was going to stop her now. She stumbled into the opening and yelled "Yes" as she saw the truck come into full view. Megan threw herself against the truck and hugged it with open arms. Megan started to weep openly as she felt the cool sensation of the truck against her face and her hands. Megan had missed the mark of the camp, but she had found the "bright blue."

It took her a few minutes to stop crying and gather herself. She was relieved that at least she wasn't lost in the woods, she would not be alone tonight in the woods with the bears who were an ever-present worry for her, and she could bring help to Uncle Tyler.

Then she remembered that the ordeal was not over. She still had to get to the camp and call for help on the cell phone. Megan wasn't sure what direction the camp was relative to where the truck was. There appeared to be two directions where the growth wasn't as severe, and the truck had been driven in. It could have been a flip of the coin.

Now that Megan had calmed down and had some hope, her powers of reasoning kicked in very well for a nine-year-old. She didn't want to get lost again, so she picked a direction and started counting her steps. She decided that if she didn't see the camp when she got to seventy-five steps she would turn around and go back to the truck. Then she would go seventy-five steps on the other side of the truck. She started walking and counting. When she got to seventy-five steps, she decided to go to ninety steps. At ninety paces, it disappointed her not to see the camp, so she turned around.

She walked herself back to the truck and started off in the other direction. Megan got to seventy-five paces and saw nothing. She went to ninety paces and saw nothing. Now she stopped dead in her tracks as if her feet were glued to the ground. Should she go on? What happened if she went on and the camp was not there? Would she have to turn around again and go back in the original direction on the other side of the truck? Suddenly, Megan started hyperventilating.

"I saw the truck. I saw the truck. I saw the truck." It was almost like a chant. Somehow the chanting seemed to slow her heart rate. Megan was still glued in the same spot. Finally, she picked up one foot and moved forward. Then she took a second step. Right then she was shuffling her feet, and she wasn't keeping track of the number of her steps.

Mercifully, the camp came into view.

Chapter 77

Megan ran toward the tent and then into the tent. Uncle Tyler had told her that his cell phone was wrapped up in a backpack. Megan jammed her hand into the backpack and didn't find it. She then started throwing things out of the backpack until she found the cell phone. She got up and tried to run outside but tripped over the contents of the backpack now lying on the floor of the tent. She got up and fell a second time as she got tangled up in a pair of sweatpants. She flung the sweatpants off to her right and finally got herself out of the tent.

She pushed the on button and waited for the phone to boot up. The phone was charged, and came on, but she had no service. Megan ran to her left holding the phone up to see if she had service. Nothing! She ran farther away from the tent, but still nothing. Then she pivoted and ran in the other direction.

"C'mon, c'mon, please let there be bars on the screen." Still nothing. Now Megan was getting frantic, because she didn't know which way to go.

She went back in the original direction she had tried, but still with no success. She let the cell phone drop to the ground as she fell onto her knees and started crying. The emotion she was feeling was desperation, only that was too big a word for a nine-year-old.

"Mommy, where are you? I'm so scared. I don't know where I am or what to do. Why did you and Daddy have to die and leave me? If you hadn't died, I wouldn't be in the woods with Uncle Tyler. I would be home with you, and we would be reading a story together. Why did you have to die?"

Megan continued sobbing for a few minutes and then as the crying stopped, she felt a little better.

"I guess I could stay in the tent tonight and there's food here for me to eat. Maybe Aunt Sheryl will come looking for us if we don't come home tonight. We have the sleeping bags and blankets so I would be warm until they find me. But I'm scared about the bears."

Megan had just about talked herself into staying at the camp and waiting for help until a final thought crept into her brain. Just as she had talked out loud to herself to stay in the camp tonight, she now said out loud, "But Uncle Tyler. I have to help him. He's depending on me."

Now another idea crept into her head. If she found the car keys, she could drive the truck back to the main road and get help.

Megan ran back into the tent. "I have to find those car keys," Megan said out loud. The thoughts were coming into her head so fast that she was saying them out loud as if there was someone else around to hear her. "Where would Uncle Tyler keep them?"

The floor of the tent was a mess with all the things Megan had thrown out of the backpack. Megan looked around and saw a second backpack. She dove for it and grabbed the zipper and yanked it open. She shook the backpack hoping to hear the keys jingle, but she didn't hear anything. She again started throwing the contents out of the backpack. When the backpack was empty, Megan threw it on the ground in disgust.

Now she looked around the tent. There were a hundred places Uncle Tyler could have hidden the car keys. "Why would you even hide the keys when there's no one around?"

Megan's frustration was growing by the minute. She had been walking much more that she was used to, and she had cried off and on since she left Tyler. Her adrenaline had been pumping for a while now and as it wore off, she was tiring. Her energy was flagging.

She realized she had wasted time going around the camp in a wide circle for a while instead of being able to go right to it. She found the truck first and then had to take a few tries to find the camp. Then just when she thought things would be alright because she found the cell phone, there was no cell service. Now she couldn't find the car keys.

Megan went over to the air mattress and kicked it and kicked the sleeping bag. Nothing jingled. There were a pair of Tyler's jeans that she picked up and fished around in the pockets. Nothing again.

"Okay, so where are these stupid car keys?" It was dawning on Megan that she was wasting time. Everything was a hassle, and it was taking a long time to do everything. It was preying on her mind continually that she was afraid that it was going to get dark and she'd be alone in the woods, and worse still that Uncle Tyler was pinned down and hurt in the woods.

She looked at the coolers and opened them, and there wasn't much food left in them, but still no keys.

"Would Uncle Tyler keep the keys in the car?" Megan didn't think so, and she thought she ought to search the camp more first. There was a six pack of iced tea and a six pack of beer both held in their own separate cardboard containers. Megan realized how thirsty she was again. She didn't realize that every time she had a good cry, she was making herself dehydrated.

She reached the six pack of iced tea and as she tried to pull a bottle of iced tea out of the container, the whole container moved. Now she heard the jingling. "You hid the keys in the iced tea!"

Chapter 78

Megan grabbed the keys and the bottle of iced tea and now ran to where she now knew the truck was. She started going to the passenger side of the truck and then realized what she was doing. She switched sides and moved to the driver side. She pushed the button on the key and the door unlocked. Megan climbed up into the driver's seat and put the key in the ignition. She turned the key and the truck purred to life.

There was yet another obstacle that Megan hadn't thought of. Tyler's truck was large, and she wasn't tall enough to see over the steering wheel. She thought about it and didn't know what to do. She couldn't drive if she couldn't see, and this truck was substantially larger than Uncle Jake's car.

An idea hit her. Now she opened the door and jumped down on the ground. She ran back to the tent and started picking up the clothes she had thrown on the ground. The pile was sticking out in all directions in her arm. Megan was hoping the pile of clothes was going to be enough to make her sit up high enough to see over the steering wheel. She tripped over a pants leg as she ran but managed to keep her balance. She dropped a sweatshirt, so she had to stop to pick it up. That caused more clothes to fall, and it forced her to stop.

Megan's excitement was both a help and a hindrance. She was finally on a roll and she thought close to getting out of the woods. These woods were now a place she hated. She wanted to go home more than anything else. She didn't want to be alone, and she didn't want the burden of being the only person responsible for getting help for Uncle Tyler.

As she opened the truck door, the pile of clothes fell again and this time she kicked the door. The shooting pain in her toe told her this had not been a good idea. With the pile of clothes on the ground, it became finally became clear to Megan that she needed to make the pile of clothes neater so that she could make the pile higher. Megan's heart was beating so fast in her chest, that she couldn't catch her breath.

She rolled the clothes into as tight a pile as she could and put them on the driver's side seat. She climbed in and hoped that the pile was high enough. It wasn't great, but it was just high enough.

Megan remembered the conversation she had with Uncle Tyler on their way up here on Friday. He had asked her if she thought she could drive the truck with a clutch, which she didn't know how to do. But she also remembered that he had showed her there was a sports feature which didn't require the use of the stick and the clutch. Megan wasn't sure where the sports feature was, so she tried a few buttons on the dashboard. Those were not the feature. Then she remembered that Uncle Tyler had pointed to the center console. She pushed the button, and she saw the word "sports" show up on the dashboard.

Now she moved the center stick shift out of park. The car jumped forward as she moved the center stick shift into drive. She jammed on the brakes, and she had whiplash as the car came to a sudden and violent stop. The next problem that shot into her mind was that Uncle Tyler had driven the truck to where it now stood. He hadn't turned the truck around, so she was going to have to back the truck out. This presented more of a challenge than Megan had bargained for.

Chapter 79

Tyler was starting to have cramps in his back and his other leg from lying in one position for so long. He has shifted as much onto his side as he could to take the pressure off his impaled leg and to try to get the shirt underneath his leg to make as much of a tourniquet as he could. He now tried to shift his weight again to take some pressure off his back and his good leg.

He shifted what he thought was ever so slightly, and the pain in his leg did not increase. He now ventured to move a little more, and the pain shot up through his leg into his lower back. He screamed out in pain. It took him a few minutes of trying to take deep breaths and lying completely still for the pain to lessen somewhat. As this point, he wasn't sure what was worse. If he lay still, the pain in the impaled leg was constant, but not too bad. It was more than a dull ache, but it wasn't a shooting pain. Right now he thought it was as someone hitting his leg with a drumstick. It wasn't as bad as getting hit with a hammer, but the constant throbbing was wearing him down. The pain was relentless.

The weather had warmed up since this morning, and he was sweating. Tyler didn't know if this was from the sun beating down on him or if it was from the pain. Worse still, Tyler was afraid that the sweating was from loss of blood and that he was going into shock.

He reached out and touched the water bottle. He opened it and took a swig. He knew he had to ration the water since he didn't know how long he would be here.

He made one more attempt to move a little more and take the pressure off his back and other leg. After his last attempt at moving, he knew it would be bad, so he decided to do it now so at least the rest of his body was not in pain as well. He took a deep breath and put his arms under his body to try to help him move in the direction he wanted to go.

"Okay, on the count of three, I'm going to do this."

He took a deep breath. "No, on the count of five, I'll do it."

Finally, somewhere between the count of one and five, he moved. The pain was so intense that he shrieked out in pain and passed out.

Although Tyler was wearing a watch, he hadn't looked at it before he tried to move, so he didn't know how long it had been that he was out. As he came to, he looked down at his leg. The red stain on his pants had grown larger, but he thought that the tourniquet, although far from perfect, was helping somewhat. Tyler was still lucid enough to know that he was still losing blood. If this continued, and help did not arrive, he could feel the fear creep into his consciousness. The fear was so pervasive that he felt it in the pit of his stomach. He realized he could bleed to death.

There was no doubt in Tyler's mind that Megan would be rescued. When they didn't return home and Tyler was not answering his cell phone, Tyler was sure that Sheryl and Jake would contact the state police and they would start searching. Tyler didn't know if they would start the search in the dark or wait until the morning. Right now he cursed himself for not calling Sheryl to tell her that they hadn't gone to the campsite where he originally had the reservation. He wasn't sure how he would have told Sheryl where they were, since they ended up in a place that wasn't where Tyler expected they were going.

Maybe he should have tried another established campsite. Now Tyler was really cursing himself. His whole life he had done what he wanted when he wanted. He hated the rules and sometimes went out of his way to break them or defy them. Now his arrogance and his defiance of the rules might well cost him his life.

The only things that Tyler was counting on was the tenacity of a nine-year-old girl who had never been in the woods before. If by some miracle she found the campsite, then maybe she could call for help on his cell phone. He didn't know what the 911 capabilities were up here. Would they be able to track his cell phone and then find Megan? He thought that 911 would tell her to stay at the campsite. He also didn't think Megan could lead the rescuers back to where he was. He didn't know if she had found the campsite and what kind of circuitous route she had taken to get herself there.

Tyler realized that it could take a few days to find him. He didn't know if Megan would remember how long it had taken them to walk from the campsite or if she would even remember that detail. She would probably be hysterical when they found her. But it comforted Tyler that they would find her and rescue her.

He was anything but comforted because he thought he was going to die.

"Since I'm going to die, I would like to make peace with all those I have hurt. They're probably too many to mention by name, but I am sorry if I hurt you.

"Blake, I'm sorry I got Megan into this mess with me. I thought I was doing something fun with her. I know I'm supposed to take care of her and look what a shit show this turned out to be. I guess I'll be seeing you and Jackie soon, so don't be mad at me when I see you.

"We learned prayers in school, but I never paid any attention, so I never really learned all of them." Tyler now wracked his brain for some of them.

"Hail Mary, full of grace and Our Father who art in heaven." Tyler now jumbled two prayers together. Tyler stopped trying to remember the rest.

"There's something about our daily bread and lead us not into temptation and Holy Mary, Mother of God.

"Listen, God, I'm sorry for what I've done, and I hope you will forgive me and not send me to hell for being such a screwup."

Chapter 80

"I got in trouble for driving Uncle Jake's car, but now everyone is going to be happy that I drove Uncle Tyler's truck. I'm going to be the happiest to drive this truck out of these horrible woods. I bet when I get home, everyone will cheer that I drove Uncle Tyler's truck. I'm probably the youngest kid ever to drive a truck."

Megan liked the sound of the words, "when I get home." They made her feel safe in this very upsetting and precarious situation.

Megan put the truck in reverse, and the truck jolted backwards. Again, she had to jam on the brakes, and she got the same whiplash motion as before. This happened a few times before Megan got the hang of keeping her foot on the brake and easing up gently.

Megan tried to see out of the back window, but as she turned around, she was slipping off the pile of clothes, which made her too short to see. Her only recourse was to use the side mirrors. This was going to be a daunting task for her to back a truck out of the woods only using the side mirrors.

The path Tyler had taken into the woods when they first arrived was narrow, and maybe one time long ago had been a real track, but now nature had won out and it was overgrown on both sides. There was still a faint trace of a path left. One could hardly call it a road.

Since there wasn't much to guide Megan, she used the driver's side mirror since it was closer to her and gave her the best view. This course of action worked for the left side of the truck, but the right side of the truck started taking a beating almost from the start. The branches started scraping the passenger side of the truck and raked the windshield on that side as well. At the beginning, Megan ignored it, but the scraping turned to screeching, so she stopped the truck. She was now familiar enough with the stick shift in the center console that she put the truck in park and left it running. She slid off the pile of clothes and wriggled across the seat and sat in the passenger seat. She couldn't see what was happening to the passenger side door, so she pulled herself up and knelt on the seat. In that position, she could see some bad scraping of the paint to the passenger side of the truck.

"Uh, oh, Uncle Tyler is going to be mad that the right side of his truck is all scraped up. I just wish that he had turned the truck around so I could have gone forward and not have to bang up the truck."

At nine years old, Megan couldn't seem to weigh the importance of her being found and getting help for Tyler versus scratching the side of the truck.

She crawled back to the driver's seat and put the truck in reverse again. Having seen the scratches on the right side of the truck, consciously or unconsciously, she now left more room on the right side of the truck. As a result, she was hitting more branches on the left side of the truck and scraping that side as well.

Even though she was inside the cab of the truck, when a large branch hit the driver's side window, she instinctively ducked and yanked the wheel, which caused the truck to veer wildly back to the right. She pulled the wheel to the left, and the overcompensation caused the truck to hit a larger branch which broke the taillight. The sound of the plastic breaking made a distinctive sound which caused Megan to slam on the brakes and the truck came to a lurching stop. Now Megan banged her head into the steering wheel.

"Aw, that really hurts!" Even as Megan was reaching for her forehead to rub it, a bump was forming. The bump came up so fast that as Megan was rubbing her forehead, she could feel the bump swelling up.

Now Megan hit the steering wheel with her hand over and over. "I hate you. You stupid thing, you hurt me!"

It took her a few minutes to calm down, and then she started backing the truck again. There were more scratching and scraping sounds as she went. Either Megan was getting used to the sounds or she didn't care. She just kept backing up.

Then another terrible sound assaulted her ears. It was the sound of the passenger side mirror hitting something large. As Megan looked over, she saw the mirror dangling down on the side of the truck.

If this had happened at the beginning of her journey in the truck, she probably would have been upset, but now she simply shrugged her shoulders and continued on. Megan had no idea of distance, and she didn't know how far into the woods they had driven. Consequently, she had no idea of how far she had backed up and how far she still had to go to reach the road.

When the truck was only about fifty yards from the road, the track became steeper. Although Megan hadn't been going very fast, the truck picked up speed with the grade. Megan's inexperience was now going to catch up with her more than it had so far in this excursion. The right wheels went into a gulley and the truck came to a halt with an enormous bang.

The truck was listing to the right side. Now Megan was in a panic. She tried to push open the driver's side door, but with gravity and the truck listing, she couldn't open it. She tried a second time with no success, but on the third try, she was able to hold the door open with her foot. She could reach over and keep the door open to jump down to the ground.

She ran around to the front of the truck and saw what she had felt. The right-hand wheels were in a gulley about a foot deep. Megan surveyed the situation, not fully comprehending what it meant. For a more experienced driver, the thought would have been to find a tow truck to pull the vehicle out of the ditch. For Megan, her inexperience may have been a blessing. She didn't comprehend how bad the situation was.

She climbed back in the truck and sat there for a minute. She didn't know whether to try to drive the truck forward or backward. She finally decided to go forward since that was the direction the truck had come from. She put the truck in drive and gunned the engine. The truck lurched forward and then the back wheels swayed right and left. But the truck stayed in the gulley.

She tried it a second time and the sound of the wheels spinning in place was excruciating to hear. But the truck didn't move. What Megan didn't know was that the truck had moved backward enough that the back wheels were on a fairly flat space in the gulley. This allowed the truck to gain enough momentum on flat ground that with Megan gunning the engine, the truck got out of the gulley. This last burst of energy ripped a large gash in the right side of the truck on an overhanging branch.

"Yes, I did it! I did it!" Now Megan was even more determined to find the main road and get out of this awful forest.

Chapter 81

"911, what's your emergency?"

"I'm on Cross Creek Road about a half mile south of Route 41 and there's a blue truck on the road that looks like it's been in the war. The truck is all banged up, and the mirror is hanging off it and I think there's a kid driving the truck."

"Is the truck driving erratically?"

"Yeah, sort of, but as I said, the truck is all banged up, and it's not a teenager driving the truck. I think it's a little kid. You should send someone out to take a look."

"Car 39, this is Dispatch. Got a call about a blue truck on Cross Creek about a half mile or so south of 41 and the caller said he thinks it's a little kid driving. Said the truck is all banged up. Maybe it's been in an accident. Please intercept the truck and see what's going on."

Only a few minutes earlier, Megan had seen the road. She hit a few more branches on her way there, and the truck suffered a few more scratches, which at this point was meaningless considering all the other scratches, dings and dents. She backed out onto the shoulder of the road and really had no idea of which way to go. Since the truck was now pointed in one direction, that was the way she was going to go rather than try to turn the truck around. She didn't know whether she'd find a gas station or some stores, but she was now exuberant that she had made it this far to an actual road.

Before she put the truck in drive, she tried the cell phone again. She wanted to call 911. The phone had an anemic one and half bars and still no service. She flung the cell phone across the seat in disgust. "Why can't there be cell service? I was sure once I made it the road there would be service. I hate this place! Nothing goes right."

The mirror on the driver's side was still attached, but it had been pushed out of position, so when Megan looked at it, she saw the side of the truck and not what was coming from behind her on the left. She turned her head as much as she could and saw nothing coming so she pulled onto the road. Megan hadn't gone very far at all, when she saw a police cruiser pass her going in the opposite direction.

She tried to hit the button for the window, but couldn't find it fast enough to lower it to wave her hand out the window. Even though she had come this far and had made it to an actual road, seeing the police cruiser go by without being able to stop it, made her frustration boil over and she started to cry again. The tears, frustration and sheer anger didn't help her driving at all and now she was swerving back and forth in the lane.

What Megan didn't see in the mirror was that the police officer saw the truck, saw its condition, and got a quick look at a driver who appeared to be a kid. He made a U turn and came up behind the truck and put his lights and sirens on. This startled Megan beyond belief, who then was so rattled that the truck was swerving worse than before. As far as the police officer could see, the kid in the truck wasn't responding to the lights and siren to pull over. He now used his loudspeaker. "Pull the vehicle off to the shoulder of the road and turn off the engine."

It took Megan a few more seconds to do what the police officer demanded, and he was about to say it a second time when he saw brake lights come on and the truck slow to a stop. He jumped out of the cruiser while Megan was still trying to turn off the engine and extricate herself from the seatbelt and the entangled clothes.

As the police officer came up to the driver's side of the truck, he took in the scratches and scrapes all over the vehicle. The truck was a mess. Just as he was getting to the driver's door, it swung open because Megan still couldn't figure out how to get the window down. What he saw inside startled him.

Inside he saw a little girl who was filthy, with her hair uncombed and wild, with a big welt on her forehead the size of an egg and a jagged scratch on her face. A multitude of thoughts ran through his head. Was this the twenty- first century version of a kid running away from home or running from abuse and stealing a truck to do so? There was no adult in the truck and the kid looked to be about ten years old.

As she saw the police officer, she sobbed. Not crocodile tears, but wracking sobs. "It's okay, what's your name?"

Megan could choke out her name but was still sobbing. "Okay, Megan, give me your hand and get out of the truck. Do you live around here? Are you hurt?"

Megan gave him her hand and jumped down, but she was still sobbing. She had a huge bump on her forehead and a large scratch, but otherwise he didn't see any blood on her clothes and when she took a few steps, she seemed to walk fine.

"Stay right here and don't move. The officer moved a few feet away and radioed to Dispatch what he saw. "Right now she's crying hysterically, so until I can get her calmed down and get more out of her, I want you to run the plates on the truck. I don't know if it's been stolen or what. Also send EMS to check her out.

"Megan, can you calm down a little and tell me what's been going on? I want to help you, but you have to tell me what's been going on so I can help you. Let's start with, do you live around here?"

"No, I went camping with my Uncle. We went hiking, and he fell."

"Where did he fall? Is he still somewhere in the woods and hurt?"

The police officer's radio screeched to life. The Dispatcher gave him the name of the owner of the truck and said the address was in Westchester County.

"Thanks. I'll be back to you in a few seconds, but the kid says her Uncle fell and is in the woods. We may need the Rescue Squad."

At the mention of the Rescue Squad, Megan started crying all over again.

"It's okay, Megan, you made it out of the woods and because of you, we'll get help to your Uncle."

Chapter 82

EMS came upon the police cruiser and truck. The Officer gave them what info he knew about Megan and asked them to check her out in the EMS vehicle so he could walk away and speak without Megan overhearing.

"Dispatch, please patch me through to the Chief on his cell phone." In less than ninety seconds, the Chief was on the call.

"Chief, this is McDonald. I have the miracle kid with me. She and her Uncle went camping, and he fell and is lost in the woods. I got some info out of her. She found her way back to the camp, found the guy's car keys and backed his truck out of the woods where I found her. She told me she's nine and has never been camping before. She does not know how long it took her to find the camp and then how long to get to Cross Creek where I found her driving the truck. She's got a huge bump on her forehead, but otherwise seems to be okay. EMS is checking her out, and she seems totally lucid to me.

"The Uncle is hurt somewhere in the woods. She's shaken up but if EMS says she's otherwise okay, I think we need her to stay here and try to show us where the Uncle is. She says he has a tree limb sticking out of his leg, so he must be badly hurt. I need you to come down here to the scene.

"She says her parents are dead, and she lives with her aunt and two uncles. Sounds weird, but the kid is making sense, so I guess it's true. She gave me the Aunt's cell phone number which I gave to Dispatch. I think you better call them. I told Dispatch to get the Rescue Squad from the county, but they will need you to activate them."

Chief Egan listened and said he was on the way. He told Dispatch to call the Rescue Squad commander, and he got the cell phone number to call the family.

Sheryl's cell phone rang and normally she didn't answer a number she didn't know, but this number came up as Glenwood Police. Sheryl's stomach lurched when she saw it. As she answered the phone, she heard a male voice say that this was Chief Egan calling.

Sheryl sat down on the kitchen chair because suddenly, her legs were wobbly. Mike was in the kitchen with her, saw her sink down into the chair and saw her face go ashen. When she said, "Yes, Chief Egan," Mike said, "Put him on the speaker phone."

Chief Egan explained what had happened as far as they knew, and that Megan was okay, but that they knew Tyler was hurt, they didn't know how badly he was hurt or where he was. Chief Egan was not one to sugarcoat things.

Sheryl was relieved and panicky at the same time. She knew she wanted to talk to Megan, and she wanted to come up to see her. Her heart broke for what happened to this little girl. The situation with Tyler sounded dire. The emotions were raging in her head. The Chief promised to let Sheryl talk to Megan as soon as he was at the scene and that his office would give Sheryl the address so they could drive up.

As soon as she hung up, Sheryl went to hug Mike. It was a relief, and it was for strength because it seemed a lot of energy had drained out of her body.

"We need to call Jake and we need to call Beverly who is Shelby's mother to take care of Kristin."

Kristin was understandably upset when she heard about Megan and Tyler. She was even more upset that she couldn't go with them. "Why can't I go? It's my sister and my Uncle!"

It took a lot of explaining to Kristin that it would not be good for her to be in the car where her leg could not be elevated, and it was going to be difficult to get around on crutches when they didn't know whether they would be in the woods. "If your leg isn't elevated, and the swelling doesn't go down, you won't be able to play in the tournament."

"Who cares about the tournament? Megan is my sister."

Sheryl and Mike didn't know what they would find with Tyler, how long they would be up there, and if Tyler was even going to be found alive, so they thought that distance from this potential disaster might be better for Kristin.

Mike got Jake on the phone and Sheryl called Beverly to ask for her help in taking care of Kristin. Jake said he would be right home and they could leave to go upstate. Mike told Jake, "We're going to throw a few things in a suitcase in case we have to stay for a few days.

"I told Sheryl that I was opposed to this camping trip right from the start. Tyler is a flake; he has always been a flake. This whole mess just proves it. He is not a responsible adult. In fact, a little kid had to rescue him."

Mike knew there was some truth in what Jake was saying, but for right now he didn't think accusations were going to help anything.

"Look, Jake, this is very stressful, and we don't know what we're going to find. So for right now, let's try not to inflame the situation. We know Megan is okay, but I hope that they're going to find Tyler alive."

Before they got on the road, Sheryl's cell phone rang, and the caller ID said Glenwood Police again. Sheryl grabbed the phone and the little voice on the other end was Megan. Both Sheryl and Megan started to cry as they began the call.

Sheryl tried her best to get herself under control on the phone with Megan. Megan's words came out as a jumble as she tried to explain all that had transpired. Sheryl was thrilled that Megan was okay physically, but she was quickly fearful of what another traumatic event would do to Megan.

At the end of the conversation, Sheryl said, "We're about ready to leave and we'll be up there to get you in a few hours. We love you and we're so glad you're okay. Let me talk to Chief Egan again."

As the Chief came back on the phone, Sheryl told him they were on the way. She asked him again about Tyler and what their plans were.

"The Rescue Squad has just arrived, and we'll talk to Megan about what she can tell us about where they were when her Uncle fell. We don't have that many hours of daylight left, so we want to get the search started. Call me again when you're close to the Police Station, and I'll tell you where I'll be with Megan."

Laura, the EMT in charge, went to speak to Chief Egan. "Megan is okay, but we want to take her to the hospital to have her checked out for a concussion. She's got quite a good-sized bump on her forehead, and she's got another gash on her face. She's lucid, and she's answering all our questions, even through the tears. I think she's more emotionally traumatized than she is physically traumatized."

"Do you think you can give us a little time before you take her to the hospital? We'd like to talk to her and see what she can tell us about where the Uncle is. I'd like to take her back in one of our vehicles to the camp and then see where she says they hiked and he fell. That's really our best and maybe only chance to find the Uncle. She told Officer McDonald that the Uncle has a tree limb sticking out of his leg and he's bleeding. He may not have much time left if we don't find him soon."

Chapter 83

Chief Egan walked back to the ambulance with Laura, the EMT. "Megan, Chief Egan would like to talk to you."

"Megan, do you think you could show us where the camp is, so we can see where you were and help us find Uncle Tyler?"

A look of terror crossed Megan's face. "I don't want to go back into the woods ever again. It was so scary." The tears welled up in her eyes and started rolling down her cheeks.

"You wouldn't be going alone. I'd be there with you and several of the police officers. We'll take care of you, and nothing is going to happen to you. We have a huge truck, and you can sit right next to me."

"Uncle Tyler was going to take care of me and look what happened!"

"Yeah, but we're police officers and we know what we're doing."

Laura had put her arm around Megan as they started the conversation and now Megan buried her face in Laura's arm. Laura and Chief Egan exchanged looks.

"It's okay, Megan. No one is going to make you go, but it would help if you could at least point out where the camp is and which direction you went from there."

Megan still didn't take her face out of Laura's sleeve. Chief Egan was about to give up and turn to leave, and it surprised him that Laura spoke up.

"How about I come with you and Chief Egan? If you get scared, Chief Egan will take us back. Is that okay, Chief?"

"Yes, we will take you back, but Laura and I will be with you the whole time."

Laura knew she was pressuring Megan, but she also knew that Tyler might bleed out if they didn't find him soon. It came down to a weighing of risks.

"You were so brave to go alone in the woods and find the camp after Uncle Tyler fell. You were even braver to back the truck out onto the highway and get help. You're safe now with us and we want to bring Uncle Tyler back safe." A few long seconds elapsed, and nothing happened.

Slowly and excruciatingly, Megan lifted her face out of Laura's sleeve.

"My Daddy said I have to stand in the box."

Laura looked at Megan with a blank look on her face and Megan saw it. "The batter's box. My Daddy told Uncle Tyler to be brave and stand in the batter's box. You have to do things when you're scared.

"Okay, I'll go if you come with me, but if it gets too scary, I want to leave."

Chief Egan looked at Laura and mouthed, "Thank you."

Chapter 84

Megan hadn't gone very far when Officer McDonald found her on Cross Creek Road when she drove the truck out of the woods, and the muddy tracks on the road made it easy to see where she had come out. There were several police vehicles with huge tires that followed the track into the woods toward the camp. Broken branches hung askew on both sides of the track which was additional evidence of where Megan had backed the truck out. Driving in a forward direction toward the camp by police who obviously know how to drive made the trip go relatively quickly. Megan was in the second vehicle with Chief Egan and Laura, the EMT. The tent was still up and there were some clothes littering the ground. One officer went into the tent and came out saying it looked as if someone had ransacked the tent. As Megan got out of the truck, she heard him say it. She then explained that she was first looking for Tyler's cell phone, then the truck keys and then she used the clothes for height to drive the truck.

The head of the Rescue Squad, Ian Stafford, was a young man in his early forties, who looked like the stereotypical SWAT team leader. Despite his military bearing, Ian had a smile that softened that look. He also had a daughter who was a little older than Megan, so he knew he could speak to her the way he spoke to his daughter. His voice was soft and his smile welcoming.

"Hi, Megan, my name is Ian. I heard you did an incredible job of finding your way back to the camp after your Uncle fell and then getting the truck back onto Cross Creek Road. Do you think that you can point out the direction you walked with your Uncle when he fell so we look in the right direction? It's important that we don't go in the wrong direction."

Megan was still holding Laura's hand as Ian spoke to her. Her lip quivered a little as she responded. "I, I don't want to go back into the woods. It's too scary."

"Okay, you don't have to go. Can you point which direction you walked toward with your Uncle?"

Megan pointed in a direction over Ian's shoulder.

"Okay, that's good. How long do you think you walked before you Uncle fell?"

Megan shrugged.

Ian tried it a different way. "Do you remember how long it took you to walk back to the camp?"

"A really long time because I got lost."

"Where there any landmarks you remember walking either way?"

"Some red flowers."

"What kind of red flowers?"

Megan shrugged again. Ian pressed on, acting as if undeterred.

"When your Uncle told you to walk back to the camp, did he tell you to do anything?"

Megan thought about this for a minute instead of merely shrugging.

"Yeah, he told me to keep the sun on my face as I was walking back, and I would find the camp that way."

"Excellent, Megan, that tells us what direction you walked in originally and what direction you walked back. Can you remember anything else? You are doing so well."

Megan chewed on this for a few seconds and then said no.

"It's okay, something else may come to you and you can let us know. This is a super job."

Ian put his hand on Megan's shoulder and gave it a squeeze.

"Do you think you can find Uncle Tyler? He's really hurt, and I love him."

"Megan, I promise you we will do everything we possibly can to find him. Whenever I'm called to one of these rescues, I think what I would do if it was my family member. That makes me work really hard. Someday it could be my daughter or my brother and I want the rescuers to treat them like a family member. Is this your Dad's brother?

"Where's your Dad now? Is he on his way up here?"

Megan swallowed hard and said, "He's in heaven."

Ian hadn't been expecting that answer. They had not passed the info about Megan living with her uncles on to him. Ian actually flinched when he heard that answer. He didn't know how to respond to her, so what came out of his mouth came from his heart.

"I bet your Uncle is a terrific guy. He told you how to get out of the woods and he saved you. Now we're going to do our very best to save him."

Ian gave Megan a little smile and walked back toward the rescue workers and the police on scene and started giving directions.

As the rescuers picked up their gear and head out, Megan yelled to Ian.

"Ian, wait, I remember something else. We were walking, and we kept going up high so that I could get a good view of the mountains and the lake so I could draw them."

"Megan, did you actually get to do any of your drawings before Uncle Tyler fell?"

"No. We never got to the top."

"This is wonderful, Megan, because you're narrowing the area we have to search."

Ian turned and spread the map of the area on the front of the truck. He started pointing with his finger on the map.

Chapter 85

Sheryl had never felt a car trip take this long and Mike was doing seventy-five on the highway.

Not long after they started driving, Jake asked Sheryl, "What did Megan sound like on the phone?"

"She was a little weepy on the phone, but so was I, even though I was trying hard not to cry."

"And they told you she wasn't hurt?"

"She's okay. She has a bump on her forehead where she hit her head on the steering wheel when she was hitting the gas and the brakes too hard. The EMTs don't think she has a concussion, but they are going to take her to the hospital to be checked out. The rescuers wanted her to come back to the camp with them and point them in the right direction. Then I think the EMTs are going to take her to the hospital."

"So how will we know where to go?"

"I have the phone number for the Chief's secretary, and she will know when Megan goes to the hospital."

"It's pretty damn amazing that a kid who has never been camping before in her life could get herself out of the woods and get help. What did they tell you about Tyler?"

"Not a whole lot. Megan said he was on a ledge which apparently collapsed under him, and he was impaled on a tree limb.

She said he was bleeding. Not that surprising that he was bleeding. I guess it's a question of how bad."

Mike now answered. "I hope they get to him in time. If he's been bleeding for hours, it could be terrible. It could be fatal."

Sheryl replied, "Megan understands that he's hurt, but I don't think she knows his possibly going into shock or bleeding out. Kristin and Megan have had enough death in their young lives with Jackie and Blake. They don't need more."

Jake said, "You should call Dr. Moran and tell her what's gone on so far. She should know. Even if they rescue Tyler, this whole thing has been traumatic enough for Megan. If it gets worse with Tyler…" Jake let the sentence trail off and he never finished it.

"You know Jake maybe YOU should call the psychiatrist instead of me. There are plenty of occasions when you conveniently forget that you are the Co-Guardian and you let everyone else do your job. Then there are other times when you want to exert your authority." The tone in Sheryl's voice was acerbic.

Mike intervened. "Calm down, Sheryl. Everyone is stressed out right now. It won't do any good for you two to be fighting."

"I was just making a suggestion. I thought it would be in Megan's best interest, that's all. You don't have to jump down my throat."

"Okay, enough you two. Both of you put a lid on it. Sniping at each other when you're both upset is not productive. We have enough problems to worry about.

"We have to think about what to do if Megan has to stay in the hospital. Even if they check her out and she can go home, what are we going to do about Tyler? I don't know if Megan is going to want to go home or stay here until they find him. Suppose he's in terrible shape, should we airlift him to a major trauma center? Worse still, suppose he doesn't make it?"

These questions gave them something to think about and perhaps driving in silence was not the worst thing.

Chapter 86

The rescuers broke up into groups with the greater number going in the direction Megan pointed out. Ian Stafford hedged his bets and sent others in a somewhat different direction in case Megan's memory was faulty and they would lose precious time.

One of the police officers had been instructed to take Laura and Megan to the hospital so Megan could be checked for a concussion once the rescuers left the camp. At first Megan was reluctant to leave the camp because she wanted to be there when they found Tyler. Laura told Megan that she needed to be checked out in the hospital. Laura used that excuse and the fact that Megan's Aunt and other Uncle were on their way to the hospital to meet her. Laura's main reason for wanting to get Megan out of there was if they found Tyler dead and brought his body back to the camp. Even if he was alive, he was sure to look awful, and Laura didn't want Megan to see either scenario. Laura could see the fright on Megan's face. Megan clung to Laura's hand as Laura guided her toward the SUV.

The rescuers brought dogs to try to pick up Tyler's scent and their big break was that Megan had left Tyler's clothes all over the camp, so the dogs had Tyler's scent. The rescuers also had whistles with them which they would blow at intervals hoping Tyler would hear the whistle and respond. They also hoped the sound of a whistle might raise him from his lethargy.

The obvious problem was they only had a general direction from Megan, and she had no sense of how long they had been walking when he fell. However, Ian had the feeling from his conversation with Megan that they hadn't been walking all that long before Tyler fell. He was hoping his hunch was correct because every minute was precious for someone bleeding and probably in shock. The other problem was that it was going to get dark.

The rescuers were in small groups with the expectation of covering more ground that way. There were places where the vegetation was dense, and the progress was slow. For a while, the dogs weren't picking up anything. Fortunately, it wasn't cold outside.

Ian had led rescue parties that went on for days, so a few hours of searching would not deter him. What nagged at him was Tyler's condition. How long could Tyler hold out if he continued to bleed and if they had to stop the search overnight? Megan hadn't given them any detailed information about Tyler's leg, except that he was bleeding.

Suddenly, one dog started barking and straining at the leash. The dog had picked up Tyler's scent. Colin radioed Ian. "Ian, my dog is barking and straining. I think we're going in the right direction. I'll let you know."

Another ten minutes passed, and the dog was still picking up the scent. Colin told the dog to sit and gave the dog some water. He blew the whistle around his neck and listened. He and the other two men listened but heard nothing. He called Tyler's name. They listened again. Still nothing in response.

"Okay, let's move forward." The dog was eager to get going. Colin let him sniff Tyler's sweater again. "C'mon, boy, let's find him. Go."

The dog jumped up and started moving forward.

Chapter 87

Tyler was drifting in and out of consciousness. Suddenly, something jolted him awake. He didn't know what it was. Then he heard it again. Through the fog in his head, he realized it was a whistle. Tyler did his best to yell for help, but the sound that came out wasn't much.

Tyler was now fighting to stay awake and not drift off. A few minutes later, he heard it again. Then he heard something else. He heard his name. Tyler's heart rate increased. If people were near enough that he could hear his name, then they must be pretty close. He could be rescued! Tyler licked his lips and saw that he still had some water left in one of the water bottles. He gulped what was left in the bottle. He took two deep breaths and yelled as loud as he could, "Here, help!"

It wasn't all that loud, but it was loud enough since the rescuers were close. They heard it and the dog heard it and started barking wildly. Colin got the dog quiet. Now all three rescuers yelled Tyler's name in unison. Tyler heard it and his heart was racing. His adrenaline and his will to live kicked in.

He yelled, "Help" as loud as he could. But it still wasn't very loud.

A voice from above him, shouted "Tyler." Tyler was disoriented and wasn't sure if the voice was God talking to him. Maybe he was going to die even if the rescuers were close. The voice called his name again.

"Tyler, can you hear me? We're going to come get you."

"Yeah, I hear you," came the weary voice. Then Tyler started to cry.

Colin radioed Ian that they had found Tyler and he radioed the GPS coordinates to him. "He's down below us on a shelf and it looks like he's semi-conscious. I'd say he's about twenty-five to thirty feet below us, so we have to get down to him. We also need to be sure that the shelf will hold us. We're going to need a basket to get him back up to where he fell from. Can you get someone to bring that for us? We're going to need an EMT. He's probably going to need oxygen and an IV."

Ian now radioed the other rescuers the coordinates so they would all head to the spot where Tyler was as soon as possible. Ian also radioed EMS to tell them they had found Tyler and told them about needing an EMT to administer oxygen and an IV. They would need an ambulance to be on standby.

Charlie was the shortest and lightest of the three rescuers and so the other two had him tethered as he lowered himself slowly down to Tyler. They could see the area that had given way on Tyler and there were rotted trees and tree roots. The place where Tyler was lying seemed pretty sound and Charlie tested the area gingerly putting his weight step by step as Colin and Tom grasped the ropes holding him. The rescuers didn't want to have to be rescued themselves.

As the three rescuers got down to Tyler, they assessed the situation and his medical condition. They quickly applied a real tourniquet and had to decide what to do about freeing Tyler so that they could lift him off the shelf and ultimately take him to the hospital.

In a short while, more rescuers arrived on the scene, and working as a team, it looked like a choreographed event. When the two EMTs arrived, they took Tyler's vital signs and quickly administered oxygen and started an IV. Tyler was barely responsive, but the EMTs hoped the IV and the oxygen would make him more comfortable and raise his blood pressure, which was very low.

Ian spoke to the EMT, Jeff, about coordinating the efforts. "We're going to have to move him to free his leg. It's going to be very painful, so we're going to work as fast as possible. Can you give him some morphine for the pain?"

"Yes, but I can't give him very much because his blood pressure is already low. I'd like to hold off as long as possible to get as much fluid into him. Give me a few minutes notice and then we'll give him the morphine. He may very well pass out from the pain.

"We're have to stop the bleeding as much as we can as quickly as possible once you start moving him, since we really don't know how much damage there is internally to the leg."

Meanwhile, Ian's men were moving Tyler's leg fractions of an inch at a time trying to get a better look. One rescuer had brought a power saw to saw off the part of the branch that was protruding up out of his leg.

"Tell me exactly what you are going to do, so I can help and also keep the bleeding under control as best as possible."

Chapter 88

Sheryl called the Chief's secretary as their GPS said they were about a half hour away. The secretary gave them the name and address of the hospital where Megan had been transported and was now being evaluated. They reprogramed their GPS and saw that the hospital was even closer and only about twenty minutes away.

Sheryl told Mike to park the car. She didn't even want to wait the few minutes it would take to park, but wanted to get to Megan as soon as possible. As Sheryl and Jake made their way into the ER and through reception, they then found Megan in an examining room with a social worker sitting with her. There was a butterfly clip on her cheek where she had fallen on the rocks in the water, and she was holding an ice pack on the bump on her forehead which had grown progressively larger as time went on. As Sheryl and Jake walked into the examining room, they saw Megan before she saw them, since was looking toward the window. Sheryl rushed toward the bed and Megan turned just as Sheryl reached the bed. Megan would have jumped out of the bed, except that Sheryl grabbed her and hugged her. Both of them started to cry.

"Let me look at you. How do you feel?"

Through the tears, Megan said, "I feel okay, but I have a headache."

"I'm surprised that's all you have after all you've been through." Sheryl looked at the social worker and introduced herself and Jake and asked about the tests performed on Megan.

"We're waiting for the test results of the CAT scan on her head to see if she has a concussion. From what she tells us, she hit her head pretty hard. The ER doctor checked her out, and there are no broken bones or sprains. Now that you're here, I will tell the nurse's station that they can give you the test results. Megan, I'll say goodbye and hope you go home soon. You're a really brave girl."

The social worker motioned with her head toward the door to Sheryl. When they were out in the hall, the social worker said, "While Megan may be okay physically, she is very traumatized no matter what the outcome with her uncle. You should think about having her see a psychologist when you get home. I haven't heard that her uncle has yet been brought into the hospital yet, so I don't know what's happening there."

Sheryl nodded in agreement and explained that Megan was still seeing Dr. Moran. "We will call her today and let her know what's happened."

Sheryl explained about the death of Megan's parents and said, "This is going to be terrible all the way around if they don't find Tyler in time. I can't imagine that a nine-year-old should have to experience the death of three important adults in her life. I really hope for Megan and for Tyler that this ends well."

Mike walked down the hall toward them just as Sheryl was finishing the conversation, and Sheryl introduced them. Sheryl said to Mike, "Let's make sure we call Dr. Moran today and see if she thinks there is anything specific we should be doing. When we go back into the exam room, see if you can get Jake to come out and call her."

As they walked back into the exam room, Jake was holding Megan's hand and they looked to be deep in conversation.

"Have they found Uncle Tyler yet? I wanted to stay until they found him, but they made me come to the hospital."

Jake answered. "I told Megan that they're working really hard to find him and I'm sure you were a big help. These rescuers find people all the time and they know what they're doing."

"Yeah, but what happens if they can't find him?" Megan's tone was plaintive.

Jake answered that he would go to the front desk to see if they had any info on their having brought Tyler into the hospital, and because he really didn't know how to answer Megan.

Mike said he would go with Jake, but that was to prompt him to call Dr. Moran.

Megan said she was hungry, and Mike said he would check if she could have something to eat and then go to the cafeteria and bring back something for her.

When they were out in the hallway, Mike told Jake what the social worker had to say and urged him to call Dr. Moran. "Look, Jake, it would be good to call Dr. Moran and let her know what has gone on and to see what we should do with Megan in case Tyler doesn't make it."

Jake nodded in assent. "He's such an idiot, but I don't want him to die. He can't do one thing right. Megan should never have been put through this. If he had stayed at the normal campsite where he was supposed to, none of this would have happened. But this guy can't follow one rule. He should never have been allowed to take Megan alone. If he wants to be reckless with himself, let him, but not with the girls."

"Jake, we still don't know all that happened. We haven't heard the complete story from Megan, and we certainly haven't heard anything from Tyler. Don't jump to conclusions."

"Are you kidding me? He took Megan to some place out in the middle of nowhere they never should have been. She's not an experienced camper. She's a little girl who's never been in the wilderness and he put her life in danger as well as his. Don't try to placate me. He is unfit to be a parent and I'm the only one who seems to get that. You bet I'm going to tell Dr. Moran and the Court appointed Evaluator."

Chapter 89

Six Weeks Later

Jody Gibson sat in the Family Room of the house with Megan. Before she sat down, she admired the picture on the easel, which was Megan's latest drawing. Megan had been using her drawings to help her express her trauma as well as seeing Dr. Moran twice a week. Megan and Dr. Moran talked a lot about what Megan drew.

Jody had purposely waited to speak to Megan in her role as Court Evaluator and only after Dr. Moran gave the okay. Jody had originally wanted to interview Megan before anyone else but that was before the camping trip. She had now interviewed everyone else, and Megan was the last person. It also took her a long time to be able to interview Tyler. Tyler had been in the hospital with a raging infection in the wound and had been on IV antibiotics. Then he went to rehab to regain his strength and to get used to the prothesis. She had kept the Court advised of the reasons for the delay.

Jody and Megan talked about school and that Megan was going to enter two of her drawings in an art contest. There was an upcoming trip to Disney World that Megan was excited about. Finally, Jody wound the conversation around to the home situation.

"So Megan, you remember that you wrote a letter to Judge Waverly telling her that you wanted to live with Aunt Sheryl and that your Uncles were mean to you. Can you tell me what made you write that letter to the Judge?"

"Everybody told me that we have to listen to everything the Judge said. She gets to tell us what to do."

"That's true. We have to listen to her. But the Judge wants me to ask you what happened that made you say in the letter that your Uncles were mean to you."

"My Uncles were always fighting with each other and that made me scared. I wasn't scared when my Mommy and Daddy were alive."

"Did they yell at you and that made you scared?"

"Uncle Jake yelled at us, and he yelled at Uncle Tyler. Uncle Tyler sometimes yelled back at him. Mostly, they yelled at each other."

"Did anyone ever hit you?"

"No, never," came the quick response.

"Does Aunt Sheryl yell at you?"

"No. She gets Uncle Jake and Uncle Tyler to stop yelling."

The conversation went on like that for a time. Jody felt she was getting unvarnished answers from Megan. She also felt that Megan had not been coached by anyone, but she wanted to be sure of that.

Jody asked the two most important questions. "Did anyone tell you what to say to me?

"Dr. Moran told me to tell you the truth and what I wanted."

"So do you want to live with Aunt Sheryl?"

"No."

This answer took Jody back.

"No? Now you don't want to live with Aunt Sheryl?"

"No, I want to live with Aunt Sheryl AND Uncle Tyler."

"Can you tell me why you want to live with them?"

"I love them both. Uncle Tyler tried his best, and we had a lot of fun on the camping trip until he fell. I got to try some new things that were great. He told me the truth that there were no bears. I didn't like going to the bathroom in the woods at all. He told me lots of great things about my Daddy that now only the two of us know. I'm sorry that he lost part of his leg. I want to help him get well.

"I love Aunt Sheryl. She's kind, and she takes care of things and makes them work out. I can see how much she loves Kristin and me. I think she misses Uncle Mike because he's in Florida, but she is taking good care of us. With Aunt Sheryl around, it's sort of like when my Mommy and Daddy were around. I feel safe with her.

"Please tell the Judge that I want to live with BOTH of them. I can't pick. Tell the Judge I don't want to choose one or the other. I choose them both."

Chapter 90

After all the interviews, Jody was about to submit her report to the Court. When she was first assigned to the case, she thought this case had the potential to be interesting but quirky, but it had surpassed all her expectations. After all that had gone on, she wanted to make sure she was giving the Judge her best recommendation after all the interviews and after she had given it much thought.

She received a call from Harris Mayfield, which surprised her. "Jody, I see that you haven't submitted your report to the Court. I think the parties have reached an agreement, which would certainly play into your recommendations."

"I'm all ears. Go ahead."

"As you know, Kristin was okay with the arrangement as it was with the three adults, but that arrangement would not last much longer. It was Megan who clearly was not okay. Sheryl has been up here in New York for many months more than she originally intended. She wants to go home to Florida, and her husband Mike now has been up here for more than two months as well. They have stayed because of the situation, or should I say multiple situations. Tyler has now been home from rehab for a few weeks, but he is not one hundred percent.

"I guess this last crisis gave everyone some perspective. Apparently, they have been talking among themselves. Jake has been offered a big job in Boston that he wants to take. Jake will resign as the Co-Guardian, but only under certain conditions. Those conditions are that Sheryl will become the Co-Guardian with Tyler, and she and Mike will stay up here every other month. They will hire a full-time housekeeper so that on the months when Sheryl is not there, Tyler will have help. In the summer months when school is out, the girls will go down to stay with Sheryl and Mike in Florida. If at the time Megan turns fourteen years old and Kristin is seventeen, the girls agree that they want to live in Florida, Tyler will consent to that. Tyler won't contest that decision. It's a logical time because Kristin will be getting ready to go to college and Megan would be starting high school.

"If Tyler wants to resign at any point, he will give up any right to appoint another Co-Guardian. If the girls want to live in Florida with Sheryl, Tyler will consent to leave the house within sixty days so that they can sell it, and the proceeds will become part of the estate.

"If you want to re-interview Kristin and Megan to confirm that this is what they want, that's fine. No one is forcing anything on them. They tell me that Sheryl, Mike, Tyler and Jake sat the girls down all together and spoke to them."

"All I can say is 'wow.' The Arabs and the Israelis sat down and compromised. Who would ever thought this was possible?"

"Do you think the Judge will buy it?"

"It certainly seems reasonable, and it will stop the fighting, which she will like. There was an inherent problem of the Court doing what's in the best interests of the children, balanced against what the deceased parents put in the Will."

"Will you recommend this to the Court?"

"I would like to talk to the girls one more time, but assuming they have no objections, yes I will recommend it."

Chapter 91 Epilogue

One Year Later

Sometime the fates are unkind or seem downright malevolent. Sometimes the fates even the score, but not always.

Before the camping trip, Tyler thought that maybe he would stay on as the Co-Guardian for Kristin and Megan for about another year, because he was thinking of moving to Florida or California where the weather was warm all year. Tyler was ruling out California with all the wildfires, rolling blackouts and earthquakes.

After the camping trip, his entire perspective had changed, since he had a very real brush with death. He realized he couldn't just abandon Kristin and Megan. More importantly, he realized he wanted to be a part of their lives and he wanted them to be a part of his. His brother, Blake, was gone, but Tyler wanted to be part of a family, and Megan and Kristin were his family. Never before had this been the least bit important to him until now.

About nine months after the camping trip, Tyler approached Sheryl one night when the girls were at the movies. "Sheryl, you've been a great sport about going back and forth to Florida. I know it's been hard on you. I'm doing okay with my new leg, and I can still do the finished carpentry work. I want to stay a part of Kristin and Megan's life, so I thought that maybe we could all move to Florida."

Sheryl had grown fond of the "new" Tyler, but she was absolutely dumbfounded by Tyler's comments. So much so, that she just sat there and didn't reply. Tyler had become a new person since the trauma of the camping trip. He had come to see life and what was important, very differently.

Tyler looked panic stricken and stammered. "I, I thought you would like this idea. You could live in your own house in Florida, and you wouldn't have to keep coming up here. I'd get my own place near you and the girls could go back and forth."

"That's a terrific idea, Tyler. You're a part of our family now and it would be wonderful if we could all be together in Florida. I'm thrilled, and Mike loves having the girls with us in the summer. Brian didn't like his job in Atlanta, so he is moving back to Orlando. The girls will have a brother and Brian will have two sisters. There's enough of an age difference between them that they won't fight, and they will appreciate each other."

Sheryl had become the surrogate mother of the daughters she always wanted. Tyler would become part of the family he never cared about before, but now badly wanted. Kristin and Megan tragically lost their parents at very young ages. However, they now had love from their relatives on both sides of the family, which is what Jackie and Blake wanted if they weren't around, even if it wasn't how they tried to fashion it.

For this family, the fates more than evened the score. After a long and difficult journey, the fates smiled on this family.

About the Author

Noël F. Caraccio is a full-time practicing attorney in Westchester County, a suburb of New York City, where she has lived her entire life. She was awarded a Danforth Fellowship for graduate studies in English. She represents Credit Unions, Social Service Agencies, and clients in commercial and residential real estate transactions, as well as Trusts and Estate matters.

She has served as a director on numerous not-for-profit Boards. She is a member of the New York State and Westchester County Bar Associations. She is an avid golfer, and belongs to Bonnie Briar Country Club where she won the Women's Club Championship.

She has published two novels, *Secrets Change Everything* and *Shattered City*.

Note from the Author

Word-of-mouth is crucial for any author to succeed. If you enjoyed *Stand in the Box*, please leave a review online—anywhere you are able. Even if it's just a sentence or two. It would make all the difference and would be very much appreciated.

Thanks!
Noël F. Caraccio

We hope you enjoyed reading this title from:

www.blackrosewriting.com

Subscribe to our mailing list – *The Rosevine* – and receive **FREE** books, daily deals, and stay current with news about upcoming releases and our hottest authors.
Scan the QR code below to sign up.

Already a subscriber? Please accept a sincere thank you for being a fan of Black Rose Writing authors.

View other Black Rose Writing titles at
www.blackrosewriting.com/books and use promo code
PRINT to receive a **20% discount** when purchasing.